What Others Are Saying about Vickie McDonough and *Call of the Prairie*...

Call of the Prairie pulled me in from the first pages. Readers will cheer for Sophie Davenport, a sheltered city girl, as she struggles to triumph over the challenges of prairie life.

—*Ann Shorey*
Author, the Sisters at Heart series

Vickie McDonough's writing shines in *Call of the Prairie*, a beautifully crafted story of courage and strength—and a reminder that even when the fulfillment of our dreams seems impossible, God has everything under control. I found myself captivated by the town of Windmill and its people and felt the call of the prairie tugging at my heart.

—*Carol Cox*
Author, *Love in Disguise*, *Trouble in Store*, and *Truth Be Told*

With her signature vivid descriptions that bring the prairie to life and a cast of engaging characters, Vickie McDonough gives readers a story that will linger in their hearts. More than a delightful historical romance, *Call of the Prairie* is also a story of duty and determination, of misunderstandings and mystery, of life and love. Don't miss it.

—*Amanda Cabot*
CBA best-selling author

Vickie McDonough writes yet another historical romance that winds itself around your heart and doesn't let go. Clearly defined characters, a captivating story that moves at a good pace, and a romance that draws you in all serve to create a winning combination in her latest release, *Call of the Prairie*.

—*Miralee Ferrell*
Award-winning author of Western romance

Vickie McDonough never fails to deliver, and her heartfelt story of an asthmatic woman's plight to escape her overprotective parents and live a normal life will delight her many fans. Sophie Davenport jumps at the chance to travel to Kansas to care for an ailing aunt but is ill-prepared for what awaits her. Though breathing can be a chore at times, Sophie faces each challenge with courage and determination. Engaging, inspiring, and filled with love and hope, Sophie's story is one for the keeper shelf.

—*Margaret Brownley*
Best-selling author, *Dawn Comes Early, Waiting for Morning,* and *Gunpowder Tea*

Josh Harper may be the shortest and least physical of the Harper brothers, but he stands tall and strong as the hero in *Call of the Prairie*. I love books about romance and strong family relationships, and Vickie McDonough scores big on both counts with this Prairie Promises series. I'm already looking forward to book three.

—*Dorothy Clark*
Author, *Falling for the Teacher*

Call of the Prairie is the perfect follow-up to *Whispers on the Prairie*. This second installment in the Pioneer Promises series does not fail to inspire. Enthralling characters and another page-turning plot had me staying up well past my bedtime! Three cheers for Vickie McDonough!

—*Sharlene MacLaren*
Award-winning author

I was particularly interested in this story because I also have asthma. Vickie's book gave me an understanding of how hard it was for people to understand this condition in the late 1800s, as well as how little doctors knew about how to control its symptoms. I loved watching the hero and heroine move from a place where each felt constrained into the plans God had for them from the beginning. I walked right beside them through it all. The secondary characters were also well-developed. As always, Vickie McDonough carries her readers to a place they haven't been and reveals the setting to them like a painter layering colors to complete a masterpiece.

—*Lena Nelson Dooley*
Award-winning author, *Love Finds You in Golden, New Mexico,*
and her highly acclaimed McKenna's Daughters series

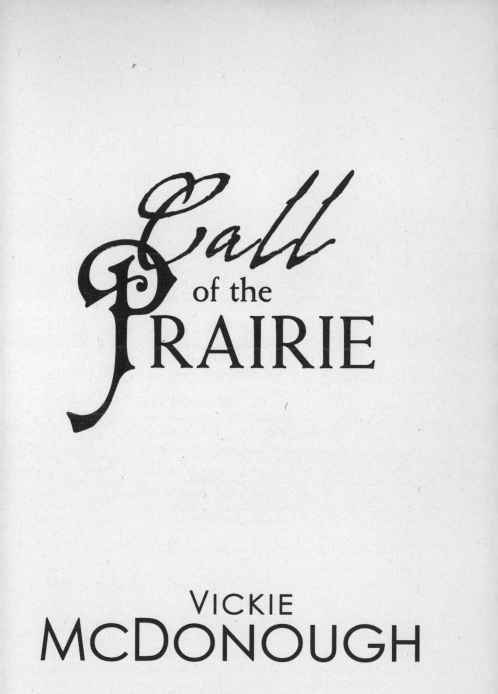

Call
of the
PRAIRIE

VICKIE
McDONOUGH

WHITAKER
HOUSE

CALL OF THE PRAIRIE
Pioneer Promises ~ Book Two

Vickie McDonough
vickie@vickiemcdonough.com
www.vickiemcdonough.com

ISBN: 978-1-60374-962-6
eBook ISBN: 978-1-60374-986-2
Printed in the United States of America
© 2014 by Vickie McDonough

Whitaker House
1030 Hunt Valley Circle
New Kensington, PA 15068
www.whitakerhouse.com

Library of Congress Cataloging-in-Publication Data (Pending)

1 2 3 4 5 6 7 8 9 10 11 **UJ** 21 20 19 18 17 16 15 14

Chapter One

April 1873 · St. Louis, Missouri

Sophie Davenport held back the curtain and peered out the front window, her heart jolting as a handsome man exited the carriage. He paid the driver, then turned and studied her house. He was taller and nicer-looking than she'd expected. She dropped the curtain and stepped back, hoping he hadn't seen her spying. She pressed her hands together and tapped her index fingers against her lips, unable to hold back her grin. Blake had finally arrived!

A knock of confidence, not apprehension, sounded at the main entrance. Sophie hurried to her bedroom door, which opened onto the main entryway, and held her breath, listening. Blake stood on her porch, introducing himself to the butler. Sophie could barely contain her giddiness. She bounced on her toes as Blake told the butler he had an appointment with her. His voice, deeper than she'd imagined, floated through the open transom window above her like a beautiful cello solo at the symphony.

She patted her hair, hoping the humidity of the warm day hadn't sent it spiraling in rebellious curls. The swish of silk accompanied her as she hurried across the room to the full-length oval mirror that stood in one corner. Pressing a hand over her chest to calm her pounding heart, she surveyed her deep purple gown. Was the fabric too dark? She'd chosen the violet silk taffeta because her brightly colored day dresses made her appear younger, but today, she wanted to look the twenty-two-year-old woman she was. Turning sideways, she checked her bustle and bow, making sure they were straight. Everything was as orderly as it could be. Would Blake like what he saw? Would he think her too short? Her light brown hair too nondescript?

Flicking a piece of lint off her bodice, she turned and faced the door. She would know soon enough. After more than a year of correspondence, Blake knew everything about her, and he had adamantly insisted that none of it mattered. He'd fallen in love with her through her enchanting missives, and he wanted her for his wife.

A vicious knock rattled the glass in the transom, and Sophie jumped. The apprehension racing through her was less about meeting Blake and more about the fact that she hadn't told her parents about him. They would have cut off her correspondence faster than their gardener could lop off the head of a snake. But it was too late now. She attempted to swallow the lump lodged in her throat, but it refused to move.

Her mother walked in, her whole face pinched like a prune, and quickly closed the door. She stood there, facing it, for a long moment, her head down, then heaved a loud, exaggerated sigh.

Not a good sign.

Finally, her mother turned. "You have a guest, Sophia—a male guest." One eyebrow lifted. "Would you care to explain to me how you are acquainted with this man, especially since neither your father nor I have ever met him?"

Sophie pressed a hand to her throat. She knew this wouldn't be easy. "His name is Blake Sheppard. He and I have been corresponding for over a year."

Her mother's brown eyes widened. "A year? But how? I've never seen a letter from him in the mail."

Ducking her head, Sophie stilled her hands and held them in front of her. "Ruthie sent and received them for me. Blake is her cousin—and a gentleman."

"A gentleman doesn't go behind the backs of a young woman's parents to contact her." Maintaining her stiff stance, her mother puckered her lips. "So, you've been deceiving your father and me?"

Wincing, Sophie turned toward the front window. "Would you have allowed me to correspond with Blake if I'd told you about him?"

"Proper ladies don't exchange letters with men they've never been introduced to, and certainly not without parental approval."

Drawing a steadying breath, Sophie pivoted to face her mother. She'd known this would be a battle. "Mother, please. Blake is a good man. Ask me anything about him."

"There's no need. We will go out to the parlor and share a cup of tea, and then you'll make excuses that will send him on his way. Is that clear?"

Sophie gasped. "But he's traveled so far, and I've waited so long to meet him." She despised the pleading in her voice. Why couldn't her parents let her grow up, like her sister? A wheeze squeaked out of her throat. She had to stay calm. The last thing she wanted was to have an attack in front of Blake.

Her mother moved closer, her expression softening. She took Sophie's hand. "You know how things are, dear. You had no business getting that young man's hopes up."

"That young man is my fiancé, Mother."

"Fiancé—why, that's absurd! You know you can't lead a normal life."

Closing her eyes, Sophie fought back tears. Why did her parents seek to limit her? Given the chance, she was certain she could be a proper wife and mother, but her parents just wanted to coddle her and keep her close. "You have to face the fact that I'm grown up. I want to live a normal life." She hurried past her mother and reached for the door handle.

"But you are not normal, dear. Your father and I only want to protect you. We couldn't bear to lose you, and you know we've come close to doing that very thing on several occasions."

Sophie shuddered at the declaration. Her mother's words rang in her ears: "*You are not normal.*" Yes, she had a breathing problem; but, as she'd gotten older, the spells had happened less often. Maybe in time, they'd go away altogether. Her parents were afraid to let her live as her sister did. If she didn't get away from them, she'd become a spinster—if she wasn't one already. She stiffened her back and pasted on a smile, trying to ignore the pain of her mother's chastisement. Blake was waiting.

She opened the door and stepped into the entryway, her gaze searching for the man she'd dreamed about so many times. Blake stood in front of the parlor sofa, speaking with her father. He hadn't noticed her yet.

"I'm sorry you've wasted your time traveling all this way, Mr. Sheppard," her father said. "But, as I've already stated, my daughter is not in the habit of receiving male visitors."

Blake's eyebrows drew together, his shoulders slumping, and he looked down at the carpet. Sophie blew out several breaths and tried to calm herself, then hurried through the entryway into the parlor, avoiding her father's glare. Her gaze latched onto Blake's, and she saw the confusion in his hazel eyes. He offered a tentative smile. "Miss Davenport, a pleasure to finally meet you."

She smiled, her cheeks warming as she curtsied. "I've looked forward to this moment for a very long time." She waved a hand toward her father, and noticed that her mother had followed her into the room. "I apologize, but I failed to tell my parents about your visit." *Because I knew just how they would respond.* "I fear they are both a bit surprised." An understatement of mammoth proportions, if ever there was one.

Sophie gathered her courage and turned to her father. "I see you've met Blake, Father." Her throat tightened at his stern stare. Another wheeze squeaked out. "B-Blake is my fiancé."

Her father's eyes widened, and his mouth dropped open. A pomegranate color climbed up his neck, turning his ears red. He turned his fiery gaze on Blake. "You presume a lot, young man. Did my daughter not inform you that she is not fully well? She is not in a position to accept an offer of marriage."

Blake cleared his throat and straightened, as if he wasn't ready to give up the battle. "Yes, sir, she told me, but I thought—" His gaze captured Sophie's, and then he glanced at the floor again. He shuffled his feet, as if he were trying to figure out a new dance step. "I thought Sophie—uh, Miss Davenport—was free to make her own decisions, sir. I'm sorry that she failed to inform you of my interest in her."

"Inform me?" Her father puffed up like a tom turkey whose hens were in danger. "A daughter doesn't 'inform' a father that she is planning to marry a stranger. A decent fellow seeks permission *before* approaching a man's daughter."

Blake swallowed, his Adam's apple bobbing. "I'm sorry, sir."

As if an angry fist clutched Sophie's throat, she felt it closing. She expelled a wheeze, and Blake shot a glance in her direction. Her father's tirade blended with the words her mother had uttered, causing an ache within her so painful, she didn't know if she could bear it. She was losing Blake, and they'd only just met. Was she doomed to live with her overprotective parents the rest of her life?

No!

She wouldn't.

She'd fight for Blake. He was worth it.

She opened her mouth to defend her fiancé, but the sound that came out more resembled the bleat of an ailing goat than her own voice. Humiliation blistered her cheeks.

Blake took a step backward, away from her, his handsome face drawn in a scowl.

"You see, Mr. Sheppard, the slightest excitement can set off one of my daughter's attacks." Father turned to Sophie's mother. "Ring for some coffee, if you will. It seems to help our Sophie's spells."

Spells. Attacks. What would Blake think?

Sophie held out her hand to him. Instead of taking it, he cast another worried glanced at her father. She sucked in another wheezy breath, struggling to stay clam in the midst of such turmoil. The room tilted. Sophie closed her eyes until the spinning stopped. All was silent for several long moments, except for her screeching breaths.

When her eyelids fluttered open, Blake met her gaze with an apology in his eyes. She knew in that moment she'd lost him.

He sighed. "Perhaps I have been too hasty. I sincerely apologize, Miss Davenport, but I must withdraw my offer of marriage. I hope you and your parents can forgive me for troubling you so."

Tears stung Sophie's eyes. She held out her hand again, hoping—praying—he'd take hold of it. "No, please—"

He skirted around her as if she were a leper, nodded to her mother, then snatched his hat off the hall tree and rushed out the door.

Sophie collapsed in the nearest chair and watched her dreams march down the sidewalk and out of sight. Tears blurred her vision as all hope of a future with Blake died. How could her parents be so cruel as to not even allow Blake to express his interest in her? How could they embarrass her so?

Her father walked to her and leaned over. "Try to calm down, Sophia."

She jumped up so fast, her head almost rammed his chin. He stumbled backward. The room swerved as she struggled for a decent breath. "How c-could you, Father?"

A wave of guilt washed over his face. "It's for your own good, you know."

She clutched the end table for support for a moment, then stumbled past him.

He took her arm. "Here, let me help you, precious."

"No! Please." She yanked away. "I can...take care of...myself. I'm a grown woman, and you both need to f-face that fact." She inhaled a decent breath and then charged on, by pure willpower. "I'm twenty-two and not your little girl anymore. Stop sheltering me...let me live my life. It's mine to live, not yours to stifle."

The flash of pain in her father's eyes only made her feel worse. Her shoes tapped across the entryway as she hurried back to her room—the former library, where her parents had relegated her, as if she were a pariah. She shut the door and collapsed on her bed, wanting to cry but knowing that doing so would only make breathing harder. She slammed her fist against her pillow. "Why, God? Why can't my parents let me grow up?"

She'd had such hopes. Thought that when her parents met Blake, they'd see what a quality man he was. But they hadn't even given him a chance. Could she have been mistaken about him? She smacked the bed, a futile outlet for her frustrations and disappointments. Blake hadn't bothered to fight for her one bit; he'd fled out the door the first chance he'd gotten. She'd tried to prepare him—to warn him about her episodes—but she must have failed.

She barked a cough that sounded like a seal she'd once seen at the menagerie in New York City's Central Park. Sophie pushed up into a sitting position, in order to breathe better. Blinking, she attempted to force away her tears, but new ones came like the spring rains that flooded the banks of the Mississippi River. Why had God cursed her with this hateful condition?

The door opened, and her mother entered, carrying a tray. Coffee. She despised the foul-tasting stuff, but it was thought to be helpful to people with asthma, as were garlic, whiskey, and a number of other nasty-tasting concoctions.

"How are you, dear?"

Sophie slid back down on the bed and turned to face the wall. She didn't want to talk—couldn't talk.

"Don't be that way. You need to drink this coffee."

She shook her head.

"Turn over, Sophia." Her mother's tone left no room for refusal.

She obeyed but didn't look at her mother. Instead, she started counting the thin, blue lines in the wallpaper—all nine hundred sixteen of them—as she'd done a thousand other times. Focusing on the task would keep her from weeping and from lashing out in anger.

Her mother blew out a loud breath, then held out the coffee cup. "Drink this."

Sophie shook her head. "Doesn't help." She sucked in a breath, thankful that this episode was a mild one and already beginning to pass, in spite of the day's traumatic events.

Her mother set the cup back on the tray with a loud clatter and stared across the room. "Whatever made you do such a thing? Don't you know that young man must have spent hard-earned money to come here? Taken time away from his job, assuming he has one? You gave him false hopes, Sophia, and now he's wasted a year of his life pursuing a woman he can never have."

Sophie clenched her eyes shut, losing count of the lines. Did her mother not care that her heart was breaking?

Guilt nibbled its way into her mind like a mouse in a sack of grain. She hadn't thought how things would affect Blake if they turned sour. She'd been so certain everything would work out in their favor. So certain that she could persuade her parents to let them marry, that she hadn't considered the negative side. But her mother was right about one thing. Blake had taken leave from his job as bookkeeper for a shoe factory in Chicago so that he could travel to St. Louis to meet her. He had wasted his time and money to come here.

And it was all her fault.

She sucked in a sob.

Her mother patted Sophie's shoulder. "There, there. Things will work out."

Yes, her father would go back to running his company. Her mother would attend her social clubs and church functions. Her sister would continue as a happily married wife and soon-to-be mother, while Sophie would continue her boring existence as a lonely spinster living in her parents' home.

The bed lifted on one side as her mother stood and quietly left the room. After the door closed, Sophie sat up and stared out the window, at the very place she'd first seen Blake. She hated feeling sorry for herself, and she normally didn't, but today, her emotions were raw.

She rose from the bed and crossed the room to her desk, where her Bible lay. She picked it up and hugged it to her chest as she gazed out at the garden. Bright yellow butterflies flitted from flower to flower. A big bumblebee disappeared in a clump of pink azaleas. The beauty of God's creation never failed to cheer her, even on the saddest of days.

Sophie blew out a loud sigh. "Forgive me, Lord, if I've been selfish." She hugged the Bible tighter. "But please, Father, make a way for me to break free from my parents. To prove to them—and to myself—that I can stand on my own. That I can take care of myself. And please, Lord, if it be Your will, send me a man someday who will love me for the woman I am and overlook my...flaws."

Tears pooled in her eyes, and her throat tightened. "But if it is Your will for me to remain in my parents' home and to never marry, help me to accept that and to be content."

If that was the Lord's will, He certainly had a monumental task ahead.

Chapter Two

Sophie untied her straw hat and placed it on a hook on the hall tree. Laboring in the garden for several hours had brightened her day, as it always did. Sweat had dampened her bodice, and far too much dirt had collected around the hem of her wrinkled dress. Tired but content, she pressed her fists to her back and stretched, working out the kinks. The pile of mail her father had laid on the entry table next to the hall tree beckoned her, and she thumbed through the envelopes. As usual, there was nothing addressed to her.

Sighing, she laid the mail back down and entered her bedroom. Three weeks had passed since the disappointing day of Blake's visit. He hadn't written—not that she had expected to hear from him again. Unfastening the buttons on her work dress, she pondered again whether she had made a mistake in not writing to him one last time.

Her soiled dress dropped to the floor, and she welcomed the coolness of one less layer of clothing. Perhaps she should rest, but she was sick of resting. *Rest. Sew. Rest. Read. Sleep.* Her life held such little purpose. If only her parents would allow her to do more.

Sophie glanced at the bed, then turned to her wardrobe, selected a pale blue day dress, and put it on. Though she didn't particularly care for sewing, it was preferable to spending another hour in bed. She walked to her sewing basket but then snatched a book from one of the walnut bookcases lining the wall instead. She'd read every book on those shelves, numerous times, and longed to ask her father to pick up several new novels from the library. But ever since Blake's visit, she hadn't wanted to ask him for anything. Her relationship with her parents had been strained by that event, and she didn't know how to repair it.

In the parlor, she took a seat near a window and opened the book. A light breeze drifted in, making the curtains dance and cooling her warm skin. The book lay in her lap, but she couldn't stir up enough interest to read it. She hated self-pity, but she'd been wallowing in a quagmire of it for weeks. Her mother had grown so tired of trying to cheer her up that she'd taken off for Boston to visit her own mother. Her father had pretty much avoided her after muttering a quick apology that dreadful day Blake had visited—an apology for possibly having been too harsh on the young man.

Possibly.

As if he wasn't certain he had been too harsh but felt he needed to say something to cheer her up.

It hadn't worked. She hadn't realized how much she'd been looking forward to a life with Blake until the dream had been lost. A heavy sigh blew past her lips.

How did one break free of quicksand? Free of the doldrums she'd been wallowing in? Gardening had worked only for the time she'd been outdoors and busy. Not even prayer had helped.

Footsteps pulled her gaze to the sidewalk in front of their house. Her father turned into the yard and strode up the walkway. Sophie glanced toward her door across the hallway but knew she couldn't get there before he came inside. Besides, she wouldn't succumb to such childish behavior as hiding, even if she wasn't in the mood to see him just then. She opened her book and stared at the pages.

Her father walked in, and she heard him rifle through the mail. Then he came into view, pausing at her bedroom door. He glanced down at a paper in his hand, then lifted his fist to knock.

Curious, Sophie straightened. "I'm here, Father."

He spun around, waited a moment, as if unsure of something, and then crossed the room in her direction.

She glanced at the paper curled in his hand. What could it be that would send him home from work in the middle of the day?

He glanced at his hand again, then pursed his lips and peered out the window before looking back at her. "I've received a telegram from Maude."

Sophie hadn't seen her father's older sister in years. Maude and her husband, Sam, had settled in eastern Kansas, in a small town called Windmill, and had returned to St. Louis only once, when Sophie was twelve. Uncle Sam passed shortly after the end of the war, but her aunt had stayed in Kansas. "How is she?"

Her father's lips twitched. He dropped down onto the end of the sofa, his brow creased. "Not good, I'm afraid."

"Oh?" Sophie laid the book aside. "I hope it isn't serious." She couldn't help wondering what type of medical care was available in a small frontier town.

"She fell and broke her arm. She's asking me to send someone to help her."

"Will you telegram Mother, then?" The trip from Boston to Kansas would be a long one, especially since her mother had arrived in Massachusetts only three days ago.

"No. I don't want to take Ellen away from her mother so soon. Your grandmother is getting older, and they need to spend time together."

Sophie thought of her pregnant sister, who'd normally be the next potential candidate to help her aunt. "Surely, you can't be thinking of asking Pam to go. Traveling wouldn't be good for a woman in her condition, and I doubt Henry would be agreeable to the idea, even if Pam was."

"I concur."

Sophie's eyes widened. That was the first thing they'd agreed on in weeks. She raked her mind. Who else could he be thinking of sending? One of their house servants? But none of them would want to leave their families. She couldn't imagine him going himself. "So, will you hire someone to help her, then?"

He stared at her for a moment. His blue eyes softened, and she saw his throat move as he swallowed. "Actually, I was thinking about sending you."

Sophie's heart lurched, and she sat up straighter. Had she heard correctly? "Me?" She hated the way the word croaked out.

He nodded. "I've thought long and hard about this, and I'm still not sure it's the right thing to do. I'll worry about you the whole time you're gone, but I think you deserve a chance to get away from here, even if you mother would disagree." He waved his hand in the air.

Sophie scooted to the edge of her seat. Maybe God had heard her pleas, after all. "I can do it, Father. And I promise to be careful and not overexert myself."

He gazed at her as if not wanting to let her go. "You know that your mother and I try to protect you so much only because we love you. There were so many times when you had asthma attacks when you were young that we thought we'd lose you." He blinked his glistening eyes. "I couldn't bear that."

Sophie moved to the sofa and took her father's hand. "I know. I'm sorry that I've been such a bear these past few weeks. Please forgive me."

"You were hurting. There's nothing to forgive."

Excitement bubbled up inside her. "When will I leave?"

"How soon can you be ready?"

She sucked in a breath as she quickly considered all she'd need to pack. "How long will I be gone?"

He shook his head. "I don't know." A tiny grin lifted his lips. "Once your mother hears what I've done, she'll probably hop the first train to Kansas, so it may be a short visit."

"I don't suppose you could wait a week or two to tell her, could you?" Sophie grinned and wiggled her brows.

"It would be a huge disappointment to your grandmother if she curtailed her visit so quickly."

"That's true. Grandmother does look forward to Mother's visits."

Her father pursed his lips. "She'll have my head."

Sophie clutched his arm. "It will all work out, Father. I trust you to do what you think best." She jumped up. There was so much to be done. "Wash day was yesterday, so Thelma will be doing the ironing today. I can be ready to go as early as tomorrow, if that will suit you."

"Let me check the train schedule. I'll get you a ticket for the first departure available." He stared at her for a long moment. "Are you certain you're up to this?"

She took his hands. "Oh, yes. I know I am."

"Promise me again you'll not push yourself too hard."

She nodded. "I promise."

"Let Maude's servants take care of the house, the cooking, and all the laborious tasks. You'll only be there to make things easier on my sister. Read to her. Help her if she can't reach something. That's all. Is that clear?"

"Yes, Father."

He nodded. "I'll contact the marshal and get the name of the local doctor, so I can make sure he knows how to treat a person with asthma. He should be made aware of your condition."

Sophie winced. Even though she wanted to object, she kept quiet, not wanting to say or do anything that might make him change his mind. She bounced on her toes, then forced herself to stand demurely, even though she longed to spin in a circle and shout to the world that she was finally leaving home. She was getting the opportunity to prove she was capable of being on her own.

God had truly answered her prayer in a most unexpected manner.

⌒

Late April 1873 · Windmill, Kansas

"Uncle Josh!" Josh's nine-year-old niece, Corrie, ran into the parlor as he lowered the window. "The train is coming, and Toby is still in the outhouse. We're gonna miss it!" Tears filled her eyes. "We won't get to see Pa if we miss the train."

He squeezed her shoulder. "We won't miss it, sweet thing. Wait here. I'll get your brother." He strode through the back door of the small house he rented in Windmill just as his nephew burst out of the privy. The door flew back and banged against the structure's exterior with a loud clatter.

"Done!" Toby's brown eyes lit with excitement. "I heard the train."

"Wash your hands while I make sure the rest of the windows are closed. Then we need to hop on down to the depot. And don't get all muddy."

The boy nodded and ran to the water pump while Josh headed back inside. He grabbed the pitcher of milk off the table, dumped the contents out the back door, and set it on the counter. He closed the window, his excitement building at the thought of being home again. The spring day was perfect for a ride on his horse. He glanced around the tiny kitchen. All was in order.

Though he enjoyed working in the small town, going home to Harpers' Stage Stop was always special. His stomach grumbled, reminding him of his ma's delicious cooking—cooking he would have the joy of savoring all weekend.

A sharp tug pulled his jacket catawampus. He straightened it and glanced down. Corrie stared up with stern blue eyes. "Stop your lollygaggin', Uncle Josh. We're gonna miss the train."

He grinned and tweaked her nose. "All right. Let's go."

"Toby!" The girl spun toward the back door and bent halfway over, as if the stance strengthened her yell. "We're leavin'! Better come or get left behind."

When Toby didn't respond to his sister's taunt, Josh marched over to the back door and looked for him. Where was that boy?

The front door banged open. "Race you to the depot."

"Hey! No fair cheatin'." Corrie whirled around, nearly knocking Josh down in her efforts to get past him.

Chuckling, he closed the back door, then strode through the house and grabbed the satchel waiting on the settee. As he walked toward the depot, his gaze took in the small town. In the square, the blades of the windmill for which the town was named rotated lazily. For the most part, the town square was deserted, but tomorrow, farmers and ranchers would fill the grassy area, hawking their produce and livestock. Josh enjoyed shopping there for fresh fruits and vegetables on the weekends he didn't return home.

A loud blast of steam signaled the train was nearing the station. He quickened his steps, even though he had plenty of time. He nodded at a couple of people he recognized as customers from the bank—Mr. Amsted and Mr. Blair, if he was remembering right. Both men were fairly new to Windmill. Mrs. Purdy, the wife of the mercantile owner, was sweeping the boardwalk in front of the store. He pinched the brim of his hat, smiling at her. "Morning, Mrs. Purdy."

"And a pleasant morning it is, Mr. Harper." The plump woman smiled. "You and the children have a safe trip home. They raced by here half a minute ago."

Josh jogged up the depot steps and searched for his niece and nephew. Corrie stood in line at the ticket window, frantically motioning for him to hurry. Toby stood at the very edge of the platform, leaning forward, watching the train chug toward him. Josh's heart jolted. He loped across the platform, dodging a trio of men, and grabbed the boy by his shirt collar, pulling him back just as the engine passed. "Toby, how many times have I told you not to do that?"

"I was countin' the whistles."

Josh shook his head. What did that have to do with anything? He dearly loved Toby and Corrie, but sometimes he wondered if they wouldn't be better off—safer—living at home with their father, instead of staying in town with him so they could attend school. He knelt and took Toby by the shoulders. "That's a very dangerous thing you just did."

Toby's brown eyes veered away from Josh's, toward the hissing train. The boy lifted his hand, as if he meant to touch the locomotive. Josh hauled him into his arms. "Toby. Stop being so foolish. You can get hurt—bad—doing things like that." Aaron had already lost his wife, Della. Josh didn't think his older brother would survive if something happened to one of his children.

The boy finally ducked his head. "Sorry, Uncle Josh."

The brakes screeched, and the train shuddered to a stop with a loud whoosh. Josh set Toby down but kept a firm hold on his hand.

"Windmill, Kansas!" The conductor's voice echoed out an open window, rising a notch in volume with each syllable he hollered. He opened the door, lowered the steps, and moved back to allow the passengers to disembark.

Tugging Toby by the hand, Josh hurried over to Corrie, who was next in the ticket line. The woman in front of him left, and he stepped forward.

"Heading home again?" The ticket clerk waited for his nod, then stamped three tickets, as he'd done on a dozen other Friday afternoons.

"Yep. Can't hardly wait to eat Ma's cooking." Josh paid the minuscule fee for the short trip to Harpers' Depot, where his father or one of his brothers—most likely Aaron—would be waiting with a wagon. "Thanks, Charlie."

As he stood alongside the train, waiting for the passengers to finish exiting so he could board, a young lady who looked only four or five years older than Corrie stepped off the train, a lacy handkerchief pressed tight against her nose and mouth. She held an expensive-looking satchel, and her dress, though wrinkled from travel, shouted quality and seemed far too mature for her slender, youthful frame. Her gaze darted to the left, then jerked in the other direction, where several dozen head of cattle bellowed as they were loaded onto a freight car. Her eyes widened. So much dust had stirred up that you'd think a windstorm had blown through. Josh imagined that the scene surprised those who were unfamiliar with the smell and dust involved in loading cattle. He watched the train, waiting for the girl's parents to debark, but no one followed her. It appeared she was traveling alone. He glanced at Corrie, who was turning down Toby's shirt collar. Josh couldn't imagine allowing her to take a trip by herself, even if the train had a first-class ladies' car.

Josh looked back at the young traveler. She stood, swaying, in front of the doorway, barely off the train, blocking the exit. Her face paled, and she struggled to breathe. The other passengers had to turn sideways in order to squeeze past her. She received scowls from two thin men, but a heavy-set man lumbering down the steps didn't act as if he'd stop.

"Stay here. Both of you." Josh eyed his niece and nephew, then hurried forward and reached for the girl, just as she stumbled.

"Here, allow me to assist you, miss." He hoped his tone was gentle enough to not frighten her.

Her gaze jerked up to meet his, and he stared into the most amazing pair of dark brown eyes he'd ever seen. She lowered the handkerchief and wheezed out something, but with the loud ruckus of the bawling cattle, he couldn't make out what she said. Seeing her face uncovered, he realized that her features weren't those of an adolescent but rather a lovely woman's. He guided her to a bench and lowered her onto it. She laid her head back against the depot wall, and her chest lifted in short jerks as she fought for breath. Josh hated to leave her alone. He searched the platform for someone who could help her, but the passengers who'd just arrived were already descending the depot steps. He patted her shoulder, then jogged to the ticket window. "Hey, Charlie. There's a woman out here who needs help. Can you fetch the doc?"

He glanced back at the woman. She held one hand against her throat and shook her head. "No doctor," she mouthed. Then she closed her eyes and leaned her head back again.

"Sure thang, Mr. Harper," Charlie said. "The train's about to pull out, so I'm done here." The thin man headed for his office door.

Josh glanced at the train. The few passengers had boarded, the last of the cattle had been loaded, and Corrie and Toby stood waiting. But what about the woman? He didn't want to leave her as she was, but he couldn't disappoint his whole family. Surely, Charlie would be back with the doctor any minute.

Josh hurried back to the woman's side. "How are you feeling?"

"Fine," she croaked out. "Go."

"All aboard!" the conductor shouted.

"C'mon!" Corrie waved her hand like a flag flapping in a heavy breeze.

Josh wavered. The gentleman in him hated leaving a woman in distress, but the children needed to go home and see their father.

Living in town had been a hard adjustment for the youngsters, who'd been raised on a ranch.

The woman sat up and lowered her handkerchief. Eyes as dark as the night sky gazed up at him. Her skin was as pale as Corrie's porcelain doll, but he had no way of knowing if that was her natural color. She swatted her hand in the direction of the train. "I'm doing better. You need to go."

A porter lugged a large trunk across the platform. "This belong to you, miss?"

She nodded and stood. "I'd like to leave it here"—she took a slow, deep breath, her hand splayed across her chest—"until…I can arrange…transport."

She did seem better now, and the porter was there.

"You coming, Mr. Harper?" the conductor called.

"Hurry." Corrie bounced on her toes, hand still waving.

Something rooted him where he was. The woman—he'd guess her age to be around twenty, if he discounted her size—offered him the tiniest of smiles. "Your children are waiting, sir."

He nodded and turned to the porter. "You'll stay with her until the doctor comes?"

"I don't need a doctor," she insisted. "I just wasn't prepared for all the dust."

Josh kept his gaze on the porter, in spite of her objection. The man nodded. Josh pulled a coin from his pocket and flipped it to him. "See that she gets to her destination." He tipped his hat to the woman. "I do hope you fare better, ma'am, but if you have problems with dust, Kansas is not the place to come."

The train's whistle screeched, making the woman jump. Josh jogged toward the door and lifted Corrie aboard. Toby jumped up the steps before Josh could snag him. He took a final peek at the woman, then stepped aboard.

As the train shuddered and crept forward, Josh ushered the children to a seat, then glanced out the grimy window. The woman pulled something from her handbag, dropped it into the porter's hand, and walked toward the depot steps. Josh's body went rigid. Where was she going? Didn't she have the sense to wait for the doctor? She'd nearly fainted, for heaven's sake.

He fell back against the seat, receiving an odd glance from Corrie. Toby sat next to the window, drawing pictures with his finger in the scum on the glass. Josh blew out a heavy sigh. It was no business of his if the woman was too stubborn to accept help. He closed his eyes, but even with them shut, a pair of beguiling coffee-brown eyes peered back.

Chapter Three

Sophie walked down the depot steps, taking her first glimpse of the small town. She hadn't expected her aunt to live somewhere so quaint. With its all-dirt streets and mostly faded wooden buildings, Windmill resembled a town in a dime novel she'd once read. The tallest structure in town, evidently the very thing it was named for, was a windmill similar to the ones she imagined littered the fields of Holland. A cylindrical wooden base, painted white, rose straight up two stories, then tapered to a red cone-shaped roof. The long arms spun lazily on the light breeze, adding charm to the rugged town. Two-thirds of the way up, a fence railing encircled the structure, and if she wasn't mistaken, a person could walk around the second story.

She inhaled a precious breath of oxygen, thankful her wheezing had stopped and the fierce grip on her chest had lessened. That had been a close call. She wouldn't be much help to her aunt if she spent her first few days in bed because of a severe asthma attack. She thought of the concerned eyes of the man who had helped her—a rather handsome man, with a finer cut of clothing than was worn by most of the men she'd seen so far. His turmoil over leaving her had been evident in the deep blue depths of his gaze, but he'd made the right decision. She wouldn't keep him and his children from their journey. Why had his wife not been traveling with them? Was he perhaps a widower?

Sophie shook her head. No matter. As nice as he'd been, she didn't want another man hovering over her, as her father always did. This was her chance to experience freedom. To make her own choices for a change.

On the far side of the street, two men hurried down the boardwalk in her direction. One carried a leather bag—the doctor, she was certain. She didn't want to start out with the man thinking her a weak woman in need of care—or, worse, writing to her father, if he was the same physician Father had contacted. She crossed the street on the opposite side from the men and strolled down the boardwalk. Since the ticket clerk hadn't seen her, she hoped he wouldn't realize she was the woman he sought. Thank goodness she hadn't fainted. That would have been a horrible way to start her adventure.

She shifted her satchel to her other hand and entered a small mercantile. The woman behind the counter was busy with another customer. Once Sophie's eyes adjusted to the dim lighting, she surveyed the shelves. The store stocked basic supplies but offered precious few specialty items, such as the hand cream she preferred or the pretty, ready-made dresses that many stores in St. Louis offered. Maybe she'd be lucky enough to find a dressmaker in town, if she needed something new.

"Can I help you with anything, ma'am?" The store clerk, a heavy-set woman with gray hair and kind light blue eyes surrounded by round gold frames, ambled toward Sophie. "I'm Myrtle Purdy. My husband, Arlis, an' I own this mercantile."

"A pleasure to meet you, Mrs. Purdy. My name is Sophie Davenport. I actually don't need anything today, but I'm sure I will some other time."

"You plannin' on settlin' in Windmill?" The woman straightened some cans on the shelf beside her, curiosity sparking in her gaze.

"For a short while, at least." Sophie was afraid to get her hopes up that she'd be here for long. Once Mother learned that Father had allowed her to travel to Kansas with no escort, other than a kind matron they'd met at the depot—who'd gotten off several stops ago—she'd be on the warpath.

"Forgive me for snooping, but is there a Mr. Davenport?" Though the woman apologized for the intrusive question, there was no regret in her curious gaze.

"No, ma'am. I'm not married." Sophie's cheeks warmed as she remembered how close she had come to being Mrs. Blake Sheppard—before her hopes had been crushed and stomped into the carpet—and her mood darkened. "I was wondering if you could direct me to Maude Archer's house."

"Oh, do you know Miss Maudie?" The woman pursed her lips and shook her head. "It's a pity what that poor woman has gone through just to survive since her husband died."

Sophie was beginning to think Mrs. Purdy must be the town gossip. Still, her heart clenched at the mention of her aunt's troubles. Maude hadn't mentioned enduring any hardships in her letters, other than her recent accident. Sophie longed to ask the woman what she was referring to, but she didn't want to delay her arrival at her aunt's. She would know soon enough. "Is her home far from here?"

Mrs. Purdy chuckled. "No, dear. Right down the street, second house past the bank."

Sophie smiled. "Thank you. I imagine I will be seeing you again soon."

Mrs. Purdy nodded. "I hope so. Stop in any time, and bring Miss Maudie, if she's feelin' well enough and can get away from her charges."

Sophie nodded and picked up her bag, her mind taking off on another tangent. What did the woman mean by "her charges"? Stifling her curiosity for the moment, she waved good-bye and started down the boardwalk. Across the street, right in the middle of the big town square, the windmill spun lazily in the light breeze. Grass spread across the square, divided into sections by wagon tracks. How odd. Why would people drive across the grass when the square was surrounded on all sides by dirt streets?

Another question with no answer. More businesses encircled the town square, but as far as she could tell, the town had only four streets lined with one- and two-story buildings, mostly made of wood or stone. She could see a doctor's office, a land office, two saloons, and other places of business with signs too small to read from across the street. She continued on, passing a boardinghouse and one of the smallest banks she'd ever seen. A church steeple rose up at the end of the street, but the windmill still boasted the honor of being the town's tallest structure.

A horse-drawn wagon was parked across the street, with two men standing behind it, talking. Several horses, heads hanging, were tied at various hitching posts along Main Street. Though the small town was rugged, it was also quiet, so unlike the noisy thoroughfares of St. Louis. The peacefulness of the quaint prairie town called to her, as if welcoming her to stay awhile.

Her aunt's house was another issue. Stopping out front, she took a moment to catch her breath and pat her hair. The wood on her aunt's front door and the house's façade was weathered and splintered, the whitewash barely showing in a few places. Her father would not be pleased with the condition of the home, but there was nothing Sophie could do about that. Loud thumps and a squeal sounded on the other side of the door, startling her. Clutching her satchel tighter, she cocked her head and listened.

"No! Stop!"

Sophie gasped. Someone in her aunt's house was in distress. She glanced down the street, trying to remember if she'd seen a police department. The sound of a scuffle drew her attention back to the house.

"No-o-o. That's mine."

A child's voice? Tossing aside proper protocol, she threw open the front door and stepped inside. A blond boy bounced on her aunt's sofa, holding a worn cloth doll high in the air. A dark-haired girl stood on the floor in front of the sofa, jumping up and down, trying to rescue the doll.

The boy stopped his bouncing and gawked at Sophie. "Hey, you can't just barge in here."

Sophie's bravery shriveled. What if she'd gotten the wrong house? "Does Maude Archer live here?"

The boy shook his head. "Huh-uh."

"Yes, she does." The girl pivoted, her unkempt braids flying around, one smacking her chest, the other whacking her back. "That's Miss Maudie's real name."

"If this is Maude's house, what are you two doing here?"

The boy jumped off the couch and tossed the doll at the girl. "We live here. Who are you?"

Sophie blinked. Why would there be children living in Maude's home, especially when her aunt was injured enough to ask for help? "What do you mean, you live here?"

The girl cradled her doll as a mother would her baby. "We live here sometimes, so we can go to school. Then we go back home when the school term is over."

Sophie wanted to ask more, but she would hold those questions for her aunt. The boy marched up to her, hands on his thin hips. "How come you moseyed on in without knockin'?"

"I...um...." Sophie's cheeks warmed. "I thought someone in here needed help."

The boy laughed and slapped one knee. Though he couldn't be more than ten years old and was just a few inches shorter than she, he had an older manner about him. "Help? A li'l thang like you?"

Sophie straightened her spine. "You might be surprised. Now, would you please tell Maude that her niece has arrived?"

"Oh, *you're* the relation she sent fer." He crossed his arms. "We ain't got no need of your help, so you can go back where you came from."

Sophie sucked in a gasp at his rudeness and despicable grammar. "Are you Aunt Maude's spokesman?"

The girl giggled. "Nah, he's just bossy."

He scowled over his shoulder at the girl. While he was distracted, Sophie stepped further into the room and closed the door. The boy spun back, turning his frown on her.

"I'll tell Maude that you're here." The girl hurried past him, then clomped up the stairs dividing the parlor from the dining room.

"So, you're stayin'?" The boy frowned and crossed his skinny arms.

Sophie nodded, trying to understand why he would resent her presence.

"Sure hope you can cook." He trudged down the hall and out the back door, slamming it so hard, the windows rattled at the front of the house.

Sophie lifted her hand to her nose and turned into the parlor. The house smelled musty, the air tinged with the pungent odor of spoiled food. She surveyed the room. Along one wall sat a sagging sofa upholstered with fabric so thin, the stuffing poked out. A cane-back rocker, with so few strands on its seat and back that it reminded her of a balding man with only a few sprigs of hair, battled a faded chair for ugliest piece of furniture in the room. Between the chairs sat a drum table with a hurricane lantern sitting on it, globe askew. Sophie straightened it and then walked out of the parlor to see who was coming down the stairs. An older girl, probably in her early adolescent years, walked into the parlor, appraising her. Sophie tried not to squirm under her gaze, which was more curious than stern.

"Are you really Miss Maudie's niece?"

Sophie nodded and smiled, hoping to ease the girl's concerns. "I am. My name is Sophie Davenport, and Maude is my father's sister. He sent me here to assist her."

The girl's thin lips quirked to one side, as if she, too, questioned Sophie's ability to assist. "I'm Hazel."

"Do you live here?"

She nodded. "Miss Maudie said to show you up to her room."

Sophie followed Hazel up the stairs and down the hall, which opened to a small sitting area. Past that, they turned into a bedroom. The drapes were drawn, a narrow space between them allowing a smidgeon of light into the dim room. Maude lay on a double bed, her broken arm in plaster and resting on a pillow. A chair sat next to the bed, facing the headboard, as if someone used it often to sit with her.

"Is that really you, Sophia?" Maude stretched a thin, white hand toward her.

Sophie smiled and stepped past Hazel, who leaned against the door frame, as if afraid to venture into the room. "Yes, it's me, Aunt Maude." She set her satchel on the chair and took her aunt's cold hand. Her heart lurched at the sight of how thin and pale the woman was. She'd only broken her arm, so why did she look as if she'd endured a long, debilitating disease?

Maude squeezed her hand. "You've matured so much since I last saw you, dear."

Matured. Not grown. The odd comment wasn't lost on Sophie. Well, she hadn't really grown much. At just five foot one, she was the shortest in her family and among her few friends. Even Hazel, who had to be ten years younger, was a good inch taller than she.

"I'm so glad you've come. I thought your father would send your mother—" Harsh, rattling coughs halted Maude's speech for a moment. She grabbed a handkerchief and wiped her mouth. "If not Ellen," she continued, in a voice hoarser than before, "then your sister."

Of course, her aunt hadn't expected to see *her.* Was she disappointed? Sophie shifted her feet and tugged her hand back. She wasn't used to touching people, especially sick ones. Her parents had kept her so isolated that she'd never been comfortable being familiar with anyone besides her immediate family. She couldn't help wondering if she would have been ill at ease holding Blake's hand. Ah, well. She'd never know now.

Suddenly, it dawned on her that, since arriving at Aunt Maude's home, she hadn't seen a single adult other than her aunt. Where were the servants? And what had that boy meant about hoping she could cook? Apprehension clawed at her chest, and her throat tightened. She walked over to the window, opened it more, and stuck her head out, trying to get her breathing under control. What had she walked into? The situation was far more dire than she had expected.

She gazed past the buildings at the open prairie beyond. One could see so far here, with no tall buildings blocking the view. Her eyes followed the dirt road out of town as it wound through nothing but grass. On the horizon sat a few, small trees, but the land looked so desolate—so lonely. She swallowed hard.

Was she up to the task of caring for her aunt and three children?

Was this rugged land a place where she could find her independence?

Or would she be better off catching the next train back to St. Louis?

No.

She'd begged her father to give her a chance to prove she could live without continuous hovering and coddling. She could do this. Had to do it.

She ventured back to her aunt's bedside. Her mounting questions needed answers before she would know how to formulate a plan for success. "Aunt Maude, why are there three children living with you?"

Her aunt opened her eyes and smiled. "Not three, dear. Five."

~~~

"Lookie! There's Pa!" Corrie stood at the window of the slowing train, bouncing on her tiptoes and waving.

"I see him too." Toby rose to his knees on the bench beside her and pounded on the window.

Josh patted his nephew's hand. "Shh. Just wave, so we don't disturb the other passengers."

The train shimmied and bumped to a stop with a loud whoosh, and the children rushed to the door. Chuckling, Josh grabbed his satchel and followed them. He ushered them out of the way so that the conductor could open the door and lower the steps, and then they all walked out into the bright morning sunlight.

His brother Aaron scooped up his children, one in each arm, in spite of their size, and hugged them. The old snake of jealousy that Josh had battled much of his life raised its ugly head. He loved his brothers, but he wished he was taller and broader, like Aaron and Ethan. But instead, he'd had the misfortune to take after a shorter, less brawny ancestor.

Aaron set the kids down and strode forward, a huge smile on his face. He enveloped Josh in a bear hug, slapping his shoulders and effectively cutting off the snake's head. "How's life in town?"

Josh let the tension release from his shoulders. "The same. Not too busy most days, swamped on others."

Aaron took the satchel from Josh's hand. "Same here, although we're usually rushing around to get everything done. We miss having you here to help."

At least the money he earned had helped see his family through the transition time. He had to admit, if only to himself, he liked working in town—dressing up to go to work in an office instead of laboring in the sun, sweating, and coated in dust by the end of the day. He suspected that his family would have preferred him staying at the ranch, but then, who would the children live with during the week?

Corrie grabbed Aaron's hand and tugged him toward the buggy. "C'mon, Pa. I want to see Grandma."

"And I want some cookies." Toby jumped off the side of the small platform.

Aaron chuckled. "Grandma will want you to eat the lunch she made first."

Josh jogged down the platform steps of the first watering stop west of Windmill. There was no depot here, just a water tank with a small windmill that pumped water from the nearby pond. A chain dangling down the side of the tank bounced in the breeze, clanking against it. The boiler man had already tugged the spigot arm over the water tender. He jerked the chain to begin filling the train's reservoir.

Climbing into the buggy, Josh gazed out across the grassy plains his family owned, marveling at how much things had changed at Harpers' Stage Stop since the train had reached this part of Kansas. His family still had a few stage lines that stopped for passengers and crews to enjoy a meal or spend the night at their home, but much of the stage business had dwindled because of the availability of train service. He was proud of how his family had adapted, investing in cattle in hopes of competing with Texans who drove their herds across Indian Territory to the cattle towns like Abilene.

Aaron nudged his shoulder. "How come you're so quiet? Thinking about a woman?" He chuckled.

Josh shook his head, but in that second, his thoughts zipped back to the young woman at the depot. Had she gotten the help she needed? Why had she been traveling alone, especially if she was given to fits like the one he'd witnessed? "I was just thinking of all the changes that have gone on around here." *And a certain woman.* "Anything new happening?"

"No, not really." Aaron guided the wagon along the trail. He glanced over his shoulder at his children, sitting at the back of the wagon, legs dangling. A proud, fatherly smile pulled at the corners of his mouth. He turned forward again and leaned closer to Josh. "Any problems with those rascals?"

"No, not really," he echoed his brother's response. "Toby is Toby. He still gets in trouble at school sometimes, but nothing you wouldn't expect from a boy his age with his energy."

"Don't be afraid to discipline him if it's warranted."

Josh winced. He hated spanking his nephew. Corrie rarely needed much more than a stern stare, but Toby could be a handful, and Josh knew he ought to keep a tighter rein on the energetic boy. But he would rather sit him down and help him see the error of his ways than spank him.

"I know you, Josh. You're a mercy person. You're all about forgiving, but sometimes tough discipline is needed. Remember how Ma used to wallop Ethan and me? We turned out pretty good."

"I have to admit to taking some joy in seeing you two getting into trouble so much." Josh grinned.

"Well, we can't all be bookworms like you."

He had missed the good-natured sparring between brothers. He didn't regret his choice to move to town and work at his uncle's bank, but he still missed the close camaraderie of his family, not to mention his ma's cooking. His stomach grumbled at the thought.

Before the wagon pulled into the yard, the back door of the main house flew open, and his ma and sister-in-law, Sarah, rushed out. Pa exited the barn, waving.

"Grandma!" Corrie stood in the back of the wagon, waving.

"Sit down before you fall," Aaron said.

Josh heard a thump and turned in the seat. Toby had hopped off the back of the wagon and landed facedown on the ground. The boy jumped up, dusted off his hands, then raced into his grandma's arms as the wagon slowed to a stop.

Aaron shook his head and rolled his eyes at Josh. "I don't know what keeps that kid from getting broken bones all the time, but I'm grateful that the good Lord keeps watch over him."

"You and me both." Josh hopped down and rounded the horses, eager to give his ma a hug.

After embracing her grandson, she released him and patted his head. "Let me greet my son."

Toby stepped aside and stopped right in front of Sarah, his face level with her round belly. "Holy cow! You sure been eating a lot, Aunt Sarah."

Sarah's lightly tanned cheeks grew a rosy red. Josh chuckled and glanced at Aaron, taking delight in his brother's embarrassment. "You get to explain that, Brother."

Aaron's throat moved as he swallowed. "I was hoping not to have that talk for another ten years or so."

"What talk?" Toby galloped around the family in a circle.

Josh shook his head as his family snickered. It felt good to be home again.

Chapter Four

Five children?" Sophie pulled the chair closer to the bed and sat.

Aunt Maude nodded. "Yes, but not all the time. The others are usually here after school until their uncle gets off work. Then he comes and collects them. Quite adorable children, those two, but the boy can be a handful."

"Where are they now?"

"Every other weekend, they go home to visit their father."

Sophie frowned, trying to understand. "Why do they live with their uncle if they have a father?"

"So they—" Maude erupted in another round of coughs that jerked her thin body. Sophie snatched a handkerchief from a nightstand by the bed and handed it to her aunt. Maude dabbed her watery eyes, then wiped her mouth and cleared her throat. "So they can attend school."

Sophie helped her take a drink from the glass of water on the nightstand. "Don't they have a school where their father lives?" She knew young ladies were often sent away to finishing schools, but those were usually back East, not on the prairie.

"No. There isn't a school where they live. That's why I keep the children." Maude fell back against the pillow.

Sophie looked around the dark room, wondering what she should do—stay by her aunt's side, as her father had instructed her, or see what the children were doing? And why, of all people, was her ailing aunt boarding children? Surely there were others who could do that task.

Maude opened her eyes. "Make sure the children go to school."

Sophie blinked. Did her aunt not know what time it was? "It's Friday afternoon, Aunt Maude. Classes should be over by now, shouldn't they?"

"Oh, that's right…." Her aunt's head lobbed to one side.

"She does that sometimes—falls right asleep when she's talkin'."

Sophie turned in the chair to look at Hazel, still standing in the doorway. The thin girl's light brown hair hung limply around her shoulders, and her sad brown eyes stared at the bed. "She just gets worse and worse. I dread goin' to school and leavin' her all day." She gave Sophie a weak smile. "It's good that you've come to help."

Sophie stood and tiptoed from the room, joining Hazel near the landing at the top of the stairs. "I thought my aunt was only suffering from a broken arm."

Hazel shrugged and stared at the floor. "It was rainin' that day she fell. She went out to fetch some firewood while we was at school, and no one found her till we got home. I reckon she took sick from bein' wet and cold."

"How long was she outside before someone found her?"

Hazel lifted one shoulder again. "Don't rightly know. I couldn't find her when we got home from school, so I went out to check the privy and found her at the bottom of the steps. She must have slipped." The girl kicked the stair rail. "It was Mikey's fault. He was supposed to bring in the firewood before school, but that boy don't do half of what he's told."

Sophie glanced over the railing to the entryway. Where had Mikey gone? And what about the other girl? What was her name?

"Amanda's movin' her stuff so you can have her bed. There's two of 'em in our room. Her and me can share."

Sophie smiled, despite her apprehension at not having a room to herself. She hadn't shared a room since she was a young girl. "Thank you. That's kind of you."

Hazel quietly walked back down the hall and paused in the doorway of the room across from Aunt Maude's. She pointed away from the stairs. "Mikey stays in that other room, just past Miss Maudie's."

They entered the girls' room. Despite the old furniture and faded wallpaper, it had charm. A chiffonier with a faded mirror that needed to be resilvered rose up on the wall opposite the two beds, and a bench with a padded cushion under a window would make a nice place to read—if she had any time for that. Amanda hung a dress on a peg, then turned and stared with wide blue eyes.

There was no room for her trunk. How was she going to manage that?

"You can have the wardrobe," Hazel said. "We don't neither one have that many dresses." She opened the doors, unleashing a stale odor, and took a single dress off a hanger and hung it on a peg next to Amanda's dress. "I'll fetch your satchel from Miss Maudie's room."

Sophie didn't know what to say to Amanda, since she'd rarely been around children. Thankfully, Hazel returned right away with her bag.

"You're pretty, but you ain't very big."

"Amanda! Hush now."

The younger girl's gaze darted to Hazel. "Why? What did I say?"

Hazel leaned down and whispered in her ear, "You said she was short."

Biting back a chuckle, Sophie smiled, hoping to reassure both girls. She walked to the bed and opened her satchel. "Well, it is true."

"Maybe so, but it ain't polite to point it out like that."

She pulled out her nightgown, unrolled the garment that she'd used to cushion her hand mirror, and laid them all on the bed.

The girls gasped. Amanda strode forward, reaching out to touch the gold scrolling that edged the back of the mirror, encircling a lovely needlework pattern of purple, lavender, and yellow pansies.

"It's so pretty."

Hazel grabbed Amanda's arm and tugged it back. "Don't touch the lady's things."

Sophie didn't want to correct Hazel, but she also didn't want to alienate Amanda. "I really don't mind, as long as you're careful."

Hazel's gaze collided with hers, as if checking to see if she was speaking truthfully. Sophie smiled and held out the mirror. "Go ahead. Take it."

The older girl reached out her hand, a bit shakier than Sophie was comfortable with, but she passed the mirror to her.

"Ma has one, but it ain't this purty." Hazel ran her finger over the gold scrolling.

Amanda frowned. "Pa sold my ma's mirror after she passed. Wish he would'a let me keep it."

Sophie's heart ached to realize that the girl had already lost her mother. "I'm sorry to learn that your mother is gone."

Shrugging, Amanda walked over to the bench seat and flopped down, staring out the open window. "It was a long time ago. I wish I didn't have to leave Pa just so I can go to school."

Sophie couldn't help wondering how long was "a long time" to a child so young. She wasn't sure how to respond to Amanda, so she concentrated on unpacking. She set the empty satchel and a dirty dress on the bottom shelf, shut the door, and glanced around the room. Both beds were made but held far too many wrinkles. Maybe the girls had been sitting on them.

A loud bang downstairs made Sophie jump. "What was that?"

"Probably just Mikey. Him and Toby are always slammin' the doors." Hazel lovingly laid the mirror on the small table next to Sophie's bed. "Boys are so noisy. I have two older brothers—they don't go to school, 'cause Pa needs them to help on the farm—who are just as loud."

Clomping up the stairs heralded Mikey's return. He stopped in the doorway, gawking. "You still here? How come you ain't started cookin' yet?"

"Mikey!" Hazel shook her head, hands on her hips. "Don't be so rude."

The boy wilted at the older girl's scolding, which Sophie found intriguing. "Well, I'm hungry."

"You're always hungry."

"So?"

"Let me go downstairs and see what I can find to fix for supper." Sophie moved toward the doorway, wondering what the children would say if they knew she'd never cooked anything. Meal preparation wasn't something she'd had to think about at home, because they had servants, including a cook, and her mother had always wanted her to stay away from flour dust, fearing it would set off an attack. Now she realized what a detriment it was to not know how to make even a simple meal.

In the kitchen, she looked about the small space with dismay. Dirty dishes and empty jars littered the countertops and spilled over onto the table, and the room had a sour smell to it. She opened the back door to usher in some fresh air. As she surveyed the backyard, her anxiety rose at the sight of the privy tilting a bit to the right. Birds flitted about a small tree with bright green leaves at the back of the yard, and a handful of white and yellow wildflowers lifted their faces to the sun. Behind the house was an alley and, past that, another row of houses. With the open prairie nearby, it seemed odd to her that that the houses would be situated so close to one another. It was like that back home, in St. Louis.

Crossing her arms, she turned back to face the mess. Was she really up to the task?

She had to be. Her aunt and the children were counting on her. But she didn't have to tackle this mess alone, especially when none of it was her doing. Back in the parlor, she found the girls sitting on the sofa, looking at advertisements for corsets in a worn newspaper. Sophie smiled. "Aren't you two a bit young for those?"

The paper snapped shut, and two pairs of surprised eyes gazed back. The girls' cheeks turned bright red.

"We…uh…was just lookin'," Hazel said.

"Trust me, you don't want to have to wear one of those confining contraptions any sooner than you have to."

"Do you wear one?"

"Amanda!" Hazel stiffened. "You don't ask ladies questions like that."

Amanda ducked her head and glanced sheepishly up at Sophie. "How're you s'posed to find out if'n you don't ask?"

"You just don't find out, if'n you have to ask a rude question." Hazel huffed a loud breath, as if explaining to Amanda was a great burden.

"There are some questions that are better not asked, Amanda. But, in this case, I don't mind answering. I do wear a corset." She wouldn't say that it was specially designed to open in the front, so it could be removed quickly when she had an episode. "I wouldn't mind showing it to you one of these days, if you're still curious about it."

Amanda beamed at her, then turned a haughty look on Hazel. "See? She don't mind."

Sophie thought it best to change the subject. "Where did Mikey get off to?"

"He went out on the porch." Hazel nudged her chin toward the front door.

Sophie peeked at the open window as she crossed the room and reached for the door. Had the boy been listening to their talk of corsets? She halfway wished that her aunt had taken in only girls. At least she knew what to expect from them, having grown up with a sister. But what did one do with boys?

Mikey stood in one corner of the porch, holding up a twig and angling it toward a spider sitting in its web. Sophie's eyes widened. What did the boy plan to do with such a creature?

No good, of that she was certain. "Mikey!"

He jumped, flinging the stick into the yard, and spun around, ears red. "I was…uh…just riddin' the porch o' spiders."

The ornery smile he flashed did little to convince Sophie he told the truth. More likely, he was collecting the critter so he could scare the girls—or her. She swallowed the lump in her throat. "I need you to draw some water and bring it into the house."

His gaze narrowed. "Why?"

Sophie lifted her brows in the same manner her father did when he wasn't pleased with her questioning him. "Because the dishes need to be washed."

Mikey relaxed a smidgeon. "I ain't washin' no dishes. That's women's work."

"Hmm." Sophie tapped her lips, scrambling for a response. "Did you eat from any of those dishes?"

"Yes. So?" The boy kicked a rung of a sad-looking rocking chair.

"Would you like to eat from them again?"

He shrugged. "I reckon."

"Then they need to be washed—and everyone will help. The task will be done before you know it, and it will free me up to prepare supper, so we can eat sooner."

At the mention of food, the boy perked up. "Oh, all right." He spun away and hopped off the side of the porch, then ran to the back of the house.

Sophie glanced up at the sky. "Give me patience and wisdom."

After disposing of the spider, she returned to the parlor. "Mikey is getting water, and once he does, we need to get to work on those dishes," she told the girls. "I'm going to run upstairs and talk to Aunt Maude for a minute. I'd like you two to scrape the dishes and put them to soak."

The girls eyed each other but rose from the couch and went into the kitchen without voicing an objection. Sophie blew out a sigh, thankful she did not have to fight them. If she established her authority early on, maybe things would go fairly well.

She hurried upstairs and into her aunt's room. She longed to cover her nose at the foul stench of the chamber pot but didn't want to offend.

Maude's eyes opened, and a smile lifted one corner of her mouth. "I can't thank you enough for coming, dear."

Sophie hoped her aunt wasn't too disappointed that her mother or sister hadn't come in her place. "I was more than happy to do so." Mere words couldn't express her delight in getting away from home, even though the situation here was far different from anything she could have imagined. "I was wondering what I should prepare for our evening meal."

Aunt Maude's lips pressed together, and she turned her face away. "I'm afraid there isn't much. That's often the case at the end of the month."

"I'm sure I can manage to find something."

Maude turned back to face her. "I hope so, dear. The children have pretty much been on their own for the past wee—" Raspy coughs interrupted her.

Sophie handed her aunt another handkerchief. There were only two clean ones left. She wrinkled her nose, and a shudder coursed through her at the thought of washing the soiled ones. But it had to be done.

Maude calmed and cleared her throat. "Once the children's fathers pay for their keep, the first of the month, I generally stock up on supplies."

"Let me worry about the meals, and you get some rest." Sophie smiled, hoping to relieve her aunt's concerns. She still had the money her father had given her, and she'd go to the mercantile and purchase supplies, if need be.

"Thank you. I am quite tired." Maude closed her eyes, and Sophie tiptoed out of the room.

A niggling worry wormed its way into her mind. Father would be upset to learn the sad state of his sister's house and the grave nature of her condition. But if Sophie wrote and told him, he would send her mother and make Sophie return home to her confined existence.

Maybe she should wait to tell him. Yes, it would be best to wait a day or two and see how things worked out. She'd have a better picture then, and maybe her aunt would rally.

And, if she were really fortunate, perhaps the father of the other two children would decide he missed them so much that he would choose to keep them home with him. She crossed her fingers, hoping dearly that would be the case.

⌒

As he walked away from the schoolhouse on Monday afternoon, Josh glanced over his shoulder at his nephew, who poked along with Mikey. Toby was always a bit cranky the day they left the ranch for the short train ride back to town. The boy missed his father and the rest of his family and wanted to stay instead of returning to school, but he was resilient, and by the end of his first day back to school, he'd usually turned his attention to something else. Right now, it was seeing if he could create a bigger dust cloud than Mikey.

Josh snapped his fingers. "Toby, stop dragging your feet. You're getting your pants filthy." *Filthier* was more like it. How did the boy get so dirty in just a few hours? "I need you to hurry today. I have an appointment at the bank in five minutes."

"I don't know why you don't let us walk to Miss Maudie's by ourselves, Uncle Josh." Corrie gave him a peevish glance, similar to the one his ma gave him and his brothers when she was displeased with their behavior. "We're nearly grown up. Well, I am, at least."

"I'm bigger'n you. Older too," Mikey snarled, then took off running, Toby chasing after him.

Josh shook his head. Yes, his niece was maturing, but his nephew still had a long way to go. Josh worried about the day when young men would start coming around to visit Corrie. The pretty girl had her father's dark brown hair and her mother's bright blue eyes. She would be quite a beauty when she reached womanhood. Hopefully, she'd be back home by then, no longer his responsibility. Let Aaron deal with besotted beaus. Josh was doing well to get the kids fed, clothed, and to school on time. He really ought to consider hiring a housekeeper and cook, but he hated to spend money on such luxuries.

He quickened his steps as he approached Maude Archer's house. The poor structure needed a good painting. He'd been meaning to recruit some other men to help the injured widow but kept getting distracted by bank business or the children. This Sunday, he'd talk to some of the townsmen and see if he could get a crew together for an upcoming weekend. Maude had a rough enough time as it was, caring for so many children at her age, and now she'd broken her arm. He knocked on the door, still not comfortable allowing the youngsters to simply walk in.

The door opened, but instead of Maude, a short girl—no, woman—glanced up at him, a curious smile on her pretty face. Then it hit him—this was the woman from the depot. What was *she* doing here?

"May I help you, sir?"

"Uh...who are you?"

Her thin brows dipped in a frown. "I'm Sophia Davenport, Maude Archer's niece. And you are?"

"Josh Harper. I'm the president of the Bank of Windmill."

"Did Aunt Maude have an appointment with you?" Her gaze darted to Corrie, and she smiled, but when she looked back up at him, her pleasant expression disappeared.

Josh wrestled with what to do. The woman he'd witnessed at the depot had been struggling for each breath, but the one in front of him seemed perfectly fine, albeit slight and small. Why, she wasn't any taller than Hazel, the oldest girl who lived here. He shuffled his feet, unsure what to do. How could someone so tiny manage five children and help her aunt, too?

He cleared his throat. "Is Miss Maudie available?"

"No." The woman shook her head, and then her eyes widened. "I mean, she is here, but she's indisposed."

He thought that by now Maude would have rallied. Yes, a broken arm was painful, but the last time he talked with Maude, she had assured him that, with Hazel's help, she would still be able to continue watching Corrie and Toby for the few hours he left them there after school. Miss Maudie was elderly, but she'd always been a spunky woman. It was hard to imagine her so sick that she'd take to her bed. "Isn't she better?"

"Are you a friend of hers?"

"I'm her neighbor." Josh glanced down the street at the bank, hoping he wouldn't be late for his appointment.

"I see." Miss Davenport frowned. "My aunt is feeling poorly today."

"I'm sorry about that." What now? He couldn't take the children with him. His appointment was too important. His only option was to leave them here—at least for today.

His niece stepped forward. "I'm Corrie." She pointed at the corner of the porch, where Toby and Mikey had cornered a frog. "That smaller boy is my brother, Toby. We stay here after school."

Understanding dawned on the woman's face, but she didn't look quite as happy as she had when she'd first opened the door. Just as he suspected, she dreaded having more youngsters to watch. Josh sighed inwardly. He hadn't wanted to leave his niece and nephew with Maude in the first place, but Toby caused too many problems for Josh to keep him at the bank, even for just a couple of hours. And there were precious few, if any, women living in town who wanted to watch two more children, especially for the pittance Maude was willing to accept for a few hours' care.

"Well, come on in, children." Miss Davenport stood back, but Mikey jumped up and raced in front of Corrie.

"Hey!" Corrie yelled, as Josh caught her to keep her from falling.

Mikey ran upstairs, then leaned over the railing and stuck out his tongue. "I beat you."

Toby frowned, slipped in the door, and headed for the stairs. Josh sent the older boy a scolding stare. Someone needed to take him in hand and teach him some manners, before Toby started mimicking all of his bad traits.

"Hazel and Amanda stayed late to help Miss McMillan clean up the schoolhouse," Corrie told Miss Davenport. "They'll be here soon." She waved at Josh and settled on the old settee. "See you later."

Miss Davenport glanced up at him, her expression uncertain. "It was nice to meet you, Mr. Harper. I'll be sure to take good care of Corrie and Toby."

He stared at her for a moment, then finally nodded, turned, and strode toward the bank. It wasn't until he heard the door click shut that he realized he hadn't said a word to her after mumbling that he was sorry to hear Miss Maudie was ill. She must think him a buffoon.

Chapter Five

What an insufferable man! Was he always so rude? Or was it just the surprise of encountering a stranger instead of Aunt Maude? Sophie leaned against the closed door. Mr. Harper didn't like her, nor did he want to leave his niece and nephew with her. That was obvious.

Something in the back of her mind struggled to grasp a thought she couldn't quite reach. Had she seen Mr. Harper before? The man would probably be quite handsome, if he ever smiled—and those brilliant eyes reminded her of the intense blue flame of a coal fire. She pushed away from the door, needing to greet the new children, when realization dawned. She halted and sucked in a sharp breath. He was the man from the depot—the one who'd helped her and nearly missed his train as a result. She struggled to reconcile the kind, concerned man she'd met the day she'd arrived with the curmudgeon who'd just left. Had he judged her less than competent because of the reaction she'd had to all of the dust? Sophie lifted her chin. Regardless, she would prove to him that she was capable.

She glanced at the sofa, where Corrie was seated. First, she had to convince herself that she could care for so many children. Sophie smiled at the girl, hoping to relieve her concerns at being left with a stranger.

"I like your dress," Corrie said. "Purple is my favorite color."

"Why, thank you." Sophie filed the compliment away, in case she had future need of it, and sat in one of the side chairs. "You have very pretty eyes. They're almost the same color as your uncle's." In spite of Mr. Harper's lack of civility, Sophie couldn't deny he was a fine-looking man. And those eyes—so penetrating, she felt they could see clear to her core, searching out and finding her insecurities and inadequacies. She gave her head a shake to rid her mind of the picture. "They look lovely with your dark hair and light complexion." With Corrie's coloring, anyone who didn't know might think she was her uncle's child, as Sophie had initially assumed.

Corrie straightened, her eyes sparkling. "You really think so?" She picked up one long braid and glanced down at it. "Grandma says I have my ma's eyes."

Sophie wondered about the girl's mother. She must be dead if Corrie's grandma had needed to explain the physical similarities of mother and daughter. Her heart ached for the child. How hard it must be to lose your mother and then to leave your father and stay with a stuffy uncle all week.

"Toby's got the same color eyes that my pa has. Brown. But his hair is blond, like Ma's. I wish I could remember what she looked like."

Sophie squeezed Corrie's hand. The last thing she needed was the girl crying over her mother. "I bought a pound cake at the mercantile and some canned apples. I thought we could slice some up for a snack to hold you over until dinner. Would you like to help me prepare it?"

Corrie nodded. "Toby will be happy you have a snack. He's always hungry."

Sophie chuckled. "It must be a male thing. I've noticed that Mikey is also starving most of the time." She stood, and Corrie did, too.

The girl reached out and took her hand. "I like you. I'm glad you came to help Miss Maudie."

Sophie squeezed back. "Me, too. I can tell we're going to be good friends."

Clopping footsteps echoed on the porch, the door opened, and Hazel and Amanda entered. Amanda lifted her head and sniffed. "What smells so good?"

"There's some soup simmering on the stove," Sophie said.

"We stayed to help Miss McMillan." Hazel's thin brows dipped, and she nibbled her lower lip as she gazed at Sophie. "I hope that was all right. Maybe we should've asked you first."

Sophie smiled and hugged the girl's thin shoulders. "Of course it's all right. Corrie explained why you'd be late. That's very kind of you girls to offer to help your teacher. I'm sure she appreciates it after a long day."

"I wanted to help, too." Corrie frowned. "But Uncle Josh was in a hurry to get back to the bank. He has another meeting to attend." The girl rolled her eyes.

"Maybe you can assist the teacher on another day, when your uncle has more time. Why don't you go wash your hands and faces, and then we'll have a treat?" Sophie watched the girls scamper off to obey. Taking a deep breath, she picked a flat, frayed pillow off the floor and set it on the sofa, then hurried to the kitchen. She'd managed to survive the weekend with no disasters, other than burning a pan of biscuits and scolding Mikey for getting into things he shouldn't, but today was the first time she had all five children under her care. Peering out the open door, she smiled at the girls washing their hands at the pump. But where had the boys gotten off to? She'd heard them come down the stairs while she was talking to Corrie, but they were nowhere to be seen now. Mikey might be old enough to gallivant around town alone—so he said—but Toby wasn't. And she was certain Mr. Harper wouldn't appreciate her allowing him to do so.

First, she would get the girls settled at the table with their snack, and then she'd look for the boys. As she approached the counter where she'd left the pound cake and jar of apples, she paused. The apples were gone, and the cupboard drawer that held the silverware was partially open. Sophie quirked her mouth. *Mikey.* Blowing out a loud sigh, she removed the cake from the basket she'd taken to the store, cut three generous slices, and placed each one on a plate. She wrapped up the remaining cake and looked for a place to hide it. The upper cabinets were too high for her to reach, so she placed it behind a big bowl on the bottom shelf of the cupboard and then shut the door. Unless she was mistaken, the boys had snacked on the apples. They would get no cake.

The girls hurried back inside and crowded Sophie, obviously anxious for their treat. Amanda frowned. "I thought you said there'd be apples too."

Sophie brushed her hand over the top of the girl's head and noticed the other girls' worried expressions. "I did, but it seems a mouse has snatched them."

Hazel's brows turned downward, matching her lips. "Mikey took them, didn't he?"

"Yes." Corrie crossed her arms. "He's a rat, not a mouse."

Amanda giggled and nodded.

"Never mind that. Grab a plate and have a seat at the table. I'll go see if I can find the boys."

"Look beside Mr. Harper's shed," Hazel volunteered.

"Uncle Josh built Toby a fort there." Corrie pinched off a corner of her cake and slipped it into her mouth. "Mmm."

Mumbling a prayer for strength, patience, and wisdom, Sophie marched across her aunt's backyard. The green grass and tiny white flowers with yellow faces strewn throughout the lawn eased her mood, but as she approached the fort, she heard boyish snickers that unsettled her.

"That was a good idea, sneakin' that jar of apples," Toby said.

"Maudie's niece is so dumb, she prob'ly won't even notice."

That ignited Sophie's ire like a flame to dried leaves. She flung the fort door open and peered inside. Both boys jumped. Two pairs of wide eyes and syrupy faces stared back.

Toby puckered up. "It was all Mikey's idea." He looked down at the dirty spoon in his hand and yanked it behind his back, but the half-empty jar of stewed apples remained encircled by Mikey's legs, obvious evidence of guilt.

Mikey elbowed the younger boy. "Snitch!"

"Ow!"

"That's enough." Sophie stuck out her hand. "Give me the jar."

Mikey frowned but handed her the container and his sticky spoon. Toby dipped his head, also handing her his utensil.

"Now, get out of there and come back to the house."

Toby immediately crawled out and had the sense to look dismayed. Mikey's expression remained belligerent, but he obeyed her and exited the fort. Both boys dragged their feet all the way to the house. Sophie's mind raced. Should she punish them? She'd never reprimanded a child before, other than to scold her sister for "borrowing" something from Sophie's room when they were young. What should she do?

The boys plodded back into the kitchen, and she followed. Mikey paused at the table, staring at the girls' plates. "Hey, what's that?"

"Pound cake." Hazel pressed her lips together and lifted her head smugly.

"And you don't get none," Amanda crowed.

Toby stood next to his sister, frowning at her empty plate, then glanced at Sophie. "How come?"

She lifted her eyebrows. "Why do you suppose?"

The boy ducked his head. "'Cause what we did was bad."

Corrie wagged her finger under her brother's nose. "Toby Harper, you should be ashamed of yourself. Just wait until Uncle Josh hears about this."

Toby's lower lip wobbled, making Sophie wonder what his cranky uncle would do. Was the man a harsh disciplinarian? Would he beat the boy?

She lifted her shoulders, telling herself it was none of her business. "You boys go out and wash up, then I want you to...." *What?* The only thing that came to mind was the punishment her mother had always enforced on her. "Go to your room and think about what you've done."

Mikey had the audacity to grin right before he spun around and raced toward the stairs.

"Mikey! Come back here!"

He ignored her, but Toby obeyed and headed outside to the pump. Should she have given them a harsher punishment? What was she going to do about Mikey? She turned toward the counter so the girls wouldn't see her indecision. If only she'd had some advance notice about the children. But, honestly, what difference would that have made? There were no books on becoming the instant guardian of five children.

⌒

Josh stared across his desk at the desperate farmer. The lunch he'd eaten an hour ago churned in his gut, and his palms were sweaty. He hated this part of his job, but he had a responsibility to his uncle and the other investors to make sound decisions and to abide by the rules they'd set up. "I'm sincerely sorry, Mr. Baker, but your loan is six months past due. Unless you can catch up on the payments in the next two weeks, I have no other recourse than to repossess your farm."

The father of six ducked his head. His fists clenched the arms of the chair, and his chest rose and fell in an exaggerated rhythm.

Josh tensed. He'd only had to foreclose on a couple of properties in the year he'd been president of the bank, so he was never quite sure how the news would be taken.

Mr. Baker let out a long sigh, then looked up, not as shaken as Josh had expected. "I reckon that'll be good news to my Tillie. She's missed her folks somethin' fierce since we moved here. I gave it my best shot, and I reckon the good Lord's answered my prayers as to what to do." He stood up and held out his hand. "We'll be gone in two weeks, Mr. Harper. An'thin' that's left behind can be sold to pay on the note or given away."

Josh stood and reached across the desk to shake the man's hand, more than a little amazed at how he'd taken the news. Josh's family members were God-fearing people who believed that the Lord ordered their steps, but he wasn't certain that any of them—himself included—would have taken such dreadful news as easily as Mr. Baker had. "I wish you well, sir. I'm sorry I couldn't do more to help you."

Mr. Baker shook his head. "Weren't your fault."

He shuffled out, and Josh fell back into his chair, thankful to have the confrontation over—not that it had been much of one. He didn't understand why God would allow a husband and father to lose everything he'd worked so hard for, but then, hadn't his own family been forced to make adjustments? He thought back to the days when a half dozen stagecoaches would come by Harpers' Stage Stop each week to change out horses and allow passengers and drivers to eat one of his ma's fine meals. Those were fun days. Josh always enjoyed meeting new people and hearing their news. Sure, he had to serve meals, clear tables, and even wash dishes, at times, but he looked forward to the stage's arrival. Now that the train ran from eastern Kansas all the way to Colorado, only two stagecoaches stopped each week. If not for the family's wise decision to raise cattle and stock horses, they might well have lost their land, just like Mr. Baker.

He glanced at the clock on the mantel across the room. Time to collect the children. He closed his window, shut his office door behind him, and walked over to the teller's cage. "Ready to go, Mr. Franklin?" Josh donned his slouch hat.

"Yes, sir. Everything's in the safe."

"Good." Josh closed the door to the bank's safe, checked that the window locks were secured and the lanterns out, and then followed Mr. Franklin outside, locking the heavy door behind him. "See you tomorrow."

The Mondays after his trips home were always the hardest. He missed his family, the ranch, and Ma's cooking, but getting back to Windmill still felt good. Today—at least, for the past few hours—he'd had a difficult time focusing on work and not worrying about Corrie and Toby. He'd contemplated finding someone else to watch them, but since the school term would be over in just a few weeks, he hoped things would work out at Miss Maudie's until then.

His boots thudded against the boardwalk and down the steps. Traffic on Main Street had thinned some since he'd eaten lunch at the café. Most businesses closed shortly after the bank, and folks headed home. At least he wouldn't have to scrounge up supper or spend money at the café, since Ma had sent home a picnic basket filled with goodies. He glanced at the house he rented as he passed by. It needed painting almost as badly as Maude's.

Josh slowed as he approached her house. Would Miss Davenport scowl at him again, as she had when he'd dropped off the children after school? With those intriguing sable eyes and light brown hair, she was quite attractive. He smiled as he remembered how she'd lifted that fetching chin and her eyes had sparked at him. She may be small in stature, but she seemed fiercely determined to care for the children and her aunt. Maybe he'd been too hard on her.

A high-pitched scream—Corrie's scream—yanked him from his thoughts.

⌒

A girl's scream ricocheted through the house, and Sophie jumped, almost dropping the pan of biscuits she was sliding into the oven. She shut the door and rushed out of the kitchen, through the dining room, and into the parlor. The front door flew open, and Mr. Harper marched in, without so much as a knock. His gaze raked the parlor, landing on the children.

Corrie and Amanda hopped up and down on the sofa. Mikey stood in front of them, holding up something gray, with Toby hovering right beside him. Sophie narrowed her eyes, focusing on the creature in Mikey's hands. She lifted a floury hand to her bodice, in hopes of calming her racing heart. Surely that wasn't—

"A mouse!" Corrie shrieked. "Help us, Uncle Josh."

"Mikey, stop that!" Sophie started toward the boy, then paused, lest he turn the critter toward her. The girls continued jumping, and she hoped they wouldn't drop through the bottom of the rickety sofa. She could hardly blame them, but she had to regain control. Mr. Harper was watching. "Children, please settle down."

Mikey ignored her, as if she hadn't even spoken. He lifted the dead rodent closer to Amanda, and the girl uttered a shrill screech, then fell back against the sofa, her head hitting the wall.

Mr. Harper latched onto the boy's shoulder, turning him around. Mikey's eyes widened. Toby slithered over to the chair in the far corner and sat down, hanging his head.

Sophie stepped as close to Mikey as she dared. "Mr. Harper, I'm perfectly capable of disciplining the children."

He turned toward her, a deep scowl marring his handsome face. His hand continued to clutch Mikey's shoulder. "Are you? Is this your idea of maintaining an orderly home? Allowing this boy to terrorize the girls?"

She noticed he'd exempted his nephew, even though Toby looked to have been Mikey's accomplice and had seemed to be enjoying his antics. Sophie straightened, hoping to appear a tad more imposing. "Of course, I don't condone such behavior. I was trying to cook supper, and I didn't know Mikey had a mouse until I came in here to see what the ruckus was all about."

"If you can't maintain control over children, perhaps you shouldn't be caring for them." His blue eyes pierced her, just as his declaration did.

She knew better than anyone that she had no business overseeing youngsters; but, when thrown into a desperate situation, a woman managed the best she could. Her throat tightened. She took several breaths, trying to force the tension from her body. "I'm sorry that I disappoint you, Mr. Harper, but you care for two children part of the time. Surely you understand that you can't keep an eye on them every moment."

His hard expression softened the tiniest bit, as if she'd made a valid point. Still, she had to do better—would do better.

He turned his glare on Mikey and shook the boy's shoulder. "Stop harassing my niece." Almost as an afterthought, he glanced toward the sofa. "And the other girls. Men are supposed to take care of females, not antagonize them."

If Sophie thought he'd give her any leeway, considering this was her first day caring for all five children, she was wrong.

"If you hope to keep caring for Corrie and Toby, Miss Davenport, you must find a way to keep these children corralled."

She started to respond, but a soft wheeze escaped. Afraid he would notice, she merely nodded.

He dropped his gaze. "Take that rodent outside, Mikey, and find a place to bury it." He didn't let go of the boy's shoulder until they reached the door. Then Mr. Harper crossed the room and lifted the two girls off the couch. He hugged his niece but gave his nephew a stern stare. "Let's go home."

Toby jumped up, ran across the room, and raced out the door. Corrie, her panic over now that her uncle had rescued her, smiled and waved good-bye to Amanda. At the doorway, she hesitated, peeking around the corner, before following her brother.

Sophie wondered if Corrie was making sure Mikey wasn't waiting to surprise her. Probably a wise idea. She lifted her gaze to Mr. Harper's, wishing she had someone to rescue her.

"Have a good—and quiet—evening, Miss Davenport."

The second he was out the door, Sophie inhaled. With the drama over and the irate man gone, the tension practically dripped off of her. She sat on the sofa and tugged Amanda close. "I'm sorry."

Amanda leaned her head against Sophie's arm. "It ain't your fault. Mikey's a numbskull."

Taking hold of Amanda's hand, Sophie turned to look at the child. "Amanda, I know Mikey frightened you, but it's impolite to call him names."

The girl scowled and shrugged one shoulder. "He's mean. I wish he never came here." Amanda pulled away, stood, and jogged up the stairs. Sophie heard a door slam.

Staring out the front door, which was still open, she blew out a sigh. She was so unprepared for all of this. Mr. Harper was right to say that she had no business caring for children. What did she know? She'd spent over half of her life in her room, shut away from everyone, as if her parents were ashamed of her affliction. Tears stung her eyes. Closing them, she fought for control. Crying only caused her nose to run and made it harder to breathe. Crying had never helped a thing.

She'd wanted everything to be in order when Mr. Harper picked up the children tonight. For some reason, she'd wanted to prove to him that she was capable.

But she had failed.

Still, she wouldn't return home unless her parents insisted on it.

She had to find a way to make the children obey, to cook decent meals, and to tend to her aunt and the house. Oh, and she mustn't forget the laundry. She was in a quagmire of quicksand that was sucking her down. She rose and walked to the door, looking up at the vivid blue sky. "Help me, Lord. Show me how to control the children and to do all that needs to be done here."

How had frail Aunt Maude handled so many rowdy children? Maybe that was the key—she needed to talk with her. Right after supper was over, she would consult her.

Sophie sniffed. Was that smoke? She scanned the street but saw no sign of a spiraling gray plume. She turned back toward the kitchen. "Oh, no! My biscuits!"

Chapter Six

Josh paced the parlor, searching for the right words to say to Toby, who sat, hunched forward, on the couch. He hadn't exactly been antagonizing the girls, but he'd looked as if he was enjoying in their plight. *Give me wisdom, Lord.*

He dropped down beside his nephew, clasped his hands between his knees, and sighed. "Toby, you know better than to harass your sister and the other girls."

"But Uncle Josh, I didn't do nuthin'. It was Mikey." Toby stared at him with innocent dark brown eyes—eyes that so resembled Aaron's. If not for Toby's lighter hair, he would be the spitting image of his father at this age.

Another pair of deep brown eyes—eyes the color of milkless coffee—stared back at him in his mind, filling him with regret. Josh ducked his head. He hadn't been much of a gentleman, and he'd lost his temper—something he rarely did—and been a bad example to Toby and Corrie. His mother would be appalled and disappointed with his behavior. Fidgeting almost as much as Toby, Josh blew out a loud breath. He owed Miss Davenport an apology for ranting like he had.

"Are we done?"

Josh drew his gaze back to his nephew. "No, young man, we are not. Maybe you didn't hold that mouse, but you did nothing to stop Mikey, and if I'm not mistaken, it looked like you were enjoying his taunting."

Toby's face scrunched up. "But he's bigger'n me. And he can be mean."

"I understand that, but it's a man's duty to protect women— um, girls. I expect you to protect your sister and not do things to upset her."

"That don't hardly seem fair. She picks on me."

Josh thought back to his ma's many talks with his brothers and him about how a man should be respectful of women, always act a gentleman, and put their welfare before his own. No matter how much a woman annoyed him, a gentleman should never lose patience with her. He pursed his lips. His ma had never met Miss Davenport. How was it that he could run a bank and deal patiently with angry, sometimes irrational, customers, but that snippet of a woman set him off like a flame to dynamite?

That woman simply had to do a better job corralling the children before one of them got seriously hurt. If he had any other options, he'd move them to another home until Miss Maudie was better. Josh shook his head. He'd been so upset, he hadn't even asked about her.

Toby fidgeted beside him. Better keep focused on his task. "Toby, you need to learn to be nice to the girls, even if they aren't nice to you. And I don't want you to get into any more trouble with Mikey. Is that clear?"

"Yes, sir." The words sounded as if they'd been pulled from mire. "Can I go now?"

"After you set the table and bring in a bucket of water."

Toby stood and kicked the sofa leg. "Settin' the table's Corrie's job."

"Since you participated in teasing her, I think it's fitting for you to do her chores tonight."

The boy's eyes widened, and then he ducked his head. "Yes, sir."

Josh grinned and pulled him into his arms. "I love you, you know that?"

"I reckon."

Toby shuffled off, and Josh gazed out the window. He was so ill-prepared to father these kids. They ought to be home with Aaron, but they needed an education. With Sarah pregnant and Ma too busy to teach them, the choice had been made to send the children to school in town. It wasn't an uncommon thing for farmers and ranchers who lived miles from town to board their children so they could get their schooling.

But he still felt incompetent—and he'd been caring for them for months. No wonder Miss Davenport was having trouble. She had between three and five children to care for, while tending to an ailing aunt, as well as the house. He should have been more patient and understanding. He knew Mikey was rabble-rouser. Ever since the boy had moved in four months ago, things at Miss Maudie's had been chaotic. Toby had rarely gotten in trouble before the older boy arrived.

Josh rose, walked to the window, and watched a redtail hawk swoop down onto the roof across the street.

Tomorrow, he would apologize.

⌒

Sophie flipped through the pages of the copy of *The National Cook Book* she had discovered in the pantry, hoping to find something she could prepare quickly for tonight's supper; otherwise, they'd be eating pancakes again. The children probably wouldn't mind, but pancakes weren't much of a meal, especially in the evening. Too bad her father hadn't sent Miss Hopper, the Davenports' cook, along with her. Just the thought of the tasty delights the woman prepared made Sophie homesick.

Thoughts of her garden also brought fond memories of home, but not fond enough that she was ready to call it quits here. What she didn't miss was spending much of the day alone in her room. Yes, the children were rambunctious, and the work was more than she could keep up with, but there was something quite rewarding about falling into bed exhausted each night because of all she'd done that day.

A knock on the door pulled her from her thoughts. Sophie set the cookbook on the sofa, straightened her spine, and went to open the door, expecting to see Mr. Harper come to collect his niece and nephew. Instead, it was a woman who stood there, smiling and holding a pot. She looked a bit younger than Sophie's mother.

"Good afternoon. My name is Kate McMillan. I'm a friend of Maude's, and I wanted to stop by and see how she's getting along, as well as to welcome you to Windmill."

Sophie smiled and glanced at the woman's left hand, noticing a wedding band on her ring finger. "It's a pleasure to meet you, Mrs. McMillan. I'm Sophie Davenport. Maude is my aunt. Please, come in." Her stomach gurgled at the delicious aroma coming from the container the woman held.

"Oh, here. This is some prairie chicken stew. I thought you might enjoy not having to cook supper tonight." A red hue brightened the woman's lightly tanned cheeks. "Taking care of your aunt and so many children would be a big job for anyone, but even more so for someone new in town. I wanted to help in a small way. Maude is such a sweet woman, and it hurts my heart to know she's ill."

"Thank you. That was kind of you." Sophie accepted the pot and carried it to the kitchen with Mrs. McMillan on her heels. She was glad she'd taken the time to clean up once the children had finished their after-school snack of gingerbread. She placed the pot on the stove and turned to face her guest. "How did you know I was here?"

The woman cocked her head, giving her a knowing smile. "This is a small town, Miss Davenport. It doesn't take long for news to get around."

Since her arrival, Sophie had spoken with only two people, other than her aunt and the children. Could Mr. Harper have spread the news of her coming?

"Would you care for some tea, Mrs. McMillan?"

"I would love some, if it wouldn't be too much trouble. And, please, call me Kate."

She set the teapot on the stove. "And you must call me Sophie."

Kate nodded and glanced around. "The house is unusually quiet, compared with the other times I've visited."

Sophie took two teacups and saucers from the shelf and set them on the counter. "The boys went outside to play, and the girls are all upstairs. Hazel enjoys reading to Aunt Maude after school."

"My daughter enjoys having Hazel as a student. She's quite smart."

"So, your daughter is the schoolteacher?"

Smiling proudly, Kate nodded. "Yes, this is Mary's second year."

Sophie hoped the other children didn't give Mary too much trouble. "I have to say I admire her. Taking care of the few children who live here can be…well…difficult, at times." *Most times*, but she didn't want to admit that. "I can't imagine teaching a classroom full of children."

"The trick is to maintain order and stick to a schedule." Kate grinned. "And it doesn't hurt to instill a little bit of fear into the children. Mary tends to wear her stern face to school, but she has a big heart, and it's hard for her."

With the water heated, Sophie prepared their tea and set the cups on the table, along with the sugar bowl, the butter dish, and the remaining slice of gingerbread she'd saved for herself. She slid the plate over to Kate.

"Aren't you having some?"

Sophie shook her head. "I had some yesterday, when it was hot from the oven."

"Then we'll split this piece." Kate buttered the bread and cut it in half, then pushed the plate toward Sophie.

"I hope you don't mind that it's a bit overdone." Sophie's cheeks warmed, and she glanced out the open back door. "We had a cook back home, but my mother never allowed me to work in the kitchen with her."

"Considering that, I'd say you did a fine job." Kate took a bite. "It's delicious."

"Thank you."

"I'd be happy to teach you some things about cooking...if you'd care to learn."

Sophie smiled, as relief chased away her embarrassment. "I would love that, but I'm afraid I would have to ask you to come here, since I must be close in case Aunt Maude needs me."

"That might work." Kate tapped her chin, and then her eyes brightened. "My daughter Pearl gets bored now that she's no longer in school. Maybe she could come and visit with Maude while you come to my house for lessons."

Sophie considered the generous offer a moment, then nodded. "I think that might be feasible, as long as I come while the children are in school."

Half an hour later, Sophie knew she'd made a true friend, in spite of their age difference. Kate was so friendly and chatty and fun to talk to. Sophie wrote down several simple recipes Kate shared and was excited about the possibilities of learning to cook better. She hadn't realized how much she'd missed conversing with adults. After Kate visited briefly with Aunt Maude, Sophie followed her to the front door.

"I wish I could stay longer, but my husband, Tom, will be getting home, and I need to be sure Pearl has the table set and biscuits made. That girl tends to get lost in her books if I don't keep a close watch."

"I understand how she feels. I love reading, too." Sophie wondered if Kate might be willing to loan her a book or two, but it was too soon to ask for another favor. "Next time you visit, please bring your daughters, if you can. I'd love to meet them."

"Why don't you all come to dinner Sunday after church?"

Sophie blinked. She hadn't been brave enough to take the children to Sunday services last week. "You mean, all of us? Except for the Harpers, of course."

"Sure."

She thought of her aunt. "I seriously doubt that Aunt Maude will be able to come."

"I suppose not, but you and the children have to eat." Kate stepped onto the porch. "Phoebe Gibbons is Maude's good friend. I'll see if she's up for a visit, and maybe she can sit with Maude while you all come over. Then I can send you home with food for both of them."

"That sounds very nice. Thank you." She smiled and waved good-bye, watching as Kate walked away, her blue calico skirt flapping in the wind. Somehow, having a friend in town made her load seem lighter.

A man walking down the street turned her way—Mr. Harper. Sophie sucked in a sharp breath. She hadn't seen Mikey or Toby or heard a peep from them during Kate's visit. She started to duck back inside, but Mr. Harper noticed her and smiled, tipping his hat. Instantly on guard, Sophie stiffened. She didn't need another lecture from him, although he didn't look as if he was in lecture mode today. As he stopped in front of her, he pulled a bouquet of slightly bent flowers from behind his back.

Sophie gasped and accepted the beautiful blooms of snow-white, lemon-yellow, and purple. "They're lovely. I recognize the hollyhock and oxeye daisy, but what is the name of this one?" She fingered one of the yellow flower's many petals.

Mr. Harper's lips twitched, and then he grinned, looking so much handsomer than when he frowned. "They have an animal name, like the daisies do. They're called goatsbeard."

Sophie giggled. "Such an uncomplimentary name for so pretty a flower. Wherever did you find them?"

"In my garden." He cocked his head, his blue eyes twinkling. "I've read that the roots have a flavor similar to parsnips."

Sophie didn't remember seeing a flower bed the day the jar of apples had gone missing and she'd stormed out to Toby's fort, but she'd been rather upset then, and her sole focus had been finding the boys. "Your garden must be beautiful, if these are a sampling."

Mr. Harper nodded. "There are only a few things blooming, but if we get some rain and don't have a horribly hot summer, there will be more flowers then. You're welcome to walk over at any time and enjoy them."

"I'd like that. I have a big garden back home, and I miss working in it." She would offer to pull weeds for him, but she was afraid he'd be offended that she thought he needed help.

He ducked his head for a moment, then gazed at her with resolve. "I owe you an apology, Miss Davenport. I'm not normally the ogre I've led you to believe. I never should have barged in the house or scolded you." He inhaled and glanced down the street. "I tend to be a bit overconcerned when it comes to Corrie and Toby."

He worked his mouth, as if he wanted to say more, drawing her gaze to his perfectly formed lips. His jaw carried a faint shadow of a beard, making him look slightly rugged. She could imagine him riding a horse across the prairie, his duster flapping in the Kansas breeze, more easily than she could picture him working in a bank. Strange tingles erupted in her stomach, and she dropped her gaze to his shoes. What was wrong with her?

Mr. Harper cleared his throat, pulling her gaze back up to his eyes. The pain she saw there made her want to reach out and comfort him. "Aaron—that's the children's father—lost his wife in a tragic accident several years ago. I'm responsible for my niece and nephew when they stay with me, and I don't dare let anything happen to them."

"I'm sorry to hear about their mother." Now his strong reactions made sense. He put a lot of pressure on himself, trying to keep those two rambunctious youngsters from any type of harm. "Surely, you understand that kids will be kids, especially curious boys like Toby. You can't protect them from everything."

He scowled and lowered the flowers. "I can try."

She knew far more than most people what it felt like, being confined to the house by parents or a guardian to keep you from injury. It may help prevent physical wounds, but nobody knew the emotional toll such rigidity could cause. At least he wasn't as strict as her parents. "I understand your concern, and I will try my best to keep a closer watch on Corrie and Toby." The fact that she had been visiting with Kate and was thus oblivious to the boys' whereabouts caused a tightness in her chest. "I don't want anything to happen to them, either."

He studied her for a moment, and she must have passed muster, because he nodded and lifted the bouquet toward her. "You'd better put these in water before they die."

"Thank you. I will enjoy them very much." Her fingers touched his, sending odd sensations racing through her. She lifted her eyes again to his, and if she wasn't mistaken, he'd felt something too.

The kitchen door banged open, and Sophie jumped back, as if her mother had caught her spooning with a beau on the front porch. Her heart lurched at the idea, and she almost snorted. What beau? She was certain that Mr. Harper was the last person in Windmill who'd care to kiss her.

"Uncle Josh!" Toby charged through the house and collided with his uncle's legs. The man leaned over, lifted the boy, and hugged him. The sight made Sophie's eyes sting. She couldn't remember ever running like that to her father—and Mr. Harper wasn't even Toby's pa.

Her parents had never been demonstrative with their affections, both having more stoic temperaments. She glanced at Mr. Harper's joy-filled face and heard Toby's giggle as his uncle tickled his stomach. She turned and hurried upstairs to get Corrie, hating the uncommon feelings of envy surging through her.

Chapter Seven

Carrying a tray while maneuvering the steps in a long dress was no easy task, but Sophie moved carefully, making her way to the top without tripping or spilling the tea. Aunt Maude had eaten so little of her breakfast porridge that Sophie thought a mid-morning tea, along with a slice of the apple bread she'd baked for the children's after-school snack, might give her a little strength.

At the top of the stairs, Sophie paused. The chair that sat beside the mahogany bookcase holding the hurricane lamp she lit each night stuck out at an odd angle. Had it been that way when she'd been upstairs earlier? She couldn't remember. She set the tray next to the lamp and pulled the chair away from the wall. How odd. The bookcase also sat at an angle, and behind it was a big hole in the plaster. Bits of crumbled plaster lay against the floorboard, and broken laths jutted out from the wall. Had some kind of animal—a rat, maybe—gnawed its way inside?

Her heartbeat kicked up to a faster rhythm, and she pressed her hand against her chest as she looked around the hallway. The area was wide, more a sitting room than hall. As far as she could see, there were no signs that a creature had entered through the hole. Maybe she was making a mountain out of a molehill. The hole could have been there for years. At least now that she knew of it, she could put something over the opening. She left the furniture as it was and carried the tray to her aunt's room. With her foot, she nudged the door open wide enough for her to slip inside, then set the tray on the small table beside the bed and gazed down at her aunt.

Maude's eyelids lifted and closed several times, then opened. She gave Sophie a weak smile. "I was just resting, dear. Are the children dressed for church?"

"No, they're at school now. It's Wednesday, Aunt Maude." Sophie smiled, but she was more than a little worried that her aunt was unable to keep track of the days and time, even though a clock sat on the dresser that was just a few feet from the end of the bed. But then, her aunt wasn't wearing her spectacles, so she probably could not read the time. "I brought you some tea and apple bread. Do you think you could sit up for a few moments and partake of it?"

Maude tried to push up, but she was too weak. Sophie grabbed two pillows, lifted her aunt's shoulders a bit, and positioned the pillows behind her back, elevating her. "I added half a spoon of molasses to the tea."

"Just how I like it."

"The bread is a bit overcooked on the outside, but it tastes good."

"Smells wonderful." Her aunt pinched off a bite so small, a mouse would complain, but she stuck it in her mouth and closed her eyes. "Mmm. Delicious."

She was concerned at how little food and liquid she'd been consuming. From being ill herself, she knew that she often didn't much care for sustenance during those times, but her aunt had hardly eaten a thing since Sophie had arrived. Sophie lifted the cup and held it close to her aunt's lips. "How about some tea?"

Maude took several small sips, pleasing Sophie. She offered her another bite of the bread, but her aunt refused. Wrestling with what to do, Sophie rose and walked to the window. A pleasant breeze ruffled the curtains, driving away some of the staleness from the room. *Show me what to do, Lord—how to help my aunt.*

"Would you close that, dear? It's making me cold."

Sophie did as asked, although she found it a bit harder to breathe in the stuffy room. She made another attempt to get her aunt to eat a little more but only managed to coax her to drink another swig of tea.

She sat there for a few moments, wishing she could openly talk with her aunt. She knew so little about her, other than that Maude's husband, Sam, had been the son of a wealthy couple from St. Louis. Both he and Maude came from well-to-do families and had grown up in a modern town. What had prompted them to move to the frontier to live in such a tiny community?

"Tell me about your family," Maude said, without opening her eyes.

Sophie took hold of Maude's hand. Why couldn't she remember that Sophie had already told her everything she could about her family—several times? "Oh, you know Father. He's always working or thinking about work. Mother is away visiting Grandmother. And Pam loves her role as a wife, and will soon add the title of 'Mother' to her résumé."

Maude's eyes opened. "You're going to be an aunt?"

Sophie nodded, although she doubted she would be allowed to do much more than hold the baby. Blowing out a sigh, she searched for some other item of interest to tell her aunt.

"And what about you? Surely, you've caught a young man's eye."

Sophie's thoughts zipped back to Blake's visit. But that was a day she'd just as soon forget. "I don't think I'm supposed to marry."

"Pish. A girl as caring and lovely as you needs a husband and children of your own."

Tears burned Sophie's eyes. Her aunt didn't understand the situation, and her encouragement toward matrimony only made Sophie's pain cut deeper. Her parents would never allow it.

Maude broke into a fit of ragged coughing. Tears rolled down her cheeks, and she fought for each breath. Sophie jumped up and lifted her to a sitting position, in hopes of helping her to breathe better. Through her aunt's gown, she felt a rumbling in her chest—a feeling Sophie was well acquainted with, but one that was unnatural for Maude. "I'm going to get the doctor. I should have done so before now."

After a few moments, the coughing subsided, and Maude gasped for a breath. She held up her hand. "No, but you *can* fetch my attorney."

Sophie didn't want to argue. She helped her aunt lie back down. "Will you be all right if I leave for a few minutes?"

Maude nodded and turned her face toward the window.

Sophie hurried down the stairs, untied her apron, and tossed it onto the sofa. Outside, she looked both ways, wondering where to find the attorney, whose name she hadn't thought to ask about. Since her aunt lived almost at the edge of town, Sophie turned left, toward the town square. As she passed the bank window, a thought blossomed. She went inside and was met with the scent of beeswax. To the left was a desk, where a middle-aged man with a mustache sat in front of some highly polished wooden cabinets; to the right was a teller's cage and a closed door.

"Can I help you, ma'am?" The man behind the teller's cage peered at her through metal bars.

"Yes, I'm looking for Mr. Harper. Is he in?"

The teller frowned. "Do you have an appointment?"

Sophie clenched her hands. Maybe this was a mistake. "No, but I care for his niece and nephew after school and just need to ask him a quick question."

"Hmpf. Perhaps it will be all right to disturb him." He left his cage—probably a good place for such a cranky man—and knocked on the closed door.

She wanted to turn and flee the awful man's presence, but asking Mr. Harper about the attorney would be quicker than going somewhere else and inquiring of a stranger—a stranger who didn't need to know about her aunt's business. The man working at the desk stared at her over the paper he'd been reading. Sophie turned away, facing the door the teller had entered. Moments later the man scurried back behind his fortress. Mr. Harper strode out of his office, his brows crinkled with concern.

"Has something happened, Miss Davenport?"

Sophie smiled, hoping to alleviate his anxiety. "No, not at all. It's just that my aunt asked me to arrange an appointment with her attorney, but I don't know where to find the man."

"Ah, well, that's simple." His relief was evident in his warm smile.

"I thought I might also ask the doctor to stop by." She glanced at the teller, whose gaze had latched onto them. She leaned in closer. "I'm uneasy because she isn't improving."

He offered his arm. "If you would allow me to, I will escort you."

Sophie was hesitant to touch him. She'd never actually touched a man, other than her father, except when she needed assistance getting out of a vehicle or going down a steep stairway. But she didn't want to upset Mr. Harper, who was being nice and trying to be helpful, so she slipped her fingertips around his arm, applying as little pressure as possible. She wasn't prepared for the explosion of awareness that zipped through her. It was ten times the intensity she'd felt when their fingers had brushed, just days before. Looking up, her gaze collided with his, and his expression held the same stunned look she figured her own face reflected. Heat raced to her cheeks. She was acting like a besotted schoolgirl.

Mr. Harper cleared his throat and gave his head a tiny shake. "Shall we go?"

Sophie nodded, too tongue-tied to respond. Why did her body react so to this man's touch? Would she feel the same thing from contact with any man? Somehow she doubted it, but she was too flummoxed to analyze it further.

He guided her out the door and to the left, in the direction of the train depot. They passed the town square on the right, and he paused. "This is where we have all our gatherings. I guess you've noticed the market we have on Saturdays, but we also hold our celebrations here, and even an occasional wedding."

Sophie had been to few weddings, her sister's being the main one, and no one she knew of had gotten married outdoors. Most preferred a church. Although Windmill had two, neither looked very big. Maybe that was the reason for the outdoor ceremonies.

"The only attorney in town is Arthur Wilkes, who also happens to be the mayor. When he gives speeches at local events, he likes to stand up there on the platform surrounding the windmill."

She gazed up at the structure. Her first impression of the windmill had been correct.

Mr. Harper led her across the street on the far side of the square, then slowed his pace and pointed to a bright red door set against a white clapboard façade. "This is Mayor Wilkes's office, and Doc Walton is just two doors down." He pulled out his pocket watch, popped the cover open, and glanced at the face, then pursed his lips as he slid the watch back inside his vest pocket. "I'm sorry, Miss Davenport, but I have an appointment in a few minutes, so I'm afraid I can't escort you back to Maude's."

"Thank you for your assistance, but I can find my own way back."

He nodded. "See you after work, then."

Sophie watched him walk away, still puzzled about her strange reaction. Even through his frock coat, she'd been able to tell that his arm was muscled—not soft, like she would have expected for a banker.

She blew out a sigh. What did it matter how strong he was or if she felt an attraction—if that's what it was? Her days in Windmill were numbered. Once her mother discovered she was there, she'd be on the first train east.

The early-morning sun reached through the window, touching Sophie's eyelids, pulling her from her slumber. She stretched, not quite ready to crawl from her bed, though she knew she had to. She yawned. After the doctor's visit yesterday evening and his news that Aunt Maude had pneumonia, she'd felt compelled to sit with her aunt long into the night. But after nearly falling off her chair, she'd finally crawled into bed. For the briefest moment, she almost wished she were back home, so that she could stay in bed for another hour, with no responsibilities requiring her to rise.

Yet even the lure of additional rest wasn't enough to send her packing, especially with Aunt Maude so ill. Sophie tossed aside the covers and shivered. Though it was mid-May, this morning's temperature seemed chillier than recent ones. She pushed up from her bed and noticed that Hazel was gone; she had risen early. Amanda lay sprawled across the bed the girls shared, one arm and one leg hanging off each side, the worn quilt in a pile on the floor. Sophie picked up the tattered cover and looked it over. When she was forced to return home, making a new quilt for every child would be something she could do—she'd have all the time in the world. The thought of such a time-consuming project might overwhelm some, but it made her smile. Time passed more quickly when she kept busy.

She folded the cover, then brushed Amanda's dark hair off her face. "Time to wake up, sweetie. It's a school day."

Amanda groaned, but she rolled onto her back, and her eyelids fluttered open. "Do I have to go?"

Sophie tweaked the girl's nose. "Of course you do. You want to grow up to be smart like Hazel, don't you?"

Blowing out a loud sigh, Amanda sat up and rubbed her pretty blue eyes.

Sophie shed her nightgown, hung it in the wardrobe, and donned the dress and petticoats she'd worn the day before. Wearing a dress for several days in a row had taken some getting used to, but doing laundry daily wasn't practical when she had so many other things to do. She made her bed, then picked up her brush, ready to braid Amanda's hair and fix her own. She'd discovered that she enjoyed brushing the girls' hair. It was something her mother had done for her only several times, on the rare occasion she'd come downstairs earlier than the servant tasked with helping Sophie dress. Sophie's grip on the hairbrush tightened. This was probably the closest she'd ever come to mothering a child. The dismal thought left a lump in her stomach.

She set the brush on Amanda's bed, then helped her out of her nightgown and into her light brown dress. Sophie glanced at Amanda's peg on the wall but found it empty. "Where's your pinafore?"

Amanda lifted her pillow, checked the floor, and finally peeked under her bed. "Found it!"

Sophie sighed at the sight of the pitifully wrinkled, stain-covered apron. She'd need to wash it tonight and wished Amanda had another one besides the nice one she wore on Sundays to church. Both Hazel and Amanda desperately needed new clothes. Though the girls had never said anything, she'd seen the looks of longing on their faces as they took in Corrie's pretty frocks. Maybe once she finished honing her cooking skills, she'd work on a couple of dresses. In fact, she ought to teach the girls how to sew, and learning to make their own dresses would be a good incentive. If only she could think of something industrious that Mikey could do in the evenings to keep him out of trouble.

"Let's get your hair braided." Sophie sat on Amanda's bed and patted the space beside her. The girl plopped down, and Sophie started brushing and plaiting her long hair.

"I'm hungry." Amanda squirmed.

"I am, too, so sit still, so we can eat sooner."

Sophie heard a shuffling at the door and glanced over her shoulder. Hazel stood there holding a tray.

"I made Miss Maudie some tea and porridge."

Sophie blinked, taken off guard. "You made breakfast?"

Hazel nodded, a becoming rosy shade brightening her cheeks. "I hope that was all right. You seemed extra tired and didn't even stir when I got out of bed and dressed."

Guilt gnawed at her like a mouse to a feed sack. "I sat up with Auntie for several hours last night and am a bit more tired than usual," Sophie confessed. Usually she woke before the children, but not today. She never seemed to do enough. If she spent a proper amount of time caring for her aunt, the children went without, but if she focused on the children, she feared depriving her aunt of adequate care. She realized Hazel still stood at the door, watching her. She smiled. "Thank you, Hazel. That was very kind of you."

Obviously embarrassed by the praise, Hazel ducked her head, turned, and left the room.

Sophie took several swipes down Amanda's almost waist-length hair. A sudden scream rent the air. Sophie jumped, dropping the brush. She rose and hurried to the door. Hazel backed out of her aunt's bedroom. The first thing that came to Sophie's mind was the hole in the wall. Could a rat have gotten inside, after all?

Hazel turned in her direction, her face pale. The girl's mouth worked, but nothing came out. She lifted a trembling hand and pointed, then gasped a sob and ran down the hallway.

Sophie couldn't imagine what could have frightened the girl so. She moved toward her aunt's room, glancing at Mikey's door. She could only hope he hadn't pulled a prank of some kind. Inside Aunt Maude's room, her gaze traveled across the floor and furniture. Nothing seemed out of order. The tray sat by Maude's bed, a thin line of steam rising from the spout of the teapot like smoke from a chimney. If a rat was in the room, it must be under the bed or dresser. She hiked up her skirt so that she could get down on her knees, her gaze skimming her aunt's face. It was odd that she hadn't awakened to Hazel's scream. Sophie started to stoop, but her gaze darted back to her aunt. Something wasn't right. Maude's lips had turned blue, and her face had a grayish cast.

Her heartbeat escalated as she stared at her aunt's chest. It wasn't moving. "No, no, no."

Pain lanced her heart as she dropped her skirts and moved to the bedside. She reached out with a shaking hand and touched Maude's hand. Cold.

Sophie clutched her bodice and backed away, as Hazel had. Tears blurred her vision. Maude was no longer with them.

Chapter Eight

Josh hated imposing on Miss Davenport so early in the morning, but he had no choice. Standing on the porch of Miss Maude's house, he checked both children to make sure they were properly dressed—something he should have done before leaving the house—then knocked. Miss Davenport opened the door, and he instantly sensed something was wrong. Her eyes were red and watery, and he'd never seen her appear so dismal. It was still early in the day, yet she already looked exhausted. What had Mikey done now? Or had Miss Davenport finally realized that she wasn't up to the task of caring for a sick aunt and so many children? Maybe he should take Corrie and Toby with him. But Mr. Rutherford needed to talk to him about a loan, and the man didn't need his private business broadcasted in front of Aaron's children.

Miss Davenport cleared her throat and touched her fancy lace handkerchief to her nose. "Did you need something, Mr. Harper?"

What if she had taken sick? She did have that breathing problem the day he first saw her at the depot.

She lifted her brows, as if repeating her question.

"I, uh, hate to impose, but could I leave the children with you until school starts? They've eaten and are ready to go, but I had a customer come to my door and ask to meet with me before he catches the morning train."

"Of course." Even though she sounded far less cheerful than normal, she pushed the door back to allow the children entrance.

84

Corrie and Toby plodded in, and both turned and waved good-bye to him.

"Are you all right, Miss Davenport?"

Her eyes widened, but her surprise quickly disappeared behind a mask of schooled—yet still pretty—features. "Thank you for your concern, but I'm fine. It's been a…more difficult morning than average."

Josh pursed his lips and looked past her down the hall. "It's Mikey, isn't it? Do you want me to have a talk with him?"

She shook her head, a gentle smile lifting her sad countenance. "Thank you, but it isn't that. I'd better go and make sure the children are eating."

She shut the door without even waiting for his response. He stood there a moment, trying to understand why he'd been dismissed so quickly. A sudden memory burst through his mind of his sister-in-law, Sarah, being especially cranky every so often. "It's just the way of women," his ma had explained. "Give them some time to rest, and all will be fine."

He strode down the boardwalk past the house he rented and stopped at the bank, located next door. At least he didn't have far to travel to work. His family, although they lived and worked in the same place, had to cover much more ground in between. The hard work he did on the weekends he spent at home kept him from getting too soft due to sitting behind a desk all week. He tried to not let his work interfere too much with the time he spent with the children. With their father absent, he wanted them to know they were loved and important to him.

He reached in his pocket, pulled out the key to the bank, and opened the door. After pulling up all the shades and making sure everything was in order, he gathered a loan application and his record book and moved them to the desk in the main area so he could keep watch until the teller and bookkeeper arrived. He dropped onto the chair, and it creaked from his weight.

The memory of Miss Davenport's sad face tugged at his chivalry. She had looked so small and alone this morning that he'd been tempted for half a second to pull her into his arms and hug her. But then he'd regained his senses.

Still, he didn't like seeing her so distressed. He wanted to help, but he doubted she'd accept his comfort. And, truth be told, he'd rather be sparring with her, watching her dark eyes spark with indignation, than to see her so despondent.

Quick footsteps and then a knock at the bank door forced thoughts of the lovely yet frustrating Sophia Davenport from his mind. He needed to focus on business right now, but maybe, in a few hours, he could walk down and check on her.

⌒

The moment after she ushered the children out the door to school, Sophie dropped onto the couch. The tears she'd held at bay for the past hour fell in earnest. Had she focused too much on the children's needs and not enough on Aunt Maude's? She'd followed the doctor's instructions, but should she have done more?

She hugged her middle and rocked back and forth on the sofa, unable to stop her tears. She'd never dealt with a disaster like this before, but she couldn't just sit here—and she had to stop crying before it brought on an attack. Fighting to stem her sorrow, she tried to decide what to do next. Should she go for the doctor? Or Kate?

The breakfast dishes still sat on the table. And her aunt's body still lay upstairs. Just thinking of that brought more tears. She dabbed her nostrils, then sucked in a breath so she could blow her nose, but it caught in her throat. A wheeze escaped. Sophie closed her eyes. She couldn't have an attack now.

She was alone, with no one to help her. "Please, Lord, help me. Show me what to do."

Pleasant things. Think of happy things. The image of her garden back home drifted into her mind like a butterfly alighting on a dianthus. She had flowers here, she remembered, and pushed off the sofa, taking care to keep her breathing slow, steady. On the dining room table sat the lovely bouquet that Mr. Harper had brought as a peace offering the other day. The flowers weren't as pretty now. Even though they'd been bent when he handed them to her, most had revived once she put them in water. She fingered a soft yellow petal of the goatsbeard, which reminded her of a large dandelion. A trip to Mr. Harper's garden would make her feel better, but she had too much to do.

She gathered the dishes that Mikey and Amanda had forgotten to remove from the table, and carried them to the counter. Her gaze landed on her aunt's uneaten porridge. Her chin wobbled. No! She had to stop thinking of her aunt and stop tossing accusations her own way. Her throat was starting to loosen, and she was able to breathe deeply again. Keeping busy would help. She ticked off a list in her head of all the things she needed to do. *Meet with the undertaker. Visit Aunt Maude's doctor and the pastor.*

The dishes could wait, but she needed to wire her father about his sister's death. He would be on the first train west, but for what purpose?

To bury his sister. She shook her head. As warm as the weather was growing, Aunt Maude's body would need to be buried quickly. They couldn't wait several days for her father to arrive.

That left only one reason for his coming: to escort her home.

That would be first and foremost in his mind. He would certainly be sad about his sister, but if he returned home with Sophie before his wife came back from her trip, he wouldn't have to listen to as much fussing about his foolishness in allowing her to travel to Kansas. Yes, Mother would be upset, but seeing that Sophie had survived and was fine would temper her anger. And then Sophie would return to her boring existence.

She walked to the back door and stared out. If she left, what would happen to the children? Mr. Harper would manage to care for his niece and nephew somehow, of that she was certain. But what about Hazel, Amanda, and Mikey? Sure, they could go home to their parents, but what about their education?

She untied her apron and hung it on the peg. The school term would be over in a few weeks. Would it be possible to keep her aunt's death a secret for that long?

No, that was foolish. Few things remained a secret in a small town like Windmill. But maybe she could keep the news from her father. Since he couldn't arrive in time for the burial, there wasn't much point in his traveling so far.

A spark of hope flamed to life. If she could keep things together for a few more weeks, then the children could return to their homes, and their parents would have all summer to make arrangements for their care next fall. Excitement pushed away her somberness.

But would she be sinning by waiting to inform her father of his sister's death?

She leaned against the kitchen counter and stared outside again. She wouldn't lie to him, but what would be the harm in waiting until the children had gone home to tell him?

Just a little more time on her own, to show her parents that she was normal. Capable. She could do this.

Upstairs, she washed her face in the porcelain bowl and checked her reflection in the mirror. The redness in her face had mostly gone away, but the skin under her eyes was puffy. Hopefully, no one would notice.

She visited the undertaker, Mr. Adams, and made arrangements for him to pick up her aunt's body, with a request that he come to the back door well before school let out. Next, she stopped by Dr. Walton's office, and he made his apologies for not being able to help Maude more. Lastly, she went to Reverend Douglas's house and told him what had happened.

He took hold of her hand. "I'm so sorry, Miss Davenport. We all loved your aunt, and she will be missed."

"Thank you, Reverend." Sophie looked away. "I just wish...."

"I hope you're not feeling like this is your fault."

"How can I not?" She forced herself to look at him again, sure she'd see disgust in his gaze, but she didn't. "If I'd taken better care of her—"

He shook his head. "Gerald—uh, Doc Walton came over yesterday after checking on Maude and told me she had pneumonia and wasn't doing well. He said he was surprised she'd hung on this long, and if you hadn't come to care for her and the children, he's sure she would have died sooner."

His words comforted Sophie. "Thank you for sharing that with me."

He nodded. "When would you like to have the service? You know we can't wait for your family to arrive, unless you want to go ahead and have her buried and hold the service at a later date."

Sophie's gaze drifted up the hill to the town's small cemetery, which sat a short distance behind the church her aunt had attended. "I don't want to wait. It will be easier on the children if we go ahead with the service. Mr. Adams said that if I could get my aunt c-cleaned up"—Sophie hated the way her chin trembled—"he could have the casket ready for a service this evening. Do you think that's too soon?"

"No, I don't. It won't take long to get the word out, and most of the folks who knew your aunt live in Windmill. I can be ready. If you could just give me the names of your family and some information about her past, that's all I should need."

Sophie spent a few minutes answering the pastor's questions. As she prepared to leave, the pastor's wife hurried inside with Kate McMillan close on her heels. Kate's worried expression brought new tears to Sophie's eyes.

"Oh, you poor dear." Kate pulled her into her arms, hugging her. "We'll take care of everything. Don't you worry."

Sophie clung to her friend for a long moment before stepping back. "I would appreciate your help. I've never had to prepare a body." Closing her eyes, she worked hard to control her emotions. She had far too much to do and no time to collapse or have an asthma attack.

"I want to make sure my aunt's"—she cleared her throat—"that her body is gone before the children come home from school."

Kate took her hand. "Of course."

Mrs. Douglas stepped close. "How can I help?"

Sophie thought for a moment. "Could you spread word about my aunt's passing and the service this evening?"

The kind woman smiled. "Certainly, and afterward, I'll come to Maude's place to help. When will the service be?"

Sophie glanced at Reverend Douglas.

"Would around six thirty this evening work? The sun doesn't set now until almost seven thirty, and folks will be finished with their supper."

She nodded. "That would be fine."

"Good. We will meet in the church and go up to the cemetery afterward."

Sophie wasn't sure how she'd gotten back outside. Her whole body felt numb. Her head hurt, and her eyes ached from the tears she'd shed. The pastor's words had encouraged her, but she still felt that she was somehow at fault.

Kate slowed her steps. "I need to stop at the house and leave instructions for the girls about supper, and then I'll be over. Will you be all right in the meantime?"

Nodding, Sophie smiled, hoping to alleviate her friend's concern.

"I'll see you in a few minutes, then."

As Sophie walked home, she couldn't help wondering how Hazel and Amanda were doing. She'd asked them both to keep quiet about her aunt's death, so as not to scare the other children, but one of them must have told their teacher; otherwise, how would Kate have known? Should Sophie have kept them home today, instead of making them go to school? Should she check on them?

She shook her head. Seeing her there would only upset them.

A wagon drove down Main Street, past the mercantile, in front of which several women stood, visiting. The depot at the end of the street was vacant; there wouldn't be another train today. The scene was normal—the same view you'd see in most towns, except that today wasn't a normal day.

She blew out a heavy sigh and pushed her feet into action. As she came upon the bank, her steps slowed. Mr. Harper had a right to know about Aunt Maude. She should have told him when he'd stopped by this morning, but she hadn't been prepared to share the distressing news. He would most have likely informed her that Corrie and Toby would no longer be staying with her, and she was sure he'd find some way to blame her. Too bad, because she had actually started to like the man, and not just from a physical standpoint.

Stiffening her backbone, she turned and entered the bank. The door to Mr. Harper's office was closed, so she crossed over to the teller's cage. The same teller peered out, and again, he didn't look pleased to see her. Was he just being protective of his employer's time, or did he dislike her for some reason?

"How can I help you, ma'am?"

"I need to see Mr. Harper, if you please."

His lips curved into what could only be called a smirk. "I'm afraid he had to leave town for a while."

"He left town?" What about the children? Had he mentioned his travel plans that morning?

"Yes, but he will return shortly."

"I see. Would you please inform him that Miss Davenport needs to talk with him?"

"Mr. Harper is very busy, ma'am. Surely you can talk to him about those two young mischief-makers he calls 'family' when he picks them up."

Sophie frowned. "That is not for you to decide, sir. Just give him my message."

She turned and strode out of the bank, afraid that if she didn't leave quickly, she'd spew out all the frustrations of the day on the rude teller.

At her aunt's door, she paused. Was it foolish of her to not want to be alone in the house with a corpse?

She nearly wilted at the ridiculous notion. God was with her, and He would give her the strength to get through this awful day and the difficult ones ahead. She turned the handle and went into the kitchen to heat some water. Then she'd go upstairs, get Aunt Maude's Sunday dress, and iron out any wrinkles.

With the water heating, she paused at the bottom of the stairs. She needed flowers for the grave. Would Mr. Harper be upset if she used the bouquet he'd given her?

She went back to the kitchen and studied it. Two of the flowers probably needed to be tossed out the back door, and several others were too cheery for a funeral. If she asked him, surely he'd allow her to cut some fresh ones, but his teller had said he'd gone somewhere. What if he didn't return in time for the funeral? Before she could change her mind, she found a knife and hurried outside, crossing the yard to Mr. Harper's garden. She realized she hadn't noticed it before, because of the shed and the wooden fence that blocked her view.

As she stepped around the shed, she caught a whiff of a floral scent and gasped at the beauty before her eyes. An artist's palette of floral wonder spread out before her. Crimson. Pink. Lemon.

Purple. There were many plants that had yet to blossom, but the ones in bloom were beautiful. Along the far side nearest the bank grew a row of vegetables. Yellow and white butterflies flitted around the flowers, as if struggling to decide which flower's nectar to sample. Mr. Harper must spend most of his evenings out here tending his garden to keep it in such a nice condition.

Sophie started to clip one flower, but guilt nibbled at her conscience. She went to the rear door, knocked hard, and waited. It was possible Mr. Harper had returned home and had not told his teller. Several minutes passed, and she knew she needed to get home before Kate arrived, so she returned to her task. Taking a steeling breath and whispering a prayer that Mr. Harper would forgive her, she clipped eight stems of flowers similar to the ones he'd given her, then hurried home.

After tossing out the old bouquet and filling the vase with fresh water, she washed her hands and started upstairs. As she trod on one of the squeaky steps, instead of encountering solid wood, her foot broke through, sending a loud crack ricocheting up the stairway. She sucked in a sharp breath and quickly grabbed the banister to keep from falling. She backed down two stairs and bent over to inspect the broken one. The carpet runner was loose, and there were scratches on the edge of the step, as if someone had pried it loose with the claw of a hammer. She pulled the runner away to study the problem. The right side of the step had cracked and given way, but there were scratch marks all over that piece of wood. She hadn't noticed them before, because the rug had concealed them. The step above the broken one also looked to have been tampered with. Was this an example of poor craftsmanship? Or had someone purposely damaged them?

She tested the other steps, making sure they were safe, then set a stack of books over the broken one, so the children would know to walk around it. Sitting on the stairs, she leaned against the railing. Incompetency hovered around her. She'd failed to care for her aunt properly, and now Maude was dead. Mr. Harper wasn't happy with her efforts to care for his niece and nephew, and now she'd stolen from him, albeit for a good reason. Discouragement made her eyes sting. If a more competent person had come in her place, would Aunt Maude still be alive?

Maybe her parents were right.

Maybe she didn't have what it took to live on her own.

Chapter Nine

Josh reined his horse, Chester, back toward town. Measuring, inspecting, and arranging everything for the auction at the Baker property had taken much longer than he'd expected. Disappointment still lingered in Mr. Baker's eyes, but his wife was obviously excited to be moving close to her family again. Life on the Kansas prairie wasn't for everyone. Josh was proud that his family had carved out a living with their stage stop, made popular by great home-cooked meals and his family's warm hospitality. The railroad had brought changes—good changes, for the most part. But those who refused to adapt, like Mr. Baker, were doomed to fail.

Josh glanced toward the horizon, lit on fire by the setting sun with a beautiful orange glow intermixed with shades of pink. The beauty of God's creation never failed to touch him, but he couldn't dwell on the view tonight. Corrie would be concerned because he was late picking up her and Toby. Ever since losing her mother, the girl had been especially given to worry if anyone returned home later than normal. Toby rarely fussed about that, since he was too young to remember Della's death and the trauma the family had endured, especially Aaron and Ethan. Josh didn't like remembering those sad days, but they were a part of his family's history. He guided his horse off the trail that led to the Bakers' property and reined him onto the road heading back to Windmill.

Della's untimely demise had left Aaron a twenty-six-year-old widower with two young children to raise. More than that, it had created a rift between him and Ethan and made things tense for the whole family. Josh would never forget how Ethan had blamed himself for Della's death. Though Aaron may have also felt a degree of guilt, his youngest brother had carried a heavy load of guilt for several years. Sarah—and the good Lord—had finally brought Ethan to his senses and helped him accept the truth that Della's death was an accident.

A brown rabbit zigzagging away from a low-swooping hawk low caught Josh's eye. He grinned when the fuzzy critter dove under a shrub, leaving the hungry predator to find its meal somewhere else. Had Sarah felt like that pursued rabbit at one time, with all the men who had come to the stage stop seeking her hand?

As Chester moved at an easy lope, Josh pondered how Sarah had almost caused a division between all three brothers, each of whom had vied for her hand. For a brief time, Josh had thought she was the woman for him, but he'd never stood a chance, because she'd already lost her heart to Ethan. And soon their second child would be born.

Blowing out a sigh, Josh topped a hill and saw the edge of town in the distance. He reined in his horse and gazed at Windmill, rising up on the prairie. He lifted his hat, allowing the breeze to cool his sweaty head. Thoughts of his little brother being married and becoming a father again created a longing deep in Josh's gut. He'd love to be married, but Sarah had been the only woman ever to catch his eye. A petite young lady with light brown hair and sable eyes slipped into his mind, as if arguing that point, but he shook his head. He may be attracted to Miss Davenport's beauty and determination, but she wasn't his type. He wanted someone hearty who could cook like his ma and run a hectic home like an army regiment. He was a man who liked structure, order. That was why working in town at the bank suited him, for now.

The clouds parted, sending the glint of a sunbeam shining in his eyes. He tugged his hat lower on his forehead. The sun would set soon, but he'd be home by then, and the children ready for bed. He hoped Miss Davenport had fed them supper, since he was so late getting back. He nudged Chester to a trot and then a comfortable lope. The scent of horse and dust mixed with the more pleasant fragrance of wildflowers. Too bad he didn't have time to stop and study them, to make sure he had all of them listed in his book of local flowers, with pictures and descriptions.

Miss Davenport had mentioned liking flowers. Maybe he should show her his book. Would she like it as much as Sarah had?

"Ah, what does it matter?" Josh chuckled when Chester flicked back his ears, as if he were actually listening. "No, ol' boy, I have no designs on Miss Davenport."

Sure, she was pretty and spunky. But he didn't fully trust that she was competent to care for a sick woman, a house, and so many children. Her fancy dresses screamed wealth, and most of the rich women he'd encountered among the groups at his family's stage stop expected to be waited on and seemed incapable of caring for themselves, much less other people. Maude Archer had showed no improvements under the care of her niece, and the children had been disorderly, far more so than normal. What *he* was going to do about the situation remained to be seen.

⌒

Sophie stood at her aunt's graveside with the children gathered around her. A larger crowd than she'd expected had turned out, in spite of the short notice. The girls all sniffled, Toby leaned against his sister, and Mikey sat, uncommonly subdued, under a tree a few yards away. The sun hunkered down behind the horizon, as if mourning the loss of Maude. It cast an ethereal glow across the small cemetery, almost as if creating a portal for her aunt's journey into heaven.

The pastor read a Scripture verse, but Sophie's mind was too numb to comprehend it. Aunt Maude was dead. Dr. Walton and the Reverend and Mrs. Douglas had all attempted to assure her that she wasn't at fault, and their encouragement had helped, but would her father blame her?

The pastor closed his Bible and gazed around at the crowd, closing his brief message. "Maude Archer was a good woman and a friend to all who met her. She was a petite lady with a big heart who blessed many families by opening her home to their children so they could live in town and attend school. She will be deeply missed. Shall we pray?"

Sophie bowed her head, thankful that her aunt had so many friends. Amanda leaned against her, and Sophie brushed her hand across the child's head. Somehow, she needed to contact the children's parents to let them know what had happened and to inform them that she was willing to continue watching the children until the end of the school term.

With the prayer over, Reverend Douglas stepped back and nodded to Sophie. She disentangled herself from the children, scooped up a handful of the freshly turned earth, and sprinkled it across her aunt's pine casket. Her throat tightened as tears burned her eyes. Stepping back again, she worked hard to control her emotions. Her aunt's friends might think her coldhearted for not crying, but they didn't know what tears might cost her.

She motioned to the children, and they each grabbed a fistful of dirt and tossed it into the hole in the ground.

Sophie moved back further to allow the others to pay their respects. Tears ran down Hazel's pale cheeks as she laid the flower bouquet on the ground beside the grave, and when the girl shuffled over, Sophie put her arms around her. Hazel's sobs set Amanda and Corrie to crying. Toby just hung his head, looking a bit confused. Sophie needed to get them away from here.

"Come on, children. Let's go home." What an odd feeling, telling youngsters who didn't belong to her to follow her home to a house that wasn't hers—or theirs. Mikey rose and dragged his feet as he walked down the hill ahead of her, with Toby on his heels.

"Miss Davenport."

Sophie glanced back to see Mr. and Mrs. Purdy approaching her, followed by several people she hadn't met. She turned to the children. "Go on home. I'll be there in a few minutes."

Three pairs of teary eyes gazed up at her. Maybe the girls were afraid to go in Maude's house without her.

"C'mon, you all." Hazel straightened, wiped her face with her sleeve, and took hold of the younger girls' hands.

Mrs. Purdy paused beside Sophie. She touched Sophie's arm, gaining her attention. The plump woman's pale blue eyes were filled with sadness. She huffed several breaths. "We were so sorry to hear about Maude. She was such a dear."

"Thank you."

Mrs. Purdy nodded and handed Sophie a jar. "Rhubarb jam. Maude bought this for the children when she could. They all loved it."

Sophie accepted the gift. "That's very kind of you."

Her husband glanced up from studying his boots. "If you need anything, you let us know." He pursed his lips, then escorted his wife down the hill.

A woman Sophie had seen at church stopped beside her and held out a basket. "I'm Louise Snider. I baked some bread and a few other things to help out."

Sophie smiled. "Thank you. I appreciate your thoughtfulness."

Several other women offered their condolences and added items to Mrs. Snider's basket. They were being polite, Sophie knew, but she was anxious to return to the house and get away from so many people, all focused on her. She wasn't used to being the center of attention. The children needed her, and she was concerned about Mr. Harper. Why hadn't he come for Corrie and Toby or attended the funeral?

Finally, she was able to walk down the hill with Reverend and Mrs. Douglas and the McMillan family. Behind her, the *swish, plop* of the dirt being shoveled over her aunt's casket taunted her.

Swish, plop.

She's dead.

Swish, plop.

Your fault.

Swish, plop.

Closing her mind to the taunts, she picked up her pace, hoping distance would chase away her doubts.

"Would you like some help getting the children in bed?" Kate caught up to her, panting several quick breaths.

Sophie stopped and turned to face the small group, including Kate's husband, a big, bearded man with kind gray eyes. "I can't thank you all for the kindness you've lavished on me today. The food. The help preparing…my aunt." She couldn't say "body." It sounded too cold. Too harsh. "But the children can get themselves ready. I think it would be best if it were just us tonight. They may need some comforting or may want to talk."

"That's probably wise." Mrs. Douglas looped her arm around her husband's. "Shall we head home, Reverend Douglas?"

He smiled and nodded. Then he glanced at Sophie. "If *you* need to talk, Miss Davenport, please come see me at any time."

"Thank you."

Kate hugged Sophie, then followed her family to the left, while Sophie headed right toward Main Street. She was the only one around, except for a pair of cowboys riding up to the saloon.

The setting sun had painted the clouds a bright pinkish orange and illuminated the buildings to her right, making them look on fire. She loved the Kansas sunsets with their brilliant hues. In St. Louis, viewing a sunset was a rare event because of the tall buildings and large homes. Not to mention she was rarely outside at evening time.

The wind whispered past her ear, as if calling to her. A pair of pigeons cooed from their perch atop a hitching post, while a scruffy dog ran across the street, casting a quick glance in her direction, then disappeared between two buildings. Welcoming lights flickered in the windows of the few houses she could see at the moment, and the quiet clatter of the windmill churning in the light breeze drew her gaze to the square. Something about this quaint town set on the gently rolling hills of the prairie lured her to stay, in spite of all that had happened.

But what was there for her here?

And even if she wanted to stay, her parents would never allow it.

⌒

Josh rode into town as dusk set in. Guilt ate at him for taking so long with his task. He was deplorably late, and Miss Davenport had every right to harangue him.

The streets were quiet, except for the usual ruckus down at the saloon. His gaze settled on a woman walking alone. Miss Davenport? Surely she hadn't left the children to go for a stroll at this late hour. He tapped his horse to a trot.

As he drew near, the woman picked up her pace, then climbed the two steps to the boardwalk. At least she had the sense to get out of the street when a rider was coming. She peered over her shoulder, her concern evident.

Once again, Josh felt like an oaf. He hadn't meant to frighten her. He simply wanted to know why she'd abandoned her duties. He stopped his horse and met her gaze at eye level. "Good evening, Miss Davenport. I'm surprised to see you out this late."

"Mr. Harper." She nodded and shifted the basket she carried. "I was growing concerned. You're much later than usual."

That she'd been concerned about him—not angry—tugged at his heart. His family loved him, but when was the last time someone else had worried about him?

Still, she had a duty she was neglecting. "Where are Corrie and Toby?"

She glanced down the street in the direction of Maude's house. "I sent the children home a few minutes ago."

Josh frowned. Where had they been at this hour? "Windmill is a relatively quiet town, Miss Davenport, but surely you realize that women and children shouldn't be out at dusk without an escort. Certain riffraff come to visit the saloons each evening."

She lifted a hand to her throat. "Yes, of course. But there were...um...extenuating circumstances." She looked down at the boardwalk.

Curious, Josh dismounted and patted Chester on the rump. The horse needed no more encouragement. He trotted down the street, then turned in between Josh's house and Miss Maudie's. Josh hopped up the steps, and Miss Davenport backed away as he drew near. "Might I ask where you've been?"

A myriad of expressions crossed her pretty face in the waning twilight, foremost of them sadness. She wrung her hands and seemed to have trouble looking at him.

His heart thumped hard. "Did something happen to one of the children?"

"No!" She shook her head, quick to reassure him, then heaved a sigh that came from deep within. She rested the basket on a porch rail and lifted her pain-filled eyes to his. "There's no easy way to say it. Aunt Maude died today."

As if a bullet had hit his torso, Josh lifted his hand to his chest to stem the pain. Kind, sweet Miss Maudie was gone? "What happened?"

"She died in her sleep. The doctor thinks pneumonia put added stress on her heart and that it gave out." Her lovely eyes glistened more than usual. "She'd eaten very little over the past few days, even though I encouraged her to try to consume more. Hazel took a tray up to her early this morning, and Aunt Maude—she was dead." Her eyes blinked several times.

A gamut of emotions raced through Josh. Miss Maudie hadn't been the same since her fall, but had she been worse than she'd let on? Had watching Corrie and Toby, as well as the others, been too much? His gut tightened. What if he was partially to blame for her death? He should have found someone else to keep the children, though he didn't know who. Miss Maudie had looked more fragile the last time he'd seen her, right before her niece arrived, but he'd chocked it up to pain from her broken arm and weakness from the cold she'd caught.

"I know this upsets you, Mr. Harper. I'm terribly sorry. I can't help feeling this was somehow my fault."

A gust of wind whipped her skirts against his pant leg and carried the rowdy music from the saloon their way, intruding on his grief. Miss Davenport sounded so alone that Josh almost pulled her into his arms. She sniffled but didn't cry. He settled for lightly touching her shoulder. "I partly blame myself."

"You? Why would you say that?"

"Because I allowed Miss Maudie to convince me she was healthier than she seemed. I shouldn't have let her talk me into leaving Corrie and Toby with her after her accident, but I did so partly because I knew she needed the income."

"Speaking of the children, I really need to get back to them."

"Of course." He took the basket from her and offered his arm.

She eyed it as if it could do her harm, then slowly lifted her hand and tucked it in the crook of his arm. Her light touch created an odd stirring in his gut, but he didn't dwell on it. He had too many other things on his mind. They walked in silence. As they passed the bank, he paused at the door, receiving a curious glance from Miss Davenport. He shook the handle, making sure it was securely locked—a habit he'd fallen into since assuming the position of president. As they continued on, something gnawed at the back of his mind. "You still haven't explained why you're out so late."

"Oh, my apologies. Because of the warm temperatures, and to make things easier on the children by avoiding a long delay, Reverend Douglas thought it best to have a quick funeral, so he held it this evening."

"I missed the funeral?" Josh stopped again. "Why didn't you inform me of Miss Maudie's death this morning? I never would have ridden out to the Bakers' place if I'd known."

"I was too distraught to explain this morning, when you showed up early with Corrie and Toby." She removed her hand from his arm and stepped to the side. "Later, I went to the bank after visiting the pastor, but you weren't there. The teller said he'd let you know that I needed to see you."

Gritting his teeth, Josh wondered why Walter Franklin had failed to pass along that important message. He certainly would have delayed his trip in favor of being here to comfort his niece and nephew. He would have a talk with Mr. Franklin in the morning.

"I guess you never got my message."

Josh shook his head and started walking again. He needed to get to the children and ensure that they were all right. Tomorrow, he would start looking for someone else to watch them. "I'll find a replacement to care for Toby and Corrie as soon as I can. When do you plan to leave?"

Miss Davenport halted at Maudie's door and gazed up at him, the light from the window illuminating her face. "I have no plans to leave at this time, Mr. Harper. You're more than welcome to continue bringing the children here—that is, unless you find me incompetent to care for them." She hiked her chin, and her sad eyes flashed, but not before he recognized the lingering self-doubt.

Josh wished he could reassure her, but how many times had he thought that very thing? When he'd first met her that day at the depot, she had seemed so frail. And yet, here she was, matching his stare, all but challenging him to admit he thought her incapable. There was more to Miss Davenport, he suspected, than he'd given her credit for. "There's no point in making a decision now. I need to get the children home."

And he didn't want to admit that he had wondered about her abilities.

She opened the door without further comment, but he could tell that his failure to protest her insinuation had affected her. The house was unusually quiet. Corrie and Toby lay at opposite ends of the couch. His niece opened her eyes, relief evident as she spotted him.

"Uncle Josh!" She slid off the sofa and hurried toward him, reaching up.

He lifted her into his arms, and she clung to him. "I'm sorry for not being here when you needed me."

"Miss Maudie...she died." Her warm tears bled through his shirt, staining his heart. Corrie always took death hard. "I miss her."

"I'm very sorry, sweetie. I had to ride out to a farm for some business, and it took much longer than expected."

"That's okay, but I was gettin' worried."

He hugged her. "I need to put you down and get Toby, since he's sound asleep."

As he made the short walk home, Josh realized that in the next few days, Miss Davenport would have more bad news to face. Miss Maudie's mortgage had been in arrears for months, but he hadn't had the heart to put the old woman out of her house. Now, he'd have no choice but to issue a foreclosure notice. Miss Davenport thought she'd be staying awhile, but when she learned about the situation, she would have no choice but to return home.

So, why did that thought bother him?

Chapter Ten

Sophie shuffled down the steps in the early-morning light. She'd gotten precious little sleep last night, thinking about her aunt, the children, and home. She ought to notify her father about Aunt Maude, but she knew the minute he received her telegram, he would purchase a train ticket—either one he'd send to her, with orders to head home posthaste, or one for himself, to come and get her. But she wasn't ready to leave. She couldn't leave—not until the children had finished school and returned to their homes. She refused to abandon them. And then, there were Corrie and Toby. What would Mr. Harper do with them after she left?

The sun had barely risen, but enough light shone in the windows that she had no trouble seeing her way to the kitchen. She paused at the doorway and leaned against the jamb. Was she being deceptive by not contacting her father? What would it hurt to wait a week or two? He'd already missed the funeral, and there was little he could do now, except arrange for the sale of her aunt's house; and it wouldn't sell any better now than it would in a few weeks. In fact, if she waited, she could fix up the house, so that the sale would bring her father more money—and that would please him.

With that decision made, she lit the lantern in the kitchen and stepped into the pantry, trying to decide what to serve for breakfast. Kate had given her a loaf of fresh bread, some eggs, and other food items, to make this first day after the funeral a bit easier, she had said. There had also been several tasty treats in the basket from Mrs. Snider.

Sophie lifted the lantern into the shadows and reached for the bread. She sucked in a gasp. All of the cans and crocks had been scooted to the side. The tin of tea had fallen on its side and opened, spilling leaves all over the shelf. Someone—or something—had been in here.

She'd never locked the exterior doors, because the children often made treks to the privy during the night, but maybe she should reconsider. Windmill was a peaceful town, but she couldn't be too careful, not with children in her care.

Pushing aside her worries about a possible intruder, she set the lantern on the floor, then brushed the crushed bits of tea leaves into the lid of the tin. The thought of throwing them out grated on her, but so did the idea of using them to make a cup of tea. She righted the tin and started to turn but then realized the bag of flour had been moved a foot to the left—or had she put it there the last time she'd used it? She couldn't remember.

Studying the scene, she found no indications of mice on the prowl—no holes in bags of sugar or coffee; no tiny footprints in the flour that had spilled on the floor. Nothing was missing, as far as she could tell. That meant someone must have been looking for something—something other than food. But what?

She lifted the lid of the bread box, finding everything as she'd left it. If one of the children had been hungry, surely he or she would have pinched off a piece of one of the breads her kind neighbors had given her yesterday. If a stranger had entered, why would he search the pantry and not take anything? Perplexed, she carried the tea lid to the counter, then went back for the lantern. Once the sun had fully risen and she could see better, she would clean the pantry and reorganize everything. That would help her to determine for sure if anything was missing.

An hour later, after tussling with the children to get them dressed and ready for school, all the while privately debating whether she should let them stay home a day to grieve, she plopped down on a chair in the deserted kitchen. She hoped she'd done the right thing in making the girls go to school again. Hazel was especially distressed, but Sophie had thought staying busy with schoolwork and being among her friends would erase the events of the previous day from her mind, at least temporarily. She needed to write to the girls' parents to let them know about Maude's death and to assure them that she was willing to keep the girls until the school year ended. If only it wasn't just three weeks away.

The front door flew open and banged against the wall. Mikey stood in the entrance, his blond hair mussed, his shirt half tucked into his pants.

"What are you doing back here?" She rose and walked into the parlor.

Different expressions crossed the boy's pallid face, chief among them worry. He looked up at her, but the defiance he so often wore was gone. "Some boys at school said you was gonna make me leave."

She looked him in the eye—an easy task, since he was almost as tall as she. "I'm hoping to stay until the school term is over, but that will partly depend on what your parents say."

Mikey scowled. "Don't got no parents. Just Wade."

"But he's your father, right?"

Mikey shrugged and lowered his gaze. "I reckon."

She had yet to meet Mr. Barnes, but he must care for his son, if he was willing to pay for Mikey's room and board so that he could get an education. "If your father agrees, you're welcome to stay as long as I'm here."

"You won't toss me out 'cause I'm so much trouble?"

The vulnerable expression on Mikey's face tugged at Sophie's heart. She cupped his cheek. "Of course not."

He studied her for a moment, as if gauging her sincerity, then grinned. He threw his arms around her shoulders, then released her and dashed back out the door. Sophie stood there, stunned. Maybe her efforts were making a difference.

With a smile warming her heart, she returned to the kitchen and stacked the dirty breakfast dishes as she pondered the near future. The situation was difficult, to be sure, but she'd never felt as free as she did here, with no one telling her what to do.

And what she needed to do now was to get busy.

As she ladled hot water from the stove's reservoir into a basin, she made a mental list of all she had to accomplish today. Besides washing the breakfast dishes and straightening the pantry, she thought she'd air out and clean her aunt's room and go through her dresses, to see if there were any she could cut down and rework for Hazel and Amanda. She nibbled her lip. Would they like that? Or would they not want to wear the clothes of a dead woman?

Outside the open kitchen door, a bird's cheerful chirp drew her gaze. It seemed odd that even though her aunt was gone, the world continued on. People who had attended the funeral last night had gone back to work this morning. Life went on, but a good, hardworking woman had gone to be with Jesus. Shouldn't things be different?

In truth, they were. *Just look at me.* She dearly missed her aunt—an aunt she'd just barely gotten to know—and yet, here she was, thinking of all the chores that needed to be done. She'd never lost someone close and didn't know what was expected of her. She glanced down at her dress. Navy with light blue piping, it was the darkest one she had brought with her. Should she make a black dress for mourning? Kate would know.

A loud knock at the door made her jump. She hurried through the house, hoping it wasn't someone else with food. They'd have a hard time finishing what they had already received before it spoiled. She pulled the door open. "Mr. Harper. I didn't expect to see you until this evening."

He removed his hat, revealing neatly combed hair almost the same shade as her father's dark walnut desk. Dressed in a nice-quality frock coat, pants, and vest, he would blend in well on the streets of St. Louis, except for the wide-brimmed, felt slouch hat he always wore—and his Western boots. His blueberry eyes captured hers. "I'm afraid I have some important business that can't wait."

"With me?" Sophie stepped back, embarrassed that she'd been staring at the handsome man. "Would you care to come in?"

He glanced past her, then turned, looking down the street. "It wouldn't be proper for me to come in with no one else at home."

"Oh, of course not." Sophie's cheeks ignited with heat. She would have thought of that, if she hadn't been admiring how immaculately he was dressed. "What about the porch?"

"Would it be possible for you to come to the bank? I hate to impose, but I have some papers there that I need to show you."

Why hadn't he brought the papers with him? Why didn't he just tell her what was wrong? She had hoped not to see too many people today, but the bank wasn't far, and the hour was still early. "I suppose so, if we could do it now."

He nodded. "I'll see you there, then." Before she could tell him that she merely needed to put on her hat and gloves and she'd be ready to go, he charged off like a thief with a posse on his tail.

Sophie hurried upstairs, removed her apron, and donned her hat and gloves. What could be so important that Mr. Harper needed to speak with her immediately? Her mind raced with possibilities. What if her aunt had left her some money? But then, if she'd had any extra, why was the house in such deplorable condition? Her heart jerked. What if her aunt *owed* the bank a large sum?

Sophie had little funds of her own. If Mr. Harper hoped she would pay off her aunt's debts, he would be sorely disappointed.

Sophie entered the bank, but instead of going over to the obnoxious teller, she went directly to Mr. Harper's office. His door was open, and he looked up when she paused in the entryway. He stood and nodded at her, but his pursed lips and serious expression did nothing to ease her taut nerves.

"C'mon in, Miss Davenport." He walked around his desk and held out his open palm beside the chair in front of his desk. "Please have a seat."

She sat, and while she adjusted her skirts, he walked behind her and shut the door. Her heartbeat picked up its frantic pace.

He returned to his chair, stared at a small stack of papers on his desk, and exhaled loudly. Sophie struggled to sit still. Mr. Harper's apparent reticence to broach the topic increased her anxiety. Whatever the news, it couldn't be any worse than what she'd already faced.

He tapped the papers, then looked up. "There's no easy way to tell you this. Your aunt was severely behind on her mortgage payments, and the bank has started the repossession procedures."

Sophie frowned. "Why would she have a mortgage? She and Uncle Sam moved here over twenty years ago, right after Windmill was founded. How could they still owe money?"

Mr. Harper lifted a page and peered at the one beneath it. "This says your uncle paid off the original loan, but he took out another one for five hundred dollars, just two years ago. He'd paid back just one hundred dollars before his death last year, and your aunt had managed to make only a few payments since then."

"If she'd paid back so little, why did you wait until now to repossess the house?"

Mr. Harper glanced toward the window, but the red flush rising up his neck and painting his ears didn't escape Sophie's notice. "I chose to overlook it because she had nowhere else to go. She was a kind, elderly woman who provided a service to this community. I couldn't find it within myself to put her out on the street." He pinned her with his gaze. "But now that she's gone, I can no longer overlook this debt. I'll need to put the house up for sale as soon as you can vacate it."

Sophie's mouth dropped open. He'd obviously been overly gracious to her aunt, but he had no intention of giving her any leeway. "You'd put the children and *me* out on the street without even allowing for the chance to make a payment on the mortgage?"

He folded his hands on his desk. "The house does not belong to you, Miss Davenport. Not unless you wish to purchase it."

Sophie coughed, her chest tightening. She closed her eyes, searching for a response while trying to calm her tense nerves. "I only need a few weeks, Mr. Harper." The short sentence left her breathless.

"For what, might I ask?"

"For school...to end." She sucked in a breath, hating the way she wheezed. She had to get control of herself. Gripping the arms of the chair, she focused on a knothole in the wall, inhaling, slow and steady.

"I think it's in your best interest to go back to your home, Miss Davenport, wherever that is. The children can return to their parents. I'll even see to it myself."

Sophie's ire flamed to life. She hadn't come all this way and endured all that she had, only to be told to leave town. The desire to lash out at Mr. Harper sent her pulse racing. Her battle for a breath was all that kept her from saying something she'd later regret. She shot up out of her chair, sending the room listing like a ship in a storm. "I am not...leaving." Sophie grabbed the edge of the desk, fighting for each breath. "Even if I...must find... another...place...to stay."

Mr. Harper leapt to his feet. "Don't be foolish, Miss Davenport."

Gritting her teeth, she pressed her hand against her chest and shut her eyes, forcing herself to stay calm. She had to get out of there before her throat closed any more. "I'll start searching... today."

"What?" He walked around his desk and frowned. "Are you all right?"

Heedless of what he thought, Sophie opened her mouth wide, desperately needing oxygen. The tiny breaths of air weren't enough for her starving lungs. White dots of light swam in her peripheral vision. *Oh, no!* She stretched out her hand, but her legs gave way, and she fell against him.

Chapter Eleven

Josh reached for Miss Davenport, keeping her from falling on the floor, and pulled her close. Dreadful wheezes filled the room as she struggled for each breath. He stared down at her pale face, more scared than he could ever remember being. This was his fault. "How can I help?"

She motioned toward the chair. Josh assisted her over to it and lowered her down. She tilted her head back, mouth open, gasping for breath.

Josh forked his fingers through his hair. He wanted to do something—anything—to help her, but he didn't know what to do. He patted her shoulder. "Try to relax, Miss Davenport. Everything will work out. I'll find a way somehow to extend the loan."

Her face had grown as white as the daisies in his garden. Her big brown eyes held fear and pain. "C-coffee...please."

Coffee? Why would she want that now? Regardless, Josh crossed the room, opened his door, and stepped across the threshold. "Franklin! Get Doc Walton." He turned to the bookkeeper, David Samuels. "Mr. Samuels, bring a cup of coffee to my office, quickly." Josh hurried back to Sophia's side.

Thankfully, the teller didn't dawdle, as he often did. On his way to the door, Mr. Franklin skidded to a halt just outside Josh's office, his gaze latching onto Sophia's back. "What'd you do to her?"

Josh shot him a scowl. "Get the doctor. Fast!"

"But the money in my till—"

"Go!"

The man's eyes widened at Josh's shout, and then he spun on his heels and hurried to the door. Josh opened his window, hoping the fresh air might help Sophia. As he muttered a prayer for her, he spied the teller, who dodged around a buggy, then jogged his way to the boardwalk across the street. With the exception of Emma Stone, who was unwell when she'd first arrived at the stage stop with her niece—Josh's sister-in-law, Sarah—he'd never been around anyone who wasn't in good health. His family members had suffered cuts, strained muscles, and other maladies common to ranchers, but not a chronic ailment, such as Sophia struggled with. Even Sarah's aunt Emma had eventually recovered from the condition that had plagued her for years.

Mr. Samuels shuffled in, carrying a cup coffee, which had sloshed onto the saucer. The man sucked in a sharp breath when Sophia emitted a loud wheeze.

Josh took the cup from him and nodded his thanks. "Keep an eye on things, and if anyone stops in to see me, ask them to return later, if they can."

"Yes, sir." He turned to leave, then spun back around. "Excuse me, sir, but my brother has similar breathing fits. He usually sips some whiskey to get relief."

Sophia stiffened, and she stared up at Josh, the slight shake of her head barely noticeable.

"Thank you for the suggestion, Mr. Samuels. We'll wait for the doctor before attempting anything."

Mr. Samuels nodded and bustled out of the office.

Josh dumped the spilled liquid out the window, then crouched down on one knee. "Are you ready for a drink?"

Sophia eyed the coffee as if it were sludge, but she pushed up in the chair. Her breathing had improved slightly, but the effort to sit up made her breathless again. Her chest rose and fell in sharp jerks, and she pressed one hand to her bodice, coughing several times. Finally, she nodded.

Josh held the cup for her and lifted it to her lips. "Drink it slowly."

She sipped the brew, then grimaced and shuddered.

"Is it too strong?" David preferred his coffee as thick as mud, but Josh liked it less potent.

"No, hate...the stuff." She broke into a fit of raspy coughs.

Then why did you ask for it? Josh set the cup and saucer on his desk, pulled his handkerchief from his pocket, and held it out for her. She lifted her gaze to his, accepted the gift, then closed her eyes as another round of bone-wrenching coughs assaulted her. Josh's heart ached for what she was enduring. He'd thought her weak, but a weaker woman wouldn't be fighting as hard as she.

Quick footsteps tapped across the wooden floor in their direction, like a woodpecker attacking a tree trunk. Josh looked up, relieved to see the doctor.

"What happened?" Doc Walton motioned Josh aside, so he rose and stepped back.

Sophia's coughing subsided, but she started wheezing again. "She couldn't catch her breath. Started wheezing like she is now and holding her chest, then she collapsed. I managed to catch her."

"You did, huh? You must have been standing awfully close to her."

"Well, I'd just come around the side of the desk...." Josh suddenly realized the doctor was poking fun at him, and gave up trying to explain.

Doc set his bag on Josh's desk, opened it, and tugged out a stethoscope. A noise pulled Josh's gaze to the doorway, where Mr. Franklin stood, watching the proceedings with obvious interest. Josh tightened his lips, but he realized he was doing the same thing. "I'll give you and Miss Davenport some privacy. If you need me, I'll be just outside the door."

Doc nodded. He stuck the rubber earpieces of the stethoscope in his ears and leaned over his patient. Josh strode across the office, motioned Mr. Franklin back, and closed the door. His teller scowled.

"You may return to your post."

Lips puckering, the man frowned but spun on his heel, and scurried around the back of the teller cage. Mr. Samuels, looking relieved, exited the cage, but instead of turning toward his corner, he shuffled over to Josh.

The man's gray eyes held concern. "I hope the young lady will be all right."

"Thank you. I do too."

Mr. Samuels nodded and turned away.

"Wait. What else do you do for your brother when he has a breathing fit?" Maybe he could learn something to help Sophia.

Pausing, Mr. Samuels shrugged. "Not a lot we can do. Give him his whiskey and try to get him to calm down. I have heard others say that coffee helps some people, but not my brother. His attacks tend to come on when he's upset." The man pursed his lips and headed back to his desk.

Josh liked the older man and wished he'd show more incentive, but he seemed quite content with his bookkeeping. Franklin was another issue. He had been rude and condescending since the day Josh took over for the previous president—and there was still the matter of his failure to tell Josh about Sophia's visit the day her aunt died. The teller obviously resented Josh's appointment as his superior when Franklin had more experience. That fact hadn't bothered Josh's uncle Elliot, who knew how hard Josh had studied to learn all about banking. Other than having to repossess properties from struggling farmers and businessmen and deny others a loan, he liked the job all right. But he hadn't been as enthralled with the position lately as he'd been in the beginning. Perhaps banking wasn't the best career choice for him.

The door handle rattled, and Josh spun around to face the doctor.

"We need to get Miss Davenport home. Could you help me?"

Josh nodded. "I can carry her."

Sophia gasped, and the barking cough started again. Josh was almost certain she was reacting to his offer, but the stubborn lady had no business trying to walk home in her condition.

Doc placed several instruments in his bag, then looked at him. "Are you certain you don't want my assistance?"

"Yes, sir. I can manage." As petite as Sophia was, she couldn't weigh much more than Toby and Corrie added together, and he could hold both of them at the same time. He bent down and peered into her face. She stared back with wide, watery eyes, and gave a brief shake of her head. That she didn't attempt to argue with him told him the dire state she was in.

"Miss Davenport, please allow me to take you home. You'll feel much better there."

Still wheezing, she studied his face. After a long moment, she closed her eyes and gave him a single nod. Delight soared through him that she would trust him enough to let him carry her. "Take my hand and let me help you up."

She inhaled through her nose, as if preparing herself, then reached out. Josh pulled her to a standing position, supporting her with his other hand. She wobbled, but Josh bent and scooped her up before she could fall back into the chair. She sat stiffly in his arms, panting heavy breaths.

"Relax, and put your arm around my neck. It will make things easier for both of us."

Her gaze latched onto his—so close, he could feel the warmth of her breath on his cheek. His heartbeat charged to a gallop, like a racehorse shooting off the starting line. With her so close, he could see several shades of dark brown in her irises. And her eyelashes—he hadn't realized how long they were. He hadn't taken a step, and yet he felt winded.

A blush infused Sophia's pale cheeks with pink. She lowered her gaze and lifted one arm, draping it loosely around his shoulders. Her wheezing increased, as if the simple act had stressed her. Josh wished she would look up again. He wanted her to see that he would protect her. He blinked at the surprising thought. Somewhere in the course of the past fifteen minutes, something in him had changed. He no longer saw her as a weak, incapable woman, but one he wanted to see healthy and smiling again. Smiling at him.

Doc cleared his throat. "This bag of mine is gettin' heavy, and we'll get there lots faster if you move your feet." An ornery grin tilted his lips, and his eyes gleamed with mischief.

Duly chastised, Josh pulled Sophia tighter against his side and stepped forward. Franklin gawked at him as he carried her through the bank, but Mr. Samuels glanced up for only a second before returning to his bookkeeping. Josh followed Doc to the door, praying for Sophia. She had to be all right. Mr. Samuels said getting upset was often what started his brother's attacks. The thought that Josh had caused Sophia's distress and thus brought on this attack repulsed him. He should have waited until the pain from her aunt's death was no longer so raw. What had he been thinking? Sophia had lost her only yesterday.

He paused at the door, glancing once more at Franklin and Mr. Samuels. "Hold down the fort. Don't know when I'll be back."

Doc opened the door, and Josh stepped out onto the boardwalk. He stopped for a moment to allow his eyes to adjust to the brightness of the day.

"Look! Ma, what's wrong with her?"

"Shh…Jimmy, hush."

Josh turned just enough to see a young boy with his mother. Both had stopped on the boardwalk and were staring. Sophia, obviously embarrassed, laid her head on his shoulder, her hair tickling his chin. Her hat, still tied beneath her chin, had fallen off and rested against his arm. Josh pushed his feet into motion. He needed to get her home before the whole town witnessed her malady.

Sophia's body quivered as her chest shook with each ragged breath. With her head down as it was, he wondered how she could inhale at all. He safely maneuvered the steps to the ground and quickly passed his house. Birds sang, riders walked their horses down the street, and the familiar swish of the windmill's blades signaled that life continued, in spite of Sophia's struggles. The normalcy of it all irritated him.

Doc opened the front door of Miss Maudie's house, and Josh carried Sophia inside, out of view of the curious townsfolk.

"Should I put her on the couch?" Josh eyed the old sofa, knowing it would be dreadfully uncomfortable to lie on.

Doc looked at it, too, then glanced at the staircase and nudged his chin up. "You think you could manage the climb?"

Sophia lifted her head. "I…can…walk."

"So can I." Josh smiled, hoping to set her at ease. Though Sophia was fairly light, Josh wasn't accustomed to carrying this amount of weight such a distance. Still, he would manage. At the top of the stairs, he puffed out, "Which way?"

"Put her in Maudie's room," said the doctor.

Sophia shook her head as if the idea bothered her, but she didn't voice her objection, so Josh followed the doctor to a room down the hall on the right. He placed her on top of the colorful quilt and stepped back. His arms felt empty without her, so he crossed them over his chest. He wasn't leaving until he knew she'd be all right. Her breathing was still labored, her face pale.

Doc pulled out his stethoscope and bent down, pressing it against Sophia's chest. After a moment, he straightened. "Could you turn over, please?"

Sophia turned onto her left side, and the doctor placed the stethoscope against the back of her dress, paused a moment, then checked several other places before finally straightening. He turned to Josh. "I think she'll be all right, but I'd like to get her out of her tight clothes."

Sophia gasped. She rolled over again, her eyes wide, and shook her head. "No."

Josh's eyes widened too, and he held up one hand, palm toward the doctor. "Don't look at me."

Doc snickered. "I thought you could run over and fetch Kate McMillan."

"Oh. Um...sure." Josh backed out the door, embarrassed by the doctor's continued chuckles. He gave Sophia a final glance, but her eyes were closed, and one arm rested across her forehead. Those attacks must be exhausting.

He jogged down the stairs, noticing that several of the steps were loose. Maybe he could fix them soon, for Sophia. He realized that at some point today, he'd stopped thinking of her as Miss Davenport—in his mind, at least. He was so thankful the doctor had said she would be all right.

As he hurried toward the McMillans', he thought about carrying Sophia. About her arm around his neck and her head on his shoulder. About her breath touching his cheek, her mouth just inches away from his.

"Hey! Watch out!"

Josh glanced up and jerked to a halt. He'd walked right in front of a man on horseback trotting down Main Street. If the rider hadn't reined his mount to the right as quickly as he had, the animal would have plowed into Josh. "Sorry."

Josh deserved the scowl that was shot his way. He'd been so lost in his thoughts of Sophia, he hadn't even known he was in the street. He shook his head, checked the rest of the road, and hastened on.

Another thought dawned. Since this morning, he'd stopped thinking of Sophia as a weak, incapable woman, in spite of her attack in his office. Instead, he now thought of her as the woman he wanted to protect. She needed someone to watch over her. And he wanted to be the man to do that.

Chapter Twelve

Light...airy...Sophie drifted with the clouds. Blake approached, took her in his arms, and kissed her—her first kiss. It was all she'd dreamed about, hoped for. But then he stepped back, and she realized it wasn't Blake at all. Josh Harper had kissed her!

Her chest tightened, and she couldn't breathe. Suddenly, she felt as if she were falling. She jerked and coughed several times.

"Relax, Sophie. Try to breathe normally."

She lay back and tried to do what her mother had told her so many times. Forcing her eyes open, she glanced in the direction of the voice. "Kate?"

"Yes, I'm here. You had a bad fit, then finally went to sleep."

"I fell asleep?" Sophie gazed at the design in the tin ceiling tiles. "Where am I?"

"Now, don't get upset." Kate patted Sophie's arm. "You're in Maude's bed."

Sophie stiffened. "Oh. I remember." Mr. Harper had put her there, but she'd been unable to voice her objection at that moment. The thought of lying on the same bed her aunt had died in sent a shiver through her. She pushed up on her elbows, but Kate gently forced her back down.

"Doc Walton said he gave you some laudanum to help you relax. He said you must remain calm."

Laudanum. No wonder I fell asleep.

Kate fluffed a pillow with one hand and lifted Sophie's head with the other, placing the pillow behind her. "Pearl and me can change out the bedding. We just finished a new tick and stuffed it. As soon as you feel able to sit in a chair, we'll remove the old bedding and put on the new tick, along with clean sheets."

With the episode over and her breathing returned to normal, Sophie allowed the tenseness to flow out of her. She lifted her hand to her forehead, trying to remember the events leading up to her attack. She'd gone to Mr. Harper's office—and he'd said something about the house. *Oh.* "Mr. Harper said he had to repossess Aunt Maude's house and that I should go back home."

Kate wrung out a washcloth over the bowl on the bedside table, then placed it on Sophie's forehead. "Well, no wonder you became so disconcerted. The nerve of him doing that, the day after—" Kate broke off her sentence, pressing her lips tightly together, as if the mention of Aunt Maude would upset Sophie.

Her aunt was gone, and nothing could change that. But the children…and the house…. "What am I going to do?" The memories of that morning's meeting resurfaced: What Mr. Harper had said. How it had upset her. How she'd had an embarrassing episode, right there in his office. Mortification sent heat marching across her cheeks. "He carried me home, didn't he?"

"That's what Josh said." An odd grin lifted her friend's lips, and her eyes twinkled. "He caught you when you swooned, and carried you here."

"I did not swoon. He told Doc Walton he'd carry me home, and did. I was weak at the moment and didn't object. Now I wish I had." She covered her cheeks with her hands. "How will I ever face him again?" Sophie rolled away from Kate, turning toward the window. Mr. Harper had doubted her abilities from the start. What must he think of her now?

"Don't be upset, Sophie." Kate patted her shoulder. "Josh Harper is a gentleman—and a nice one, at that. Why, I could hardly get him to leave here and go back to the bank. His only concern is for your health and well-being."

And the house he wants to repossess.

Why had she dreamed of kissing him? And why had she enjoyed it?

"Your breathing sounds as if it's back to normal. Do you want to try sitting up?"

A list of all the things she needed to do infiltrated her thoughts. "I need to *get* up."

She sat and swung her legs over the side of the bed. Kate rushed to her side, looking as if she was about to have her own fit—a fit of apoplexy.

"You can't get out of bed, other than to sit in the chair—and that's only for a short time. Doc said you should stay in bed all day and rest."

Sophie tested her breathing, slow and steady, relishing her relaxed throat. Thank the Lord, the episode had passed. She looked at Kate. "I appreciate your concern and that you came to sit with me, but I've had many of these episodes, and while they leave me feeling a bit weaker than normal, there's no reason to stay in bed."

Kate's expression said she wasn't convinced.

The warm breeze drifted through the window, lapping at her arms and making her aware that she was wearing nothing but her chemise. Her heart jolted. Surely she hadn't been undressed by the doctor—or, God forbid, Mr. Harper. Just the thought brought heat to her cheeks and tightened her throat again. "What happened to my clothes?"

"I took them off. Doc thought you would breathe better without your corset and dress."

"That must have been difficult to do by yourself, especially since the laudanum had knocked me out."

"Oh, Pearl helped. She's downstairs fixing some chicken soup and biscuits for lunch. It should be ready soon."

Sophie started to rise, but Kate stopped her again.

"Tell me what you want, and I'll get it."

She hated the sense of being coddled and not allowed to do even the smallest of tasks. Yes, she'd had a severe episode of asthma, but that was partly her own fault for rushing to the bank and then allowing herself to get so upset. "I appreciate your help, but I can dress myself."

Kate sighed loudly but nodded and stepped back. Sophie rose and crossed the room to the chair where her dress, corset, and petticoat had been laid.

An hour later, she saw her friend to the front door, since Pearl had already gone home. "The soup was delicious. I can't thank you and Pearl enough for all you've done."

Kate smiled and clasped Sophie's hand. "That's what friends are for."

Sophie nodded. What would Kate say if she told her that she'd never had a close friend before? "I still appreciate you, more than you know."

Kate's brow wrinkled. "Are you certain you don't want me to stay? I don't mind at all."

"Yes, I'm fine now." Sophie smiled to ease her friend's concern. "But I do thank you for being willing."

"Just make sure you don't overdo things. There's nothing that can't wait until tomorrow." Kate turned to leave, then stopped suddenly and swiveled back. "Oh. I forgot to tell you that Josh said he'd make other arrangements for Corrie and Toby this afternoon."

Sophie nodded and shut the door, feeling as if she'd flunked an important test. Now that Mr. Harper had seen her at her worst, he'd yanked his niece and nephew from her care without even having the backbone to face her and tell her in person. And without the small income she earned for watching Corrie and Toby, she doubted she'd be able to rent another house. She slowly made her way upstairs, to the wardrobe in the room she shared with the girls, and fished out her reticule. She counted the money she had left. Four dollars. The small sum might be enough to rent a room for a week.

Dropping onto the edge of the bed, she stared out the window. What a mess she'd made of things, when all she'd wanted to do was prove she could take care of herself. Once she returned home, her mother would have a buggy full of fodder to lecture her on, and neither she nor her father would let Sophie out of the house, ever again. She exhaled a loud sigh. Self-pity wouldn't help her in the least.

She needed a plan—and she needed one fast.

⌒

"Toby! Put that down." Josh jumped up and reached across the desk for the ink pot before his nephew could create a disaster.

"Aw, I just wanted to draw."

"Not with ink, and not in my office. Sit down in the corner with Corrie and look at those books."

Toby frowned and kicked the leg of the desk. "I wanna go play with Mikey. How come we gotta stay here?"

Corrie rose and walked over to the desk. "Because Miss Sophie is sick, remember?"

"If'n she's sick, how come the others get to go over there?"

Corrie rolled her eyes, like an impatient mother. In spite of the tension cramping his shoulders, Josh fought to keep from smiling.

His niece blew out a sigh. "Because they live there, you dolt."

Josh's humor fled. "Corrie, no name-calling. Apologize to your brother."

She scowled. "Sorry."

Josh sighed. He hadn't gotten a lick of work done since bringing the kids to his office after school. Having them there was highly unprofessional, but he'd wanted to make things easier for Sophia.

He was glad that Kate McMillan had stopped by earlier to let him know she'd recovered and seemed to be fine.

He was the dolt, if anyone was. Watching Sophia struggle for each breath, and then seeing her so weak that she stumbled, had scared him half out of his wits.

He couldn't shake the memory of her face so close to his. In fact, every time he thought about it, his pulse kicked up to triple its normal pace. For a brief moment, he'd wanted to kiss her, even though it would have been highly inappropriate, given the circumstances. He'd kissed a few women—girls, really—when he was younger. But none of them left an imprint on him like Sophia had. And he hadn't even kissed her. So, why did she refuse to leave his mind?

Toby shuffled back to the corner, his brow creased with displeasure, and he dropped down. He started pulling rocks from his pocket and lining them in a row. At least he didn't have a frog or snake that would set Corrie to screaming.

A quick knock pulled Josh's gaze to the door. "Come in, Doc."

The doctor glanced at the children, then sat in one of the chairs across from Josh. "I see you have some assistants today."

He nodded. "I didn't think Miss Davenport would feel up to watching them. How's she doing?"

Doc sat back in the chair and crossed his legs. "Quite well, actually. I just checked on her again, and she had those three children sitting quietly at the table, eating some of Mable Turner's molasses pie."

"They got pie!" Toby leapt to his feet. "No fair."

Josh scowled at him and pointed his finger toward the floor. Toby's lower lip shot out, but he dropped down again. He leaned toward his sister and loudly whispered, "They got pie."

"I'm not deaf." Corrie twisted her index finger in her ear.

"I'm so hungry, my belly's growlin'." Toby stretched out on the floor, facedown, and rested his cheek in his hand, his lip still sticking out.

Focusing on the doctor again, Josh rubbed his neck, hoping his tension didn't show. "I'm glad to know she's better. What do you suppose brought on her, um"—he leaned forward and lowered his voice—"spell?" *As if I don't already know.*

"Miss Davenport suffers from asthma. It's quite common, although, from what she's told me, I suspect her case is more severe than most."

"What brings on the, um, attacks?" The word sounded harsh, but that's what they were.

Doc shrugged. "It's something we're studying. The generally suspected cause is overexertion, but some physicians speculate it's from too much dust in the air, while others believe stress might bring on the breathing problems. In Miss Davenport's case, I imagine all of those are factors."

Josh felt bad for Sophia, but there was one thing he had to know. And he owed it to Maude to learn the truth. He leaned forward and spoke softly, "Is it possible she might have somehow contributed to Miss Maudie's death?"

Drawing his lips together, Doc shook his head. "Maude died of pneumonia. It has nothing to do with asthma, which is not contagious."

"I had no idea she was so ill."

"How'd you like to have been her doctor?" He glanced at the children, then scooted to the edge of his seat. "That stubborn woman didn't listen to a thing I told her about taking care of herself, and look where it got her." He shook his head. "If anything, Miss Davenport helped her aunt, but I think Maude was too far gone to come back, even with assistance."

Relief washed through Josh. He hated asking questions about Sophia. A rock thumped against the wall, and he shot Toby another stern glare before turning back to Dr. Walton. "Miss Maudie was a stubborn woman who hid her aliments well."

Sophia had the same gumption. Josh couldn't help admiring how she'd stood up to him—more than once. Maybe he'd been too harsh on her when they'd first met.

"Yep. She was in a class of her own." The doctor heaved a loud sigh.

Josh was beginning to think her niece was cut from the same cloth.

The chinking clatter of breaking glass made Josh jump. He stood, staring in disbelief at his shattered window.

Corrie uncurled from her spot in the corner and stared. "Um… *Toby*, you're in so much trouble."

Friday afternoon, Sophie stood in the front doorway and waved good-bye to Hazel. The girl was so excited to go home for a few days that her face practically glowed. Her father probably wouldn't need to light the wagon's lanterns on their trip home. Since Amanda's father had already picked her up, that left only Mikey. Sophie felt a twinge of sympathy that his father visited so rarely. She still had yet to meet him.

The pretty afternoon beckoned to her. A brilliant red cardinal swooped down and landed on the porch railing. Its drab brown mate joined him, and the two pecked at something on the post, then flew off together. Sophie sighed. Even birds had companions. She knew her parents would never allow her to marry, but she'd held out hope that God would open that door one day.

Handsome Mr. Harper rushed into her thoughts. How concerned he'd looked during her episode. How strong he'd been to carry her home. How protected she'd felt in his arms. Tears stung her eyes, but she battled them away and lifted her chin. He was only being a gentleman, helping a lady in distress. She was the last woman he would want. And besides, she didn't need a man to make her feel fulfilled. She had the Lord to comfort and guide her.

When she returned to St. Louis, she would fill her life with projects—things that could help others and still keep her parents happy. But until that day, she had work to do.

Where was Mikey? Sophie leaned out the open doorway to check the porch, but the boy wasn't in sight. She closed the door and walked to the kitchen, expecting to see him sneaking a snack, but no Mikey. Hmm.

A loud thump above drew her gaze to the ceiling. What was he doing upstairs? With fewer children to watch, she had a list of tasks she hoped to accomplish this weekend, and she dearly wanted to make some headway in her relationship with her remaining charge. She should check on him. She placed her hand on the banister, but a knock on the front door interrupted her climb. Who could that be?

Dr. Walton and Kate had both stopped by earlier. Mr. Samuels from the bank had delivered a note from Mr. Harper, letting her know he would keep the children with him this afternoon so that she could rest. Maybe Hazel had forgotten something and returned.

Pasting on a smile, Sophie pulled open the door. A cowboy?

The man leaning against the porch post had his head down, as if studying his boots, and his hat blocked much of his face. But, as he straightened, his brown eyes lit with obvious interest. He wielded his dimples like finely hewed weapons. And that smile…. "Well, who do we have here?"

Her breath whooshed too fast for her to respond. The man oozed so much charm that if he could bottle and sell it, he'd make a fortune.

He pushed his Western hat back, revealing his handsome face. Long lashes shaded his twinkling eyes, and that pair of matching dimples kept winking at her. Though his hair was darkened with sweat, the blond strands glistened in the sunlight.

Whoever he was, he'd sure piqued her interest. Sophie straightened and glanced down, checking her apron for stains.

He cleared his throat, pulling her gaze up to his. His mouth twisted in a cocky grin. He tipped his hat and gave a brief bow. "The name's Wade Barnes, ma'am. Might I have the pleasure of knowing yours?"

"Sophia Davenport. *Miss* Davenport."

He pushed away from the post and stepped closer. "A beautiful name for an exceptionally beautiful woman."

A blush warmed her cheeks at the rascal's compliment. "Thank you, Mr. Barnes." *Barnes?* Why was his name familiar?

"Where's the old lady that watched that scalawag of mine?"

The perfect picture of the man Sophie had conjured up cracked, and her smile dimmed. "Are you referring to Mrs. Archer?"

"Partly, yes."

At his crude reference to Aunt Maude, all thoughts of flirting fled like a spooked bird. "Mrs. Archer, my aunt, is dead, Mr. Barnes. How can I help you?"

His cocky expression shifted to serious. He tugged off his hat. "I apologize, ma'am. Mrs. Archer was a feisty lady, and I kind of liked her."

Sophie's patience was dissipating quickly. "How can I help you, sir?" she asked again.

He glanced past her, and for the first time since laying eyes on him, wariness clawed up her spine. The man was a good foot taller than she and quite brawny. He shrugged. "Just come to fetch Mike. Is he here?"

"Mike who?"

At the sound of a stampede, Sophie turned and watched Mikey come careening down the stairs, his eyes shiny, as if he had something exciting to tell her. His gaze traveled past her, and he halted suddenly on the last step, his expression dulling. He pushed one hand behind his back. "Wade."

Mikey's greeting held as much excitement as a cold pancake.

Wait! Mike. Mikey? Sophie spun back around. "You're Mikey's father?"

Mr. Barnes shrugged again. "I reckon I am."

"Do I gotta go with him?" Mikey asked.

She turned to face the boy. "Don't you want to go with your father?"

Mikey looked down, instead of at the man on the porch, then shrugged, just like his father had. She could halfway understand his reticence. If he spent the weekend with his father, saying good-bye again on Sunday evening would be all the more diffi-cult, but at least this would probably be the last time they'd be parted, since school was almost over. "Your father's ridden a long way to see you. Don't you think you should go with him? I'm sure he's missed you."

"Yep. Aren't ya glad to see me, *son?*" Mr. Barnes stepped up behind her.

Mikey lifted his head, but he looked about as happy to see his father as Sophie would be if hers showed up unexpectedly. The boy hid his emotions well, which made him hard to read. She wanted so much to see him happily frolicking with the other children instead of getting into trouble all the time.

"I reckon." He spun around and headed back up the stairs.

"Hey, where ya goin', boy?" Mr. Barnes shouted in her ear.

Sophie jumped, then stepped aside, putting some distance between them.

"Gotta get my stuff." Mikey trotted to the top of the stairs and out of sight.

"That boy's grown since I last saw him."

"When was that, exactly?" Sophie turned back to face Mr. Barnes, not liking the fact that he'd stepped inside. He was a big man, even an inch or two taller than Josh Harper. If he chose not to leave, she'd never get him out. She swallowed back the appre-hension that rose in her throat.

He gazed down at her, a soft smile on his lips. "How long have ya been here?"

"Two weeks. My father got a telegram that my aunt was ill, so he sent me to care for her."

"I didn't know she was doin' poorly. She was fine last time I was here."

Sophie liked the deep timbre of his voice, but the fact that he evaded her question about when he'd last visited his son wasn't lost on her. "Aunt Maude broke her arm a month ago. Why have you waited so long to come and visit Mikey?" No wonder the boy had turned his back to his father. It must be terribly hard for him to watch the Harper children return to their uncle each night and the others go home some weekends.

Mr. Barnes shuffled his feet. "My ranch is a far piece from here, so I don't get to town more than about once a month."

Sophie relaxed somewhat. "I can understand that. At least Mikey will be able to stay home all summer."

"Uh...yep, that he will."

The boy clomped down the stairs.

Mr. Barnes looked past Sophie, his gaze unreadable. "Ya ready to go, maverick?"

"I reckon. Gotta go out back first."

Confusion gnawed at Sophie. Why didn't Mikey seem happy to see his father? Was it possible he had been looking forward to spending the weekend alone with her? To not have to compete with the other children for her attention? Things had been better between them since she'd assured him she wouldn't make him leave. But what if Mr. Harper repossessed the house?

The back door slammed, causing the windows to rattle. Sophie jumped. And then a terrible racket sounded in the kitchen, pulling her away from Mr. Barnes. At the sight of the missing back door, her mouth dropped open.

"Looks like your door fell off."

Sophie's heart lurched at the voice directly behind her, and she spun around. Mr. Barnes had followed her into the kitchen.

"Got a hammer? I can fix that for ya." His eyes twinkled, as if he would be genuinely happy to help her. "We get mosquitoes the size of buzzards around here, and that pretty skin of yours is likely to draw them like June bugs to a lantern."

Sophie relaxed at his casual chatter, her cheeks warming at his comment. Maybe she was judging him too harshly. She'd had so little experience with men, but knowing the door was off all night while she was alone was more troubling than accepting his help. "Yes, I have a hammer, and I would appreciate it if you repaired the door." She gestured toward the pantry. "I'll get the tools."

He nodded, then ambled out back and studied the doorjamb. "Looks like it just lost a hinge and pulled the other one free when the door fell. Shouldn't be too hard to fix."

"That's good to know." She watched as he lithely carried the door down the stairs into the yard and examined it. Then she turned and walked to the pantry. With the children running in and out so much, she'd almost given up hope of keeping insects out, but there were other types of varmints she wanted to avoid—namely, the characters who patronized the saloons in the evenings.

She'd been alone in the house only when the children were at school, never at night. That was one thing she'd taken for granted back home—the security her father's presence in the home had given her, even though he slept upstairs. Never had she been afraid of someone breaking in and getting to her, except during the first few nights when she was relegated to sleeping in the former library, so near the front door. Even though a maid had slept on a cot in the same room, Sophie had been lonely—and sad. Her mother had insisted the purpose of the move was to keep her from having to tax herself climbing the tall staircase every time she needed to lie down, but Sophie believed they simply hadn't wanted her coughing to disturb their sleep.

She'd been a pariah in her own home.

Pushing away the distasteful memory, she entered the pantry. Given her situation at home, one would think she wouldn't mind living alone—and part of her didn't. But another part of her missed her family, in spite of everything.

Sophie found the crate of tools on a shelf in the corner and carried it to the kitchen counter. It was a good thing Mr. Barnes had been here when the door had broken. Without it firmly attached, she doubted she would have been able to sleep a wink tonight.

She returned to the doorway and peered out. Mr. Barnes had leaned the door against the house and now stood with hands on hips, as if trying to decide on a course of action. She couldn't help admiring his fine build, his shirt pulled tight across his wide shoulders. He was a handsome man, no doubt about it. So was Josh Harper, but not in the same way. Where Josh's hair was darker and his eyes an intriguing blue, Mr. Barnes' hair was a dusty blond and his eyes like coffee with cream. And those dimples…she exhaled a sigh. Mr. Harper was more reserved and businesslike, while Mr. Barnes seemed happy-go-lucky.

"I found the hammer and some other tools, Mr. Barnes."

"Call me Wade." He winked, and a huge grin pulled at his lips.

Sophie's stomach flip-flopped. Never had a man winked at her before. Though Mr. Barnes' action was cavalier and something her mother would frown upon, it rather excited her—made her feel noticed. Pretty.

A steady pounding next door pulled her attention that way. Josh Harper stood to the side of his garden, driving a tall pole into the ground. She loved the colorful array of flowers she could see from her vantage point on the porch. If she were staying longer, she'd plant a garden of her own and even try her hand at raising some vegetables.

Mikey exited the privy and paused when he saw his father. He frowned and slammed the door. Obviously unhappy with the delay in leaving, he shuffled over, glanced up at Sophie with an unreadable expression, and then plopped down on the steps. The poor boy needed a mother—someone to love him and teach him some manners. She could do both, but her remaining time with him was short.

Another movement next door snagged her attention, and she glanced that way again. Josh Harper stood beside his shed, looking at her. The deep scowl on his face matched Mikey's.

Chapter Thirteen

Josh walked around his shed and surveyed the scene in Miss Maudie's backyard. What had happened to the door? And who was that man helping Sophia?

He pursed his lips as he battled uncommon feelings of envy. Other than when Sarah had first arrived at his family's stage stop and he'd battled his brothers to win her affection, he'd never wrestled with jealousy over a woman. And he didn't like the envy pouring through him like soured milk.

He ought to return to his work, but his feet moved forward of their own accord, leaving him no choice but to ride along or fall flat on his backside. As he drew near, Sophia's cheeks turned pink, but he wasn't sure if it was because this was the first time he'd seen her since her asthma attack or because he'd found her with a strange man.

Mikey hopped up from the step he'd been sitting on and loped toward him. "Can I play with Toby?"

Josh shook his head. "He's not here. Their pa came to town and took them riding."

"Aw, shucks." Mikey kicked a rock and sent it flying.

"Sorry."

The stranger turned, and he frowned when his gaze landed on Josh. Who was this guy, and why was he helping Sophia?

"Mr. Barnes," she said, "this is my neighbor, Mr. Harper." Her gaze latched onto Josh's. "Mr. Barnes is Mikey's father."

Josh searched his mind, but he couldn't remember Miss Maudie ever mentioning the boy's father. Still, he stretched out his hand. "Nice to meet you."

Mr. Barnes eyed the gesture, then stepped forward and shook his hand. His gaze didn't quite reach Josh's eyes. "Yep, me too."

"How long is this gonna take? I'm gettin' hungry." Mikey pushed in between them, receiving a scowl from his pa.

The man quickly adjusted his face into a roguish grin and shrugged. "Shouldn't take too long. I just need to straighten out the hinge and reset it."

"I can do it." The words rushed from Josh's mouth before he'd thought much about them. The sooner this rascal left, the better. "Go on and take your boy to dinner." He forced a smile, hoping the man wouldn't perceive him as a threat and would take his advice and leave. "I've got a nephew Mikey's age, and I know how boys are always starving."

Barnes nodded. "I reckon they are. Mike, here, nearly eats up my whole month's pay."

Mikey tugged on his pa's arm. "C'mon, then."

Mr. Barnes looked up at Sophia. He flashed a charming grin that Josh figured would make most women take notice. *He* wanted to knock it off Barnes' face. His fist curled, and then he blinked several times. Where had that thought come from? He relaxed his hand, despising how jealousy could so quickly tempt a man to do something that went against his normally peaceful nature.

Barnes stepped in front him, resting one boot on the lowest step. "If it'd be all right with ya, Miss Sophie, I'll take Mike to eat at the café, since he's about to waste away, and let Mr. Harper finish fixin' the door."

How was it that this man had the gall to refer to her by her first name? Hadn't they just met? Josh's fist closed again, and once more he forced himself to relax. He had no claim on Sophia. Until today, he hadn't even realized he'd developed feelings for her. But there was something about Mikey's father that bothered him, and he didn't want that man around Sophia any longer than necessary. Why hadn't he ever seen him before? Or heard of him?

Sophia smiled. "You go on, Mr. Barnes. I know how impatient Mikey gets when he's hungry."

The man jogged up the steps, grasped Sophia's hand, and kissed the back of it. Her eyes widened, but a pleasant grin quickly replaced her surprised expression. "Enjoy your time with your son, Mr. Barnes."

"It's Wade, remember?"

She nodded, her gaze skittering past Mikey's father to Josh. She seemed embarrassed, but he couldn't tell if it was due to the man's brash behavior or because Josh had been there to witness it. He rarely took an instant dislike to anyone, but he was bordering close to that line right now.

Sophia stepped back and almost entered the house in her effort to put distance between herself and Barnes. "When will you bring Mikey back?"

The man gazed up at the sky for a moment, then looked at her. "Sunday afternoon, I reckon. It's a pleasure to have met ya, and I look forward to visitin' with y' again." He tipped his sweat-stained hat to her, then jogged down the steps. He lassoed Josh with his gaze, and a smirk lifted one side of his face.

Josh frowned, his gut twisting. It was a good thing the man didn't visit his son often; because, if he did, Josh was certain he'd need to ask God's forgiveness for his bad thoughts on a regular basis.

As the pair rounded the corner of the house, Sophia held on to the porch rail as she glided down the steps. "Are you certain you don't mind repairing the door, Mr. Harper?"

Josh smiled. "Not at all. In fact, I'd planned to ask you tomorrow if you'd mind if I repaired the loose steps inside. I noticed them when I came downstairs after…well, you know."

Her cheeks turned crimson. "About that. I'm dreadfully sorry for having an episode in your office. It was terribly unprofessional." She lowered her head.

Once more, the thought of carrying her, holding her close, made Josh's arms tingle. He couldn't help but remember how seeing her struggle for each breath had opened his eyes and made him realize for the first time that he cared about her. Cared what happened to her. "There's no need to apologize. If anything, it was my fault."

Her gaze shot to his. "What do you mean?"

"I should have waited to tell you about the mortgage. You'd just lost your aunt, and…I was insensitive to your grief. Will you forgive me?"

She blinked, obviously taken off guard by his apology. Her lips quivered, then lifted in a sweet smile. "Of course, Mr. Harper, but I understand the urgency of the situation and your kindness to my aunt. I appreciate what you did for her."

Sophia's gratitude warmed his chest. "Since we're neighbors who see each other daily, do you think you could call me Josh?"

She hesitated a moment. "Only if you'll call me Sophie."

He'd taken to thinking of her by her formal name. "Does no one call you Sophia?"

A teasing grin played across her pretty lips. "Only my parents, when they're angry with me."

"Ah, I see. Then Sophie it is." The tenseness remaining from his encounter with Mr. Barnes rolled off his shoulders as he enjoyed the relaxed conversation. He wanted Sophie to see him as a friend—and possibly more.

"So, do you actually know how to repair my door?"

He placed his hand over his heart, pretending to be injured. "Hath the lady no confidence in my abilities?" As soon as the words left his mouth, he realized the irony of them. He'd forced Sophie to prove her worth to him—more than once.

Sophie shrugged, but the glint remained in her eyes. "Well, you *do* work at a bank."

"True, but I grew up on a ranch." He tugged the edge of the door toward him and studied the hinges. The top one was bent a bit in one corner, but the bottom one looked like it had just come loose. With so many children going in and out, it was no wonder. He should have thought to check it sooner.

Sophie leaned back against the porch rail. "I thought you lived at a stage stop."

Josh set the door against the house again. He needed to get his tools. "I did, but it was also a ranch. And a farm, if you will. We serviced the stage customers and drivers, and changed out and cared for the relief teams, but we've always raised cattle and horses, and grown most of our own food and hay for the livestock."

"I never thought about it, but I imagine many people out here do much the same, since they live so far from town. I love my flower garden at home, but I've never tried to grow vegetables. Our gardener grew onions, carrots, salad greens, and some herbs, but we bought most of the food we needed."

Josh knew by Sophie's dresses and manner of speech that she came from a well-to-do family. His family wasn't rich, but they'd never gone without and generally had the money necessary for any supplies they couldn't produce for themselves. "I guess we've grown up in different worlds." Not too different, he hoped.

A flock of geese honked overhead, and she looked up. Josh watched her, admiring the contours of her face, and the way her hair curled around her temples. But what fascinated him the most were her deep brown eyes and how they twinkled when she was excited.

"Isn't it interesting how they take turns being the leader?"

Josh had witnessed the lead goose falling back to one side of the *v* and another goose taking its place many times. "Yes, it is. I've read that it's how they rest."

Her brow crinkled. "That doesn't make sense. The goose is still flying, so why does its position matter?"

"I believe it has something to do with the force of the wind." He searched for an example and then snapped his fingers as the perfect one came to mind. "When it's especially windy here, sometimes Corrie and Toby walk directly behind me so that I block the breeze and they don't have to struggle as much."

A light sparked in her eyes, and he knew he wanted to witness that over and over.

"That makes perfect sense."

He smiled. "I suppose I'd better fetch my hammer, so I can get your door repaired before the mosquitoes come out, searching for their supper."

"Oh, I have a box of tools in the kitchen. I retrieved them for Mr. Barnes but forgot about them." She turned, then paused when Josh came up the steps.

"Allow me, please."

With a soft nod and a demure smile, she stepped back, giving him permission to enter. He quickly found the crate of tools on the kitchen counter and carried them outside. He checked the doorjamb, making sure it didn't need repair, then hopped down the stairs. "This shouldn't take long." He glanced up at the sun and noted its sinking position on the western horizon. "Aaron should be back soon with the children, and once they wash up, we're going down to the café to eat. Would you care to join us?"

Sophie gazed into Josh's eyes and saw nothing but sincerity there. After what had happened in his office, she expected him to avoid her, not offer his friendship—if that's what this was. She liked him, for the most part. Liked his easy manner, especially with his niece and nephew. Liked his pretty blue eyes. This well could be her only chance to go somewhere with a man—and the children and their father would be there to serve as chaperones. Before she could change her mind, she nodded. "That sounds much preferable to eating alone."

He rewarded her with an engaging smile. "Wonderful. Then I'll get busy."

He yanked the bent hinge off the side of the door, laid it on the porch, and pounded it with the hammer. Sophie watched, impressed with how he plowed forth and didn't hesitate. The hammer actually looked more natural in his hand than the pen in his office had. Banker. Gardener. Rancher. Carpenter. There was much more to Josh Harper than she'd expected.

The light breeze blew a tress of hair into Sophie's eyes, and she tucked it behind her ear. She brushed her hands across her skirt, then looked down, surveying her clothes. If she were going out this evening, she'd need to change into a fresh dress and fix her hair. An unfamiliar sense of excitement raced through her. She'd had few things in her life to look forward to, and she couldn't keep the smile from her lips.

"Would you mind helping me for a moment?" Josh glanced over his shoulder at her, matching her smile, and making her stomach quiver.

"Of course. What would you like me to do?"

He lowered the door so that it stood on its side. "Hold that end steady while I attach the hinge."

She hurried down the steps, did as asked, and found her gaze drawn to him. He stood so that his end of the door rested again his left thigh. As he bent over to reattach the hinge, his dark hair fell over his forehead in a boyish manner. His light blue chambray shirt blended well with the darker blue of his eyes, and his rolled-up sleeves revealed tanned arms with muscles that contracted as he worked.

He suddenly straightened, and she jerked her gaze away. She'd never actually watched a man work before and was surprised how it absorbed her interest. Josh turned and moved toward her. She released the door and backed up several steps. He grabbed for it and stood it on its side again, then made several adjustments to the remaining hinge. When he was finished, he propped the door on its end.

"Almost done. Let's get it hung." He carried the door up the stairs with no trouble, then worked it into place. He glanced at her. "Would you mind helping me one more time? It will only take a moment."

She started up the stairs. "Of course not."

He waved her inside. "Just hold up the door so I can get the top hinge attached to the jamb."

After a minute or so, he gently pulled the door from her hand, fanning it back and forth, then closed it. He turned to her and grinned. "Good as new."

"I don't know how to thank you...Josh." Saying his Christian name felt a bit awkward, but she liked it. Joshua in the Bible was a fine man, and she was beginning to think Josh Harper was, too. He had a right to be concerned about her ability to care for his brother's children, especially after their first encounter at the depot.

"No thanks needed, especially since you said you'd dine with me this evening."

Sophie suddenly realized they were alone in the house with the doors closed. "I need a few minutes to get ready."

"Of course. I'll go home and come back for you in...say, half an hour?"

"That would be fine."

He gave her a brief nod, then returned the tools to the crate. With a final smile, he closed the door and was gone.

Sophie's heart trilled as if she'd just run a race. She spun around and hurried toward the stairs. If she was going to be ready in thirty minutes, she needed to hustle.

Chapter Fourteen

Sophie moved along the clothesline and stopped in front of a pair of socks. She removed the clothespins and handed the socks to Corrie, who folded them and laid them in the laundry basket, while Sophie pulled the pins off of Amanda's Sunday dress. The rhubarb-colored frock was still damp, but that would make ironing out the wrinkles easier—a trick she'd learned from Kate. She folded the dress and laid it in the ironing basket.

"I like helping Grandma and Sarah with the laundry at home."

"That's nice. I'm sure they appreciate your help as much as I do." Sarah, Sophie remembered from a conversation at the café last night, was married to Ethan, the youngest Harper brother, and would soon have a baby. Sophie continued down the line, folding the bigger items and letting Corrie take care of the smaller ones.

The girl must resemble her mother very closely; other than her dark hair, she looked nothing like her father, Aaron, whom Sophie had met at dinner last night. In fact, with her blue eyes, Corrie bore a greater resemblance to Josh. Did it bother him that Aaron had two children, and Ethan would soon have a pair, but Josh wasn't even married? Of course, neither was Aaron, since his wife had died. What a tragedy that must have been. At least Aaron had a loving family to help him through his sorrow.

Sophie picked up the basket of clothes to be ironed. "I'll run this inside and come back for the other."

146

"I can get it." Corrie hoisted the second basket awkwardly in her arms and carried it as if it were a baby.

Pounding rumbled through the house—the very reason Sophie had chosen to do outside chores for much of the morning. About ten o'clock, Josh had appeared at her front door, the children in tow, to repair the stairs. Sophie passed through the kitchen and dining room and into the short hall, her heartbeat increasing with each step. She paused at the bottom of the stairway. Toby sat on the landing halfway up, two steps above where Josh worked, handing him nails and chattering like a magpie.

Josh finished hammering and straightened, towering over her from his perch. His face lit with a bright smile. "Hey, let me show you something I discovered. It's both odd and ingenious." He walked down two steps and waved her to come up.

"What is it?" Corrie piped up from behind her.

"I know!" Toby beamed.

Josh looked over his shoulder at the boy and lifted his index finger to his lips. "Shh. I'll tell her."

"Aw, shucks." Toby crossed his arms, his lower lip pushing out.

Sophie's curiosity took wing. "Let me set this down first." She dipped her chin toward the laundry basket.

"I'll get it." Josh jogged down the steps and relieved her of her load.

Her heart leapt as his hands brushed against hers. He walked into the parlor, deposited the basket on the sofa, and turned back toward her, smiling. Something had changed between them, but she wasn't sure what. He'd finally quit scowling at her, and she no longer felt as if she had to prove herself to him.

He reached out his hand and took hers, gently tugging her up the stairs. Corrie had deposited her basket on the hall floor and now sat next to her brother on the landing. Just before they reached the children, Josh bent down and flipped back a wooden plank, revealing the interior of the step.

"What in the world?" Sophie leaned forward to examine the hidey-hole. The piece of wood had a small hinge on the underneath side, which allowed someone to fold it back, revealing an eight-inch opening.

"It's bigger than it looks. I stuck my arm inside and reached half the width of the step."

"I've never seen anything like it. Did you find anything in there?"

Josh shook his head.

"Nothin' but beggar's velvet." Toby rested his elbows on his knees with his chin in his hands. "I was hopin' for pirate's treasure."

Sophie couldn't help chuckling at his reference to dust balls and treasure. "More likely some bandit would have stashed his loot from a train robbery."

"Like Jesse James?" Brown eyes dancing, Toby bolted upright. "Mikey's always talkin' about findin' some treasure. If'n I had some gold, I'd hide it in there."

Josh's amused gaze snagged Sophie's. "The question is, what do you want to do about it now that you know it's there? Leave it as is or nail it shut?"

She shrugged. "Seems a shame to close up something that's been so well hidden for so long. Is it unsafe as it is?"

Josh closed the flap and bounced on it. The step creaked. "It's not as strong as the others that are a solid piece of wood. If it was me, I'd nail it down. You don't want anyone tripping on it if it comes loose."

"I suppose you're right." Sophie nodded. "But are you positive there's nothing in the hole?"

Waving his hand at the opening, Josh grinned. "Be my guest."

She studied his expression for a moment, then lifted her skirt so that she could go down on her knees. She peered inside the cavity, but all was dark, except for a six-inch radius beneath the hole. She leaned down and stuck her hand inside, then glanced over her shoulder. "There aren't any spiders, are there?"

Josh tucked in his lips as if trying not to laugh. His eyes glistened. "Only big, fat hairy tarantulas."

She jerked her hand out, then realized he was teasing. If it wouldn't have been considered unladylike, she would have smacked his leg—the only part of him she could reach at the moment.

"Go on, Miss Sophie. Uncle Josh is just funnin' with you." Corrie flashed her uncle a stern look she'd probably seen her grandma use on him.

Lifting her chin, Sophie accepted his challenge, and reached into the hole. She patted her hand around, feeling nothing but wood. Blowing out a sigh of disappointment, she pulled her arm out, and Josh helped her to her feet again. "Well, fiddlesticks."

"Were you hoping for a treasure too?" he asked.

"Yes. One big enough to pay off the mortgage."

He pursed his lips, and his expression turned serious. "I wish there'd been one like that too."

Sophie's heart pounded as she stared at him and read the apology in his gaze.

"I'm hungry." Toby pressed his hands against his stomach.

"Um, I suppose I've kept you long enough." She carefully backed down the last two steps, holding tightly to the railing. "Since you've been so kind as to repair my stairs, why don't I prepare some lunch for all of us?"

"Yay!" Toby clapped, and Corrie joined him.

"You're sure it's not too much trouble?"

"No trouble at all." She smiled, then spun toward the kitchen, needing some distance from her handsome helper. The sensation she'd felt the first time their hands had touched now needed no physical contact in order to manifest, and she didn't want to think too hard about the implications. Getting her hopes up would only lead to disappointment.

Josh smiled as he hammered in the last nail on the stairs, looking forward to his second meal in less than twenty-four hours with Sophie. He'd thoroughly enjoyed last night's supper, even though Aaron had teased him the rest of the evening about being "in love."

He stood and straightened, rubbing the pinch in his back from bending over for so long. Corrie popped up from her seat next to her brother and hurried down the stairs.

Toby pulled out another nail from the sack. "Can I pound one in?"

Josh ruffled his nephew's hair. "Not now, pardner."

"Aw, shucks."

"Maybe when we go home after lunch, I can find a board for you to hammer."

"Yee-haw!" The boy jumped up, bouncing on the landing. He raced down the stairs. "D'you hear that, Corrie? Uncle Josh is gonna let me hammer some nails."

"Just askin' for trouble, if you ask me," Corrie mumbled from the kitchen door.

Toby jutted his chin out. "Don't gotta ask you. Uncle Josh said I could."

Josh shook his head and opened his mouth, ready to tell them not to bicker, when Sophie calmly walked through the doorway. "You two go out and wash your hands. Lunch will be ready soon."

Josh trotted down the stairs, hammer and jar of nails in hand. Sophie's eyes dropped to the tools, and then she glanced past him up the stairs. "Would you mind doing another small project? I hate to ask, but there's a hole in the wall—several holes, actually—and I have to admit I'm a bit nervous that a mouse or something bigger might try to get in."

Josh smiled, hoping to relieve her unease at asking another favor. "I'd be happy to. Where are these holes?"

Sophie walked closer, looking quite domestic in the faded floral apron. He was usually a good judge of people, but he'd sorely miscalculated her abilities.

"The biggest is in the upstairs sitting area."

Josh held out his elbow. "May I assist you, Miss Davenport?"

A pleasing blush stained her cheeks, and she returned his grin. "Why, thank you, kind sir."

"My pleasure." Josh matched his pace to hers, enjoying the feel of a pretty woman on his arm—no, not just any pretty woman; only Sophie. How had he become so infatuated with her so quickly, especially when he'd had so many doubts at first? Maybe it was seeing the stubborn, determined woman fighting for each breath. He felt as if someone had lit a flame of attraction within him and immediately turned it up high. All he wanted to do was help her—protect her—be with her.

The image of Wade Barnes intruded on his thoughts, tossing a bucket of water on his flickering hope. He'd wracked his brain as he lay in bed the previous night, trying to remember if he'd ever heard of the man before. As the only banker in town, he knew most of the local farmers and ranchers. But not Barnes. Maybe his ranch was closer to one of the other nearby towns—Olathe or Lenexa.

Josh suddenly realized they'd stopped in the upstairs parlor. Sophie stared at him with an odd look on her face.

"Uh, did I miss something?" Heat warmed his neck and ears. "Guess I was lost in thought."

She shook her head. "No, you didn't miss anything. The big hole is behind this bookcase." She reached for the lamp, but Josh hurried to her side.

"Allow me." His fingers hovered over hers, brushing as lightly as butterfly wings against her skin. She stared up at him with her stunningly dark eyes. Wisps of her soft brown hair had fallen loose and curled around her pink cheeks. His belly clenched.

A door downstairs banged, and Sophie jumped, tugging her hand away. She stepped back and gestured. "Um…just set it over there."

Josh did as directed, but the fact that the lamp clattered because of his trembling hand wasn't lost on him. When he'd been attracted to Sarah before she married Ethan, it had almost been a game—to see if he could win her interest before his brothers did. But his attraction to Sophie was different. Deeper. There was no competition—at least, not unless Wade Barnes tossed his hat in the ring, but he seemed more the sort to conquer and leave. Josh wanted to be around Sophie as long as she'd allow.

She cleared her throat, and he spun around.

"Lost in thought again?" A teasing glint danced in her eyes.

"Guess so. There seems to be an epidemic of it today."

"Hmm. I hope it isn't contagious."

He grinned. "My apologies. I've never been accused of being overly talkative. Ethan's the conversationalist of us three Harper brothers, but even he isn't that chatty."

"Your mother must have been lonely."

Josh scooted the chair beside the bookcase several feet to the right. "Nah, she was too busy, and she had Pa. And Corrie and Toby, once they came along."

"I bet she misses them."

"Yes, everyone misses the children." As if his comment had summoned them, Corrie and Toby raced up the stairs, with the boy a few steps ahead.

"Come back here, Toby," Corrie screeched.

Sophie cocked her head, then stretched out her hand and touched Josh's arm. "I'm sure you're missed too."

He nodded and swallowed the lump that had risen in his throat. He knew his family was always happy to see him, but their joy at seeing the children tended to overshadow his homecomings, as it should. Still, he wished there was one special woman who would come running and throw her arms around his neck, as if he were the only person in her world. He spun toward the wall, fed up with all his melancholy thoughts and embarrassed at confessing something to Sophie that he'd never revealed to anyone. He tugged the bookcase away from the wall and whistled. "That's some hole."

"Imagine my surprise when I first discovered it."

Josh leaned over, examining the scratches in the plaster and the broken lathes. "Looks more as if someone was trying to get out than in."

He heard a grunt and a loud thump behind him, and stood. Corrie and Toby tumbled across the carpet runner.

"Give that to me." Corrie clawed at Toby's fist.

"Hey, stop that—right now." Josh strode down the hall and lifted his niece off of her brother. Toby shoved something in his mouth. "What's the meaning of this?"

Corrie's face had turned red, and she looked as angry as a hen after her first egg had been taken away. "Toby stole a cookie."

Josh hoisted his nephew to his feet. "That so?"

Toby shrugged one shoulder, but the crumbly evidence dotted his lips. He ducked his head. "I reckon."

Josh blew out a heavy breath. "Thank you for your honesty, but you know better than to help yourself to dessert before a meal, especially when you're a guest in someone else's home. You know not to take food without permission."

Toby's lower lip popped out.

"You'll get no more cookies after lunch. Now, go sit in that chair until I finish."

Corrie lifted her nose in a haughty look that said "I told you so," but when she noticed the glare Josh sent her, her expression shriveled. She moseyed over to stand by Sophie. "Why are you up here? I thought we were gonna eat."

Sophie ran her hand over Corrie's head. "We are. I just wanted to show your uncle this hole in the wall."

"Looks big enough that a rat or even a possum could crawl through."

"Corrie!" Josh didn't want his niece frightening Sophie or putting images in her head that might worry her later.

He glanced at Sophie. "Is the food ready, by chance?"

She nodded. "Would you like to eat first and then take care of this? Or maybe even repair it another day? I've kept you most of the morning already."

"Let's eat, but I don't mind fixing this today. I'll need to go back to my shop first, to cut some wood to fit the hole and mix up some plaster. There's not much I can do about the wallpaper, though."

"That's all right. The bookcase hides it, anyway."

"That's true. Are we done up here?"

Sophie nodded. "Let's go down and eat, shall we?"

Josh nodded and motioned for Corrie to lead the way.

Corrie cast a quick glance at her brother, smirked, and hustled for the stairs.

Toby got a panicked look in his eyes. "Do I hav'ta sit up here and miss lunch?"

Josh was tempted to tease and say yes, just to scare some obedience into the little rascal, but instead he shook his head. "You can eat with us, but no cookies."

Toby slid off the chair, a resigned expression on his face. "Yes, sir."

Josh helped Sophie down the stairs, and they headed into the kitchen. On the counter, she'd laid out a buffet of sandwiches, sliced pickles, quartered apples, and a plate of cookies. His stomach rumbled, and she glanced at him, another smile twitching her pretty lips.

He sure hadn't expected to spend half the day with Sophie, especially with Aaron in town, but his brother had a couple of horses to deliver to a ranch nearby and hadn't wanted to take the children along. So, that had left Josh free to come over and help. And he was sure glad. Being practically alone with her had made him think thoughts he rarely allowed—thoughts of a woman who loved him, of having his own family, and of doing chores around their home. Josh banged into the doorjamb, knocking himself back a step.

Sophie snickered. "Lost in thought again?"

He rubbed the sore spot on his shoulder. "Yep. If it keeps up, I'll need a map to find my way home."

Chapter Fifteen

The congregation stood, and Sophie lurched to her feet. Her cheeks warmed as the pastor gave the benediction. She'd missed the second half of the sermon because she'd been reliving the dream she'd had last night—a dream she could never tell to a soul. Josh Harper and Wade Barnes were knights of old; each wore a shiny suit of armor and carried a shield and jousting lance. Josh rode a regal gray stallion, while Wade rode a spirited black steed. And Sophie sat in the grandstand, next to the king of the realm. The champion would win her hand. She rose, handkerchief held high, and when she dropped it, both horses shot forward as if released from a catapult. But now, try as she might, she couldn't remember who'd won.

"Why the scowl?" Kate bent to pick up her Bible from the pew but kept her eyes on Sophie. "Did Reverend Douglas say something that upset you?"

"Oh, no, not at all. I was just lost in thought, I suppose." She instantly remembered Josh saying the same thing just yesterday, and smiled.

"Must have been some heavy thoughts."

Tom, Kate's husband, stood behind her and leaned down. "I'll get the buggy. The girls went outside to socialize."

"Thank you, dear." Kate patted his bearded cheek and caught Sophie's gaze again. "Are you still coming over for Sunday dinner?"

"After all you've done for me, I should be feeding *your* family." Sophie stepped into the aisle and waved at Corrie, who stood behind her father, Aaron. The girl smiled and returned the gesture.

Kate slipped into the aisle and leaned close to Sophie's ear. "There's two mighty fine-looking Harper men over there. How about I invite them to eat too?"

"Kate!" Sophie barely resisted clapping her hand over her friend's mouth. "Shh. They'll hear you." Though she would have enjoyed sharing another meal with Josh and his brother, she didn't dare. Folks would start the rumor mill, spinning tales about them courting. "If I eat another meal with Josh Harper any time soon, the whole town will be talking."

Kate moved passed Sophie, then turned. "You didn't grow up in a small town, did you?" She patted Sophie's hand. "Honey, folks have been betting on you two since the day you arrived and Josh helped you at the depot."

Sophie's heart skipped a beat. "You can't be serious. We became friends only recently."

"Don't worry about it. Time will reveal the truth." Kate looped her arm through Sophie's. "C'mon. I'm starved."

An hour later, Sophie sat with the McMillan family at their table. Tom's deep voice rumbled a short prayer, then every head lifted.

Pearl handed Sophie a bowl of pickled beets, her blue eyes twinkling. "So, I hear you had supper with Josh Harper and that handsome brother of his. He lookin' for a wife?"

"Pearl!" both Kate and Mary responded together.

"What?" Pearl blinked, obviously surprised by the reaction of her mother and sister. "How's a woman supposed to learn that kind of thing if she doesn't ask?"

Tom chuckled as he took four pieces of fried chicken off the platter, then passed it to his wife. He bit into the crunchy meat, wisely refraining from commenting.

"Both men are too old for you." Mary sliced her biscuit in half and slathered butter on it.

Pearl stiffened and glared at her sister. "They are not. Why, the age difference between me and them can't be much different than what's between Ma and Pa."

"She's got you there." Tom looked at Mary, but when Kate pinned him with a sizzling glower, he ducked his head and concentrated on his food.

Sophie nearly laughed at the big man being so effectively put in his place by his feisty wife. Life with the McMillans was anything but boring, and so different from the quiet, formal meals she'd eaten with her parents.

"What do you plan to do now that your aunt is gone?" Mary asked her.

Kate scowled again. "Sophie's gonna think I never taught you girls any manners."

"It's all right, Kate." Sophie dabbed her lips with her napkin. "Honestly, I'm not sure. I'd like to stay in Windmill, at least until the school year is over, so that the children can finish the term before they go home for the summer."

Mary nodded. "That would be wonderful. It's so hard for children who live far from town to get a decent education." She suddenly paused and blinked several times. "I wonder what will happen to them in the fall."

Sophie shrugged. "I wish I could stay and care for them, but I've already been here longer than I expected to. Once my parents find out about Aunt Maude—"

"You haven't told them?" Kate held a chicken leg halfway between her plate and her mouth.

Shaking her head, Sophie felt the familiar tension of her dilemma. "I'm not ready to leave yet, and if they found out, they'd insist I return home immediately. Besides, telling them now won't achieve anything. The funeral is over."

"You're playing with fire, if you ask me." Kate set the chicken back on her plate, wiped her fingers on her napkin, and reached out, laying her hand on Sophie's forearm. "Tell me why Josh was at your house yesterday. I've been dying to know."

Sophie despised the heat rising to her cheeks. She shrugged. "Just repairing a few of the stairs, so the children wouldn't fall, and patching a couple of holes in the wall."

"Holes?" Kate's excited gaze jumped from one person to the other, and Sophie got the distinct impression that the woman knew something significant she'd never told her.

"Yes, there were several. I thought perhaps they'd been made by some critter wanting in, but Josh"—Sophie cleared her throat as another blush warmed her cheeks—"Mr. Harper said they were made by someone—or something—on the inside of the house." She scrunched her napkin, still uncomfortable with that theory. It made no sense.

Tom studied his wife for a moment, then swatted his fork in the air. "Go ahead and tell her. You know you're dying to."

"Oh, let me. Please, Ma." Pearl folded her hands as if in prayer and tapped her fingertips against her lips.

"Be my guest." Kate looked a bit disappointed but covered it up by taking a sip from her cup.

Pearl shifted on her chair, her eyes sparkling. "It's rumored that a treasure is hidden somewhere in Miss Maudie's house."

Sophie sucked in a sharp breath. "A treasure? What kind? And where did it come from?"

Pearl shook her head and gave a brief shrug. "No one knows, but there's been lots of speculation."

Sitting back in her chair, Sophie let the thought sink in. She considered the sad state of the pantry supplies and knew that if her aunt had possessed a significant sum of money, she would have fed the children better. Furthermore, if there had been some money, why would her uncle have taken out a loan against the house? "If

Uncle Sam and Aunt Maude had some hidden wealth, why did they live so poorly? The treasure must be that—just a rumor."

Tom leaned forward. "It might explain the holes you found in the wall."

All eyes shifted to the end of the table. Kate set her fork down on the edge of her plate with a ting. "What do you mean?"

"Miss Davenport said that the holes looked as if they'd been made from the inside. Someone's been looking for the treasure."

Both daughters gasped, then every head turned toward Sophie. Her mind raced. Had someone sneaked into the house while they were sleeping? Or had the holes been made before her arrival? Just because she hadn't noticed them at first didn't mean they had been carved out recently. The scene in the pantry burst into her memory.

"What is it?" Kate leaned forward. "Did you think of something?"

"I woke up early a few days ago and went downstairs to decide what to prepare for breakfast, and I noticed someone had been in the pantry. Jars and cans had been moved on the shelves, as had sacks of flour and sugar on the floor."

Kate gasped. "You had a break-in?"

Sophie shrugged, lifting her palms in the air. "I don't know. That's the odd thing. As far as I could tell, nothing had been taken. Just moved around."

Mary leaned forward. "Somebody was looking for something."

"Sounds like it," Tom said, his deep voice rumbling.

Pearl clapped her hands together and bounced in her seat. "Oh, this is the most exciting thing to happen in Windmill since that stray dog ran down Main Street with Mayor Ashton's hairpiece in its mouth."

"Pearl!" The color left Kate's face. "Act like the lady I know you can be and don't tell tales."

Lowering her head, Pearl leaned toward Sophie. "Well, it is," she whispered.

Tom's eyes danced, and his shoulders shook.

Kate whacked her husband's upper arm. "Don't encourage her." She sent Pearl a narrow-eyed glare, then turned to Sophie. "Do you have locks on your doors?"

"Yes, but I never use them. The town is so peaceful—and small. I never felt they were needed. And then, there are the children, and their treks outside to the...um...well, you know." Talk of privies wasn't acceptable in normal conversation, not to mention at the dinner table.

"Tom, after you take your Sunday nap, we'll go over to Sophie's. I want you to check those locks and make sure they're secure. And you"—Kate faced Sophie again—"make sure you lock up the house at night. Close and latch all of the windows on the bottom floor, and tell the marshal about your intruder."

"Do you truly think it's necessary to do all that? I'm not even sure the pantry prowler wasn't one of the children merely hunting for a late-night snack."

Mary giggled. "'Pantry prowler'...I like that. Sounds like a newspaper headline. 'Pantry Prowler Invades Home Searching for Hidden Treasure. Takes Nothing.'"

Tom and Pearl joined her in her mirth, but Kate's expression remained serious. Sophie couldn't help wondering if she had taken things too lightly. She didn't have just herself to be concerned about. She couldn't let anything happen to the children. Starting tonight, she'd make sure the house was locked up as tight as Josh's bank.

After dinner, Sophie headed home. She figured she should have at least an hour before the children returned from their weekend away. That was just enough time to make a quick search of the house. She didn't actually believe a treasure was hidden there, but her uncle had been an officer in the Great War, and who was to say he hadn't found something precious and secreted it away? And if there were a treasure, would it be enough to pay off the mortgage? Her foot caught on the hem of her skirt, and she stumbled. After righting herself, she slowed her pace. If she found a treasure, who would it belong to now?

She dashed across the street, in front of a slow-moving wagon, and passed the bank and Josh's house. Childish giggles echoed out the open windows, followed by the rumble of a man's laughter. Her stomach did a somersault as she remembered the time spent with Josh yesterday.

Last night's dream charged back into her mind like a contingent of knights on their gallant steeds. The dangerous dark knight, Wade Barnes, battling the trustworthy warrior, Josh Harper, on his dappled gray mount. The thought of the two handsome men doing battle for her heart made her feel lighter than a seedpod soaring high on a gusty spring breeze. She'd never hoped to catch the attention of even one man, much less two. Even if it was only in her dreams.

Sophie blew out a loud breath. "Oh, girl, you're a fool to hope so."

As she reached for the doorknob, she paused. Voices echoed around the side of the house. She crossed to the left of the porch and looked between her house and the next. Wade Barnes and Mikey stood outside the parlor window, a bulging canvas bag at their feet.

"Is there some way I can help you gentlemen?"

Mikey jumped, but Wade straightened slowly, a wide smile causing his dimples to flash. "So, the pretty lady has returned."

Sophie would be lying to say that his compliment didn't affect her, but she was too curious as to what they were doing to return his smile. "What were you up to?"

Wade pursed his lips, eyebrows arched, and shrugged. "Just trying to get the window open so Mike could get inside."

After the tale she'd heard at dinner, Sophie bristled. Was Mr. Barnes also planning to enter her home? "And why does he need to get into the house?"

Mr. Barnes picked up the canvas bag and strode toward her. "Ya weren't home, and I needed to hit the trail to make it back to the ranch before dark. I didn't want to just leave the boy on the street."

"Yep." Mikey trotted to his side and sent his father a narrow-eyed glance. "What kind of pa would abandon his kid?"

She wondered what the basis was for Mikey's sarcastic comment. Something about the situation didn't feel right to her, but then, she'd practically given up trying to make sense of Mikey's peculiar actions. Some families were just different. She returned to the front door and opened it. Evidently, neither of them had thought to try the door, or they'd have known it was unlocked. "Well, I'm home now. Say good-bye to your father so he can be on his way."

A strange odor wafted off Mikey, as if he'd spent the night in a pigpen, and Sophie lowered her gaze to look more closely at the boy. Dirt smudged his cheeks, and pieces of dried grass clung to his hair. Where had he been, to have gotten so filthy? Then again, perhaps she didn't want to know. "Go out back and start drawing some water. You need a bath."

He turned up one side of his mouth and groaned. "Aww. I thought I missed out on a bath since I was gone on Saturday."

"No such luck. The bedding is clean and fresh, and you'll not be using it unless you've bathed. If you hurry, you can finish before the girls return."

"But it's the middle of the day."

Sophie gave the boy a stern glare and pointed to the house. "Go on, now."

"Shucks." Mikey turned and dragged his feet through the parlor.

Sophie blew out a breath. She'd need to wash his clothes tomorrow, since he had only one other set.

The boy's father cleared his throat, drawing her gaze back to him. His clothing, while not the newest, looked clean and didn't reek like his son's. He held the canvas bag out to her. "Got something for ya."

Sophie sucked in a quick breath. Gift-giving wasn't proper unless a couple was courting or extremely close friends.

He raised a hand, palm out. "I see that refusal on your pretty lips. It's just a passel of vegetables and a hunk of beef. Consider it a gift for the children, if ya feel awkward taking it for yourself."

Food…for the children. That she could accept, especially since they needed it so badly, and she had only a few dollars left. "Very well. That is kind of you. The children will appreciate it."

His wide grin told her he was pleased with her acceptance. He set the bag inside the open door.

Though attracted to the comely man, she didn't quite feel comfortable in his presence, but she couldn't pinpoint exactly why. She struggled for something else to say. "I was disappointed not to see you and Mikey in church this morning."

Mr. Barnes's wide smile wilted before he lifted it back in place. "I reckon it just slipped my mind, since I don't get to town too often."

Disappointment settled over Sophie. If he rarely got the chance to go to church, it seemed he should make it a priority to attend whenever he could. She blew out a sigh. Who was she to lecture someone on his churchgoing? She'd stayed home many times because her mother didn't want her out in bad weather, not to mention Sophie had never been eager to face the pitying glances of the other parishioners whenever she emitted a raspy cough during the service.

Mr. Barnes stepped closer, obviously not bothered by her comment. He lifted a hand and caught a tendril of hair that had come unpinned, twisting it in a too-familiar gesture. "How about going to supper with me next time I'm in town?"

Sophie's heart fluttered like a hummingbird's wing. Had he seen her dining with the Harpers? Was that why he'd asked? A movement to her right drew her gaze away from his—a man walking his horse down the street. His head turned toward her and Mr. Barnes, and she took a step back to put some distance between them. The last thing she needed to get was a reputation for entertaining men. Still, she needed to respond to his question. "And when will you be in town again?"

"Depends." His dimples deepened and his eyes glimmered. "When are y' available?"

His charm and attention flattered Sophie. The man was so good-looking that she wanted to frame a tintype of him and put it on the wall. She set aside her prickly caution, choosing to enjoy the rare compliment. "Not until next weekend, I'm afraid, and only if all of the children have gone home for the summer."

"Can't ya leave 'em for one night? That big girl's old enough to watch 'em."

Sophie's delight fizzled. "Surely you aren't asking me to shirk my responsibilities in order to enjoy a night on the town."

He ducked his head and tugged off his hat. "Aw, you're comely, and have good manners to boot. I'm eager to spend some time with ya."

"We barely know one another, Mr. Barnes."

"It's Wade, remember? And that's why I want to have supper with ya—so we can get better acquainted."

Sophie struggled with a response. Part of her felt the need to run inside the house and bar the door, while another part wanted to accept his offer and enjoy dinner out with a fine-looking man. Still, good sense reigned. "I should know you better before joining you for a meal." She glanced into the house. "I need to check on Mikey."

Mr. Barnes nodded and set his hat back on his head. "Fair enough. See ya next weekend, then?"

She nodded, then watched his long legs take him away. She liked his calm demeanor and quick smile. He didn't seem overly caring about his son, but her father had been the same way with both of his daughters, except when Sophie wanted to do something—and then he became overprotector extraordinaire. Too bad more fathers didn't exercise as much sense in their protectiveness as Josh Harper did with his niece and nephew. He'd make a good father—and he'd even had some practice.

A reverberating clang in the house made her jump. She exhaled a loud sigh and entered the dim structure. Here she was, comparing Josh Harper and Wade Barnes on their fathering skills, while she'd already forgotten about her charge.

Chapter Sixteen

Josh stared out the window of the bank, his thoughts on Sophie. He'd never been attracted to a woman to the extent that she invaded his thoughts and affected his work. She was so pretty. So determined. So industrious, in spite of having a physical affliction that sometimes got the better of her. But the moment her attack had passed, she had gone back to work. Stubborn woman didn't even rest a full day.

He couldn't shake the sense of protectiveness that had nearly overwhelmed him when he'd held her in his arms. She was so light, and she'd seemed to fully trust him at that moment. And she'd smelled of rose water.

Glancing down at the past-due mortgage, he tapped his pencil on the page. What was he going to do about it? He didn't want to bring up the subject again and send her into another asthma attack, but he couldn't overlook it, either. The bank board was pressuring him to foreclose. His uncle had even written to him, instructing him to repossess the property immediately, even going so far as to say that the banking business was no place for softhearted men.

And that was part of the problem. Josh liked helping people, giving them loans when they needed them, but he dreaded foreclosing or chasing after someone for payment on a loan.

He leaned back in his chair and gazed out the open window. A wagon rolled past loaded with what looked like the contents of someone's home. The driver had already passed from view, so he didn't know if the folks were coming or going. A man on horseback trotted down the street, a cloud of dust floating up after him. That was something Josh missed about living at the stage stop—riding. Galloping Chester across the hilly plains, with the wind whipping his clothing and the sun warming his skin. Maybe he'd take a short ride at lunchtime today.

Mr. Samuels' shoes tapped a steady rhythm as he approached Josh's office. He paused just inside the door. "I picked up the mail while stopping at the mercantile for some ink, Mr. Harper."

"Thank you." He reached out and accepted the day's correspondence from his bookkeeper. As Mr. Samuels turned to leave, Josh thumbed through the missives. The last one made him pause. The envelope was a finer quality than most he received. His gaze settled on the embossed return address: Davenport Designs in St. Louis.

He knew of no business by that name, but his uncle lived in St. Louis, so maybe the note was tied to him. Josh used his letter opener to rip open the top of the envelope. He set aside the smaller envelope inside and unfolded the thick page, his fingertip brushing the embossed stationer's mark in the upper left corner.

Honored Sir,

I am writing this letter to inform you that I recently talked with Charles Harper, a friend and business associate of mine here in St. Louis. As coincidence would have it, I was telling him of my daughter's visit to Windmill, Kansas, and he informed me that his nephew managed the Windmill bank for him. Charles explained what a fine job you were doing there, and encouraged me to impose upon your services concerning a delicate matter.

With great trepidation and many hours of wrestling with the idea, I agreed to allow my daughter Sophia Davenport to travel to Windmill to be an aid and encouragement to her aunt, Maude Archer, who is my older sister. This is Sophia's first trip alone, as she is fragile and has suffered a lifelong infirmity. I have included a draft to cover any expenses of either my daughter or sister, as well as a smaller draft—payment for your services and confidentiality, as well as a stamp for your return missive.

I realize you do not know me, but your uncle assured me you were an honorable, trustworthy individual. Please forgive me for imposing upon your services, but I would like to request that you keep an eye out for my daughter and contact me by telegram should she become ill or endure trouble of any sort. I regret that my business commitments did not allow me to travel with her to visit my sister. I trust that you will inform my daughter that you have received the enclosed funds, but I would greatly appreciate if you would keep the details to yourself and not inform her of my request that you keep watch on her. Though she is frail and has been sheltered much of her life, Sophia has an independent nature and would not take kindly to learning of this arrangement.

I am in your debt.

Edward Allen Davenport
Davenport Designs
St. Louis, Missouri

Josh folded up the letter and peeked inside the smaller envelope to find two drafts and a stamp. He sat back in his chair, a mixture of emotions battling one another. He considered what Mr. Davenport had said about Sophie being frail and sheltered. No wonder she was over her head with all there was to do at Miss Maudie's house. And yet, she hadn't shied away from the work, as he would have expected from the woman her father described. Rather, she had embraced it. For a wealthy woman from the city, she didn't seem to mind getting her hands—and her pretty dresses—dirty, and for that, he admired her.

He'd finally stopped wrestling with the idea of her watching Corrie and Toby. She'd done well with the children; they liked her and enjoyed being with her. He had no complaints now, but he worried about her overexerting herself. She needed someone to watch out for her, but the idea of being a spy for Mr. Davenport stuck in his craw. He wouldn't be Edward Davenport's lackey. First thing in the morning, he would pen a note to the man and return the smaller draft. As for watching out for Sophie, he was already doing that. Not because someone paid him to, but because he was starting to care for the stubborn, intriguing woman.

Josh peered inside the envelope again and studied the larger draft. It wasn't enough to pay off the loan, but Sophie could use it to cover a payment or two, if she so chose, which would give them more time to find a way to pay off the balance. She would also have enough money to get by, at least for a short while.

Josh tapped his pencil on the desk. Sophie's father didn't seem to know his sister was gone. Had her letter informing Mr. Davenport of the sad news not arrived before he'd written the one Josh had just received? Ah, well. It was none of his concern.

He gazed out the window. With Sophie's aunt gone, he knew her dedication to the children was the only thing holding her here. What would happen when school ended and the children returned home for the summer? Would she leave?

He may have wished that at first, but not now. The thought of her departure left a hollow cavern in his gut.

⌒

With the children off to school on Monday morning, Sophie sipped her tea and scanned the short list of properties available for rental printed in this week's newspaper. Not much to choose from, and only two that she might possibly afford. She jotted down the addresses on the back of an old envelope. She'd clean up the kitchen, then go take a look at them.

Half an hour later, as she dumped her rinse water out back, someone knocked on the front door. Sophie quickly dried her hands, then hurried down the hallway and opened the door. On the porch stood a short man wearing a brown sack suit and holding a leather briefcase. He studied her with kind-looking hazel eyes. Her aunt's attorney. She remembered him from the day he'd visited Aunt Maude, shortly before she died.

"Mayor Wilkes, isn't it?"

"Yes, I am—or was—your aunt's attorney. I realize it's a bit early to come calling, but might I have a word with you?"

"Of course, if you don't mind sitting on the porch. All of the children are at school."

He eyed the faded rocker with the same expression the children had made at the mashed turnips she'd served with supper last night. "I suppose that will have to do. I'd hoped to talk with you last week, but I wanted to give you plenty of time to recover from your aunt's passing and your…uh…." He tugged at his shirt collar, his ears turning ruby red. "Well, you remember what happened…at the bank."

Heat scorched Sophie's cheeks. Kate had been right about everyone knowing one another's business in a small town. In fact, she was a bit surprised she hadn't heard that the attorney was planning to visit her. She took a steadying breath. "Would you care for some tea, Mayor Wilkes?"

"That sounds delightful, but, as this is a business visit, I'm afraid I must decline."

While he pulled the other rocker closer to the one by the door, Sophie turned and quickly removed her apron. She brushed back the wisps of hair that had come loose while she was doing dishes, then hurried outside to join him. When she sat, he did too, and unfastened the clasp on his briefcase. He pulled out several sheets of paper, smoothed them, then looked at her.

"As the attorney of Maude Irene Archer, it's my duty to inform you that she left all of her worldly possessions to you, her niece.

That includes her house and all its furnishings, and her bank account. Do you understand, Miss Davenport?"

Sophie's heart jolted. She owned a house! Her joy instantly faded. Did that mean she was now responsible for the debt to the bank?

Mayor Wilkes' expression dimmed. "I'd hoped that would be good news, Miss Davenport. Your aunt was so taken with you that she had me change her will just a few days before she passed."

"It would be good news, if not for some other information I received last week." She twisted her hands as she pondered how to ask her question without painting her uncle Sam in an unfavorable light. "What if my aunt owed money to someone? Is that debt now mine?"

Mayor Wilkes' thick moustache wiggled as he quirked his mouth. "That would depend on the debt and whether the person she was indebted to decided to pursue collecting said debt."

She knew there was no chance the bank would overlook the unpaid loan. She dreaded saying more, but she desperately needed advice. "What if the debt was a loan against the house?"

He frowned and sat back. "I didn't realize Mrs. Archer owed money on her home. That would certainly complicate things."

"Especially when the loan is well past due."

He nodded. "Yes, I can see that. Still, given the situation, I would expect the bank would give you some time to arrange payment of the loan, if you have the means to do so."

That was a big *if.* She knew her father had the money, but he would be surprised to learn that his sister hadn't left the house to him, and both parents would expect her to return home now that Maude was gone. "I don't suppose you know how much money my aunt had in her bank account, would you?"

He shook his head. "Sorry, I don't. You'll need to talk to Joshua Harper about that." The man's mustache danced, and his eyes lit up. "I do believe you two are acquainted."

"We are." Sophie avoided looking at the man and stared out the window. A black-and-white dog trotted along the street, head down, tongue hanging out one side of its mouth. A horse, tethered to the hitching post at the house next door, flicked its tail to one side, then the other, swatting flies. This peaceful community had stolen a piece of her heart, and she didn't want to leave.

"Well, I just need you to sign this paper to make everything official. Could we step inside to your table for a moment?"

Sophie nodded and rose. Yes, she loved this town and wanted to stay, but with no income or way of making any, how would that be possible?

⁓

Josh stood on Sophie's porch, still unsure how to approach her about the draft from her father—and the fact that it had been sent to him to deliver, rather than directly to her. He hoped she would overlook that fact and be grateful her father had provided some money.

He pressed his lips together, still somewhat annoyed that Mr. Davenport had asked him to spy on his daughter. What kind of man did that?

A rowdy stampede inside the house caused the porch to shake. He stepped back from the door, on the chance that the children burst through it, but they didn't. Through the open windows, he heard scuffling and then a squeal. He moved forward and knocked on the door. The noises inside quieted.

He heard shushing, and then the door opened, revealing a red-cheeked Hazel. She caught his eye for a brief moment, then ducked her head. "Corrie, your uncle is here."

Behind her, he spied Mikey on the sofa, holding a doll up high. Amanda stood on the floor in front of him, stretching to reach the toy. The ornery grin on the boy's lips faded when he saw Josh staring. He dropped the doll, ran across the sofa, jumped off, and raced out of the room.

"Mikey, slow down," Sophie yelled from the kitchen.

The back door slammed. Amanda cuddled her doll, tears shimmering in her eyes. Hazel meandered down the hall toward the kitchen, and Corrie tugged on Josh's trousers until he looked down.

"Toby hit Amanda, so he's sitting in a chair where Miss Sophie can watch him."

As if the news brought back a terrible memory, Amanda sucked in a quivering sob, and tears started streaming down her face.

Josh leaned against the doorjamb, already exhausted. How did Sophie deal with all the commotion for hours at a time, day after day? Suddenly, he realized what Corrie had said. "Toby hit someone?"

His niece bobbed her head, as if proud to be the one to tattle on her brother. Though he would miss the children, he was nonetheless glad that summer was almost upon them, so that they could return to the ranch.

"Where did you say Toby was?"

Corrie stepped back and pointed down the hall. "In the kitchen."

Tired from a stressful day at the bank, Josh trudged through the house, but when he paused in the doorway and saw Sophie stirring something on the stove, the domestic scene lit a flame in him. He could imagine her cooking in their home—preparing supper for him. He blinked, taken by surprise at the direction of his thoughts. He pulled his gaze away from her, hunting for his nephew. Toby sat in a chair facing a corner of the room. Hazel moved around the small table, setting a fork at each place.

"Oh, Mr. Harper's here," Hazel said, almost as an afterthought.

Sophie spun around, and her eyes widened. Something dripped off the spoon she held.

"Smells good, whatever you're cooking." Josh smiled, hoping to soften her alarm. "Hazel let me in. I hope that's all right."

"Uncle Josh." Toby slid from the chair and started toward him.

Josh lifted his brows. "Did Miss Davenport say you could get up?"

"No, but—"

Josh flicked his fingers in the air, motioning for Toby to return to the chair.

The boy scowled but obeyed. He crossed his arms. "I wish Pa was here."

The barb pricked Josh, as had been Toby's intention. "So do I."

Sophie pulled in her lips, as if trying not to laugh, then turned and set the spoon down. "Parenting is difficult, even on a good day." She pivoted back to face him. "So my mother often said."

He nodded. How many times had he felt insecure at the task he'd been given? Did Aaron feel the same at times?

"Toby, since your uncle is here, you may get up. I want you to tell him what you did."

His nephew slid off the chair, his frown deepening. "Oh, all right."

"We'll discuss it when we get home," Josh told him. "Right now, I need to talk with Miss Davenport."

Sophie's eyebrows lifted. "Oh?"

He glanced at the children, then looked back at Sophie. "Could you get away for a short walk?"

"Um…I suppose so. The children have been extra rowdy today—probably from the change of being away from their parents again. A walk would do them good." She turned to Toby. "Would you please look out back and see if you can find Mikey? Tell him we're going for a walk."

Josh took a step back. He'd meant to invite only Sophie. "I need to talk about something of a...um...private nature."

Sophie grabbed a cloth and moved the steaming pot from the stove to the warmer. Then she untied her apron and hung it on a hook. She approached Josh with a teasing glint in her eyes. "Surely, you didn't mean to ask me to take a walk alone with you, out in public. I know you wouldn't expect me to do such a thing and leave the children here at the house without supervision. What would people think?"

She had a point. He'd basically asked her to shirk her responsibility—something he'd accused her of doing in the past. He dipped his head. "My apologies."

Her smile brightened. "Apology accepted—and I'm so thankful for a chance to get the children outside for a while."

He understood. Corrie and Toby always went to sleep quicker after they'd taken a long walk or done some other outdoor activity in the evenings. "Where shall we go?"

Sophie lifted her eyes to the ceiling and tapped her lip with her index finger, drawing his gaze to her pretty mouth. When he raised his eyes to meet hers, she was staring at him, a pleasant pink brightening her cheeks. He couldn't look away from the depths of her amazing eyes. He wanted to kiss her.

Something bumped into his backside, pushing him forward. He grabbed Sophie to keep from knocking her down and took several bumbling steps as Corrie raced by.

"Sorry, Uncle Josh. You were in the way."

The three girls tromped outside, leaving the door open. Josh realized he and Sophie were alone—and he still held her in his arms. He glanced down, and she looked up, her breath mingling with his. "A gentleman would release you."

Chapter Seventeen

Sophie couldn't breathe, but it wasn't because of an asthma episode. Josh's drumming heart pummeled her shoulder. She wanted to stay just where she was, wrapped in the arms of this man she was coming to care for, but it wasn't proper for them to be alone in the house. And a nagging thought wouldn't leave her alone.

Did Josh truly feel something for her? Or was he merely holding on to her out of fear she'd have another attack?

"*You are not normal.*" The memory of her mother's haranguing comment was like throwing a bucket of dirty rinse water on her dreams. What man would want a sickly woman like her? She forced herself to look up again into Josh's sapphire eyes. "Since I know you are a gentleman, you should let me go. I promise not to collapse at your feet."

The twinkle in his eyes dimmed, his arms went limp, and he stepped away. He cleared his throat. "You're right. I'm sorry. I'll wait on the front porch until you're ready."

Sophie grabbed hold of the back of a chair as she watched him make a hasty retreat through the house. Had she completely misjudged the man? He'd seemed disappointed to release her. She wanted to believe that he might find something in her worth liking, but her mother had tromped on her dreams so many times, she was afraid to hope. And if Josh had felt something, she feared she'd doused his attraction.

Hanging her head, she exhaled a loud sigh. Not for the first time, she wished she'd been born whole—without a dreadful affliction.

But self-pity never accomplished a thing, other than to make her feel worse. Shaking off her disappointments, she walked to the back door and searched the yard for the children. Hazel and Corrie waited by the privy, but the boys weren't in sight. Rather than stand alone with Josh on the porch, she put on her bonnet and walked outside to wait with the girls. The sooner this walk was over, the better.

Ten minutes later, Sophie stood on the open prairie, a quarter of a mile from town. Even with her bonnet, she had to squint because of the sun's intensity in the cloudless sky. The boys galloped like horses, while the girls trotted around the grassy area, gathering wildflowers into bouquets. Sophie turned back to face the town, surprised to see how small the buildings looked.

"There's a large rock over there. Would you care to sit?"

She glanced where Josh was pointing and nodded, then allowed him to help her over the rough terrain. She sat on the sun-warmed boulder, keeping a close eye on her charges. The tall grass swished in the light breeze, surrounding her with the pleasant scent of freshness and flowers. The peacefulness of the prairie soothed her. Given the choice, she thought she could spend the rest of her days in this tranquil place that was so different from the busyness of the big city. "I should have thought to do this sooner. The children are having a delightful time."

"Occasionally, I'll bring Corrie and Toby out here to tire them out before bedtime, but I wouldn't recommend that you come alone, especially if you're unarmed."

Sophie's gaze shot to his. He held it but a moment before looking away. She felt she'd hurt him somehow, though she had no idea what she'd done. The only reason he could possibly feel wounded would be if he actually cared for her...but that was foolish. She wrung her hands in her lap. If only....

"I suppose we should address the reason I needed to talk with you."

She checked on the children again, then looked up at Josh. Fortunately, the sun was at her back. He tucked his hat down low, shading the top half of his face. Had the bank decided on a date by which she needed to be out of the house?

Neither of the places she'd considered renting would be big enough for her and the children. She clenched the fold of her dress, waiting for the dread announcement.

Various expressions crossed Josh's face, as if the news he was about to impart was difficult. Suddenly, he reached into his frock coat and pulled out an envelope. He smacked it against one hand, then held it out to her.

"What is it?"

"Take a look."

She took the envelope from him and peered at the mailing address. The bold handwriting was familiar—her father's? Intrigued, she peered inside, then pulled out a blank sheet of paper. A smaller page lifted on the breeze and then fluttered to the ground several feet away. Josh hurried to pick it up, then returned it to her. She stared at the draft for fifty dollars, signed by her father. Then she gazed up again. "I don't understand. How did you get this?"

⌒

Josh wrestled with how much to tell Sophie. He wanted to be honest, but he didn't want to reveal all that her father had said. "Your father sent it to me and asked that I deposit it into an account for you."

"Why didn't he just send it to me?"

Josh shrugged. He couldn't tell her about the other draft and her father's written request that he spy on her and report back to him. The news would devastate the stubborn, independent woman. "He mentioned that he knew my uncle Charles, who verified I could be trusted, so I suppose that's why he sent it to the bank."

Sophie ducked her head, and Josh wished he could see her expression, but the wide brim of her bonnet blocked it. Was she relieved that her father cared enough to send her some money?

She suddenly shot up off the boulder as if she'd seen a snake. She thrust the draft at him. "Take it. I don't want it."

He shoved his hands in his pockets and shook his head. "What am I supposed to do with it?"

"Send it back to my father."

"But it's enough money to make a payment or two on the mortgage and still have plenty to live on for a time."

Sophie crossed her arms and scowled at him. "I don't want my father's help. It would only reinforce his belief that I can't survive on my own."

"What's wrong with a father helping his child?" Josh's family was loving and supportive. If his parents heard he was having a difficult time, they'd be the first to offer help. "I don't understand why it upsets you so much."

"Of course you don't!" She sliced her arm through the air like a soldier wielding a sword.

Josh stepped back, hoping she wouldn't have another wheezing attack. Her dark eyes had widened, and the wispy curls that had pulled free from her hairpins spiraled around her face. She shook her head, reminding him of a neighbor's filly that had gotten loose one winter and hadn't liked being captured the next spring. She'd wanted her freedom, just like Sophie.

"You haven't been treated like a leper your whole life, forced to stay at home while your family attended church, concerts, and other social events they felt would be too taxing. And you probably never had your bedroom moved downstairs to the library so that you wouldn't infect your sibling, as if asthma were contagious. Or been told that you are not normal." Sophie tramped away.

Josh stood there, stunned, not so much by her outburst as by what she'd revealed. Had her parents really treated her that way, or was that merely her interpretation?

Sophie suddenly pivoted and strode back. She shoved the draft at him again. "Please take this." A wheeze followed her words. She closed her eyes, one hand resting on her chest. "I don't...want it."

He eyed the draft, then took it, not wanting to upset her further. She turned her back to him, but she couldn't hide her panting. Her shoulders jerked as she struggled to breathe.

"Children!" Josh hollered. "It's time to go home."

A chorus of disappointed "Aww's" shot his way, but the girls gathered their flowers and started toward town, walking side by side.

Mikey took off running. "Race you!" he called over one shoulder to Toby.

"Hey!" Toby chased after him.

Josh touched Sophie's arm. "Are you all right?"

She stiffened and nodded. "Give me a moment."

Josh relaxed a bit at hearing her talk without a loud wheeze. Would he ever be able to have a serious discussion with this woman and not provoke an asthma attack?

He stared out across the prairie, trying once more to understand why Sophie was so against accepting help from her father. His own family always practiced give-and-take, helping one another whenever it was needed. No one gave a thought that he might be doing more than his brother or one of their parents. Running the stage stop had been a group effort—it still was, even with Josh working in town. He'd taken the job at the bank to supplement his family's income during a time when finances were especially tight. But now that they had adapted and expanded the business, they no longer needed his financial assistance, leaving him stuck in the middle. He liked town life, but he also enjoyed living at the ranch.

Still, he felt that if he moved back there, he'd never figure out what his life's purpose was.

Josh glanced toward Windmill. The girls had reached the edge of town, but the boys were nowhere to be seen. He needed to return and decide what to do about supper, but he didn't want to force Sophie.

She stood, looking out over the prairie. What did she see? Did she think of the place as a desolate wasteland compared to the crowded city she called home?

"You must think me deplorable."

Her sudden words took him by surprise. "No, not at all. But I will admit that I can't comprehend why you resist your father's aid so vehemently."

She gracefully turned, and he was relieved to see that some color had returned to her cheeks. "You couldn't possibly understand unless you'd lived the life I have." She looked toward town. "We should be getting back."

He nodded and offered his arm. She eyed it for a moment, then accepted it, wrapping her hand lightly around his upper arm. Her touch sent a current of awareness surging through him. How was it this woman could affect him so, when, just a few weeks ago, he'd thought her incapable of caring for his brother's children?

Sophie heaved a big sigh. "I'm sorry for spewing the problems of my past on you."

Josh chuckled. "I have two brothers and grew up on a ranch. It's not the first time I've been spewed on."

Sophie's arm shook as she giggled.

He stood taller, knowing that he'd made her smile when she was troubled, and patted her hand. "I don't need to know why you don't want to accept the draft, but if you need to talk about it, I'm a good listener."

"I've never had anyone to talk to about this before. No one could possibly understand what it's like to be so coddled that you feel you'll suffocate." She stopped and looked up at him. "The only reason I was permitted to come here was that I was the only one available to help Aunt Maude. If my father could have sent someone else, he would have. My mother was already in the East, visiting her mother. My sister is due to have a baby soon, and Father had important business to attend to. I'm sure my mother doesn't yet know I'm here, or I would have received a scathing letter by now, ordering me to return home."

Were things truly as bleak for her as she painted them? If so, he could see why she fought so hard to stay here.

"I can see by your silence that I've shocked you."

Josh shook his head. "No, it's not that. I tend to be a thinker." He rested his hand on hers. "I'm sorry your life has been so… difficult."

She shrugged, her lips pressed in a tight line. "Perhaps now you can see why I'm not so eager to return to my humdrum existence. It's hard to explain," she waved a hand toward Windmill, "but there's something about this town and the prairie that feels like home to me. I love the quiet, the friendly people…the freedom one has out here."

He moved forward, dreading the end of their time together but knowing he needed to get back to the children. "I want to help. I hope you'll let me know if there's anything I can do."

Sophie stiffened momentarily but then relaxed. "That's kind of you. I'm learning that people out here help one another without a second thought. I've had people 'do for me' so much that I balk at it, but I'm realizing that I don't have to do everything on my own."

Josh smiled. "No woman—or man—can survive alone. God made us to need one another, to want to help others. It's human nature."

They reached the edge of town, and Josh slowed his pace. He hated for this time to end. If only he knew more about wooing a woman. He wanted Sophie to know that he cared, but he didn't want to scare her away.

He stopped in front of her house. "Could I ask you a question?"

Sophie nodded and stepped up onto the porch, putting them almost at eye level with each other.

"Why would your father send money for you to deposit in an account for your aunt, now that she's deceased?" His heart rate quickened. Was the money for Sophie's return trip? But no, her father had wanted him to open an account in her name. "Why did he not insist you return home?"

She ducked her head and nibbled on her lower lip. After a moment, she blew out a sigh and looked up, her pretty face framed by her sun bonnet. Her flittering gaze connected with his and held it. "He didn't insist I return home because I haven't told him yet about Aunt Maude."

⌒

Josh's forehead crinkled. Sophie nibbled the inside of her lip. Would he think her horrible for not telling her father that his sister had died?

"I couldn't see the harm in not telling him, since Aunt Maude was buried so quickly. He never would have made it in time for the funeral, especially since I was so busy arranging everything that I forgot to send him a telegram. And then, when I thought to do so, I didn't want to. I knew he'd make me leave." She heaved in a deep breath to fill her lungs again, so glad that her wheeze had disappeared.

He stared down at her, his handsome face showing no expression of judgment. "While I may not agree with what you did, I can understand your reasoning, especially after what you told me about your home life."

Sophie reached out and clutched his hands. "Thank you, Josh. That means so much to me."

He tightened his grip on her hands, and she glanced down, realizing what she'd done. She tugged free just as a loud clatter arose from inside the house. "I'd better check on the children."

She dashed through the door without waiting for him to respond. A dining room chair lay overturned on the floor. She heard a noise in the kitchen and hurried that way. Hazel stood at one end of the table, while Corrie and Amanda each knelt on a chair, all of them arranging the flowers they'd collected in two vases. The pantry door was open, so Sophie walked over to close it, but she found Toby and Mikey inside. "What are you boys doing?"

The boys jumped and spun around. Sophie looked past them but couldn't see anything that had been disturbed.

"We was just lookin' for somethin' to eat. We're hungry." Mikey crossed his arms and kicked the flour sack. Toby kept his head down, darting glances between Mikey and her. Something didn't feel right about the situation, but she couldn't pinpoint what.

"Out. Both of you." Sophie stepped back, and the two boys slunk past her. She studied the pantry, but other than a few crocks that had been moved, nothing seemed out of place. This was her fault. If they hadn't taken a walk with Josh, supper would have been ready by now, and the boys wouldn't have been tempted to hunt down a snack. "I'll whip up some biscuits and warm the stew. That shouldn't take too long."

Neither boy looked back at her before hurrying from the room. She glanced in the pantry once more, then remembered she'd left Josh on the porch. "Corrie, your uncle is ready to take you home."

"Aw, I wanted to—" Corrie glanced at Sophie, then slid off the seat. She gathered up the clump of wilting flowers that lay on the table in front of her and waved at the other girls. "See you tomorrow."

Sophie followed her through the house to the porch, where Josh still waited. She appreciated that he didn't enter without permission—at least, not since that day when she'd first arrived and he'd thought his niece and nephew were in trouble. She smiled, and he mirrored the action, then tipped his hat at her.

"Thank you for the stroll. Have a good evening."

Toby came barreling outside, and Sophie watched the three of them walk away, Josh holding Corrie's hand. A few paces up the street, Josh turned and waved, then gifted her with a tip of his hat.

Sophie nodded and closed the door. Leaning against it, she dared to let her heart dream. She could be happy in Windmill—was happy. If only her parents would allow her to stay. She could watch the children again next fall and earn income doing so, and she was a skilled seamstress—perhaps she could make dresses to sell.

And if she stayed, maybe her attraction to Josh would grow into something she'd only dreamed of.

Chapter Eighteen

Sophie shut the door to the root cellar and refastened the lock. She'd discovered the key while searching her aunt's bedroom and had hoped to find at least a little treasure in the cellar. Her fascination with the idea of a secret cache irritated her, but she'd read so many books during her dreary existence that she couldn't help wanting to find a hidden hoard. Dirty and smelling like musty air, she blew out the lantern and carried it back into the house. Too bad she couldn't have found some canned vegetables or produce stored in the cellar.

In the kitchen, she washed her hands and face in the basin she'd prepared in advance, then collected her hat and gloves, preparing to go for groceries. Maybe she could find something to purchase for tonight's dinner to surprise the children.

Sophie walked in the mercantile and waved to Mrs. Purdy. The woman smiled. "How are you doin'? I can't tell you how I miss seein' Miss Maudie. She was such a dear."

"Thank you. I miss her too."

Mrs. Purdy bustled around the counter, as quickly as her plump body could move, and enveloped Sophie in a hug. Taken off guard, Sophie wrapped her arms around the woman, gave a quick squeeze, and stepped back.

"Oh, here I go, a-carryin' on." Mrs. Purdy lifted her round spectacles and touched her index finger to the corner of each eye. Then she reached for a pin that was sticking out of her gray bun and shoved it back in. "Now, how can I help you?"

Sophie glanced around the store. "I was hoping to find something different to feed to the children for dinner. They're getting a bit tired of soup and stew."

"Well now, let me think."

Mr. Purdy stepped out from behind the storeroom curtain, carrying a crate. The man smiled and nodded at Sophie. "Dean Gilroy sold me some smoked hams this morning. Would one of those interest you?"

His wife snapped her fingers. "That's right. Ham sure goes well with mashed turnips."

Sophie fought a smile. "If I feed the children another turnip, I'm afraid they'll run away."

The older couple chuckled.

"How about some rice?" Mrs. Purdy suggested. "What you don't cook stores well and for a long time."

Remembering how she liked the rice Miss Hopper made at home, Sophie nodded. "Is it difficult to prepare?"

"Rice?"

Sophie spun toward the door, happy to see Kate, even if she was laughing at her.

Kate strode toward her. "All you do is pick out any stones or stuff and boil it. And then clean the stove after it boils over."

Sophie returned Kate's smile. "Even I ought to be able to cook that." She leaned in and lowered her voice. "How much should I buy?"

Kate smiled at Mr. and Mrs. Purdy as she walked to the shelf that held some smaller bags of rice. "One pound should be more than enough for several meals."

Sophie joined her, noting the price. "I think I'll purchase three pounds. Using some in my soup will add variety." She carried the three sacks to the counter. "I'd like one of your smaller hams, also. And do you have any butter?"

"Sure do." Mr. Purdy spun around and ducked behind the curtain again while his wife began to tally her purchase. Sophie counted out the coins needed, realizing her supply was dwindling fast. Once again, she wondered if she was being overly stubborn about not accepting her father's draft. If she allowed Josh to deposit it, she could buy whatever she wanted, even some fabric to make clothes for the children. She wandered over to the fabric section and fingered a lavender calico that would look pretty on Hazel.

A skinny man she'd seen around town walked into the store and looked around. His eyes lit up when he saw her. "Miss Davenport, I've been huntin' fer ya." He hurried toward her, pulling a paper from his pocket. "Ya got a telegram."

Sophie's heart lurched. A telegram rarely brought good news. She glanced at Kate, whose eyebrows rose, then handed the man a coin and accepted the message. She scanned the cable. It was from her mother.

Arriving in three days. Be packed.

—Mother

A tremble raced through Sophie as her heart dropped to the floor. Her days of freedom would soon be over.

Kate rushed to her side. "What is it? You look like your favorite horse just died."

⌒

Josh signed his name to the letter to Edward Davenport and laid the pen down. He scanned the missive again, satisfied with this version—his fourth attempt. Mr. Davenport probably wouldn't like the fact that he'd returned both drafts and told the man he wouldn't spy on Sophie. Hopefully the man would be placated knowing Josh appreciated the confidence Mr. Davenport had placed in him.

He stood and stretched, then crossed to the big window that overlooked Main Street. A cowboy rode past on a brown and white pinto, while a farmer in overalls drove by, going the other direction. The two men nodded to one another. Josh could hear the squeals of the schoolchildren, playing outside at recess. Down the street, a dog barked.

He enjoyed small-town life, but he missed his family. And his job had been less and less satisfying as of late. Maybe he should go back to the ranch. But then, he was comfortable here, and he liked helping people by giving them loans to improve their land or business.

Josh blew out a loud sigh and swatted a fly away from his face. He wasn't sorry that he'd come to work for his uncle, but he wasn't sure he wanted to continue. His workshop beckoned him, with its sweet-smelling pieces of raw wood. His fingers itched to pick up his engraving tools and make something nice for Sophie. He leaned on the windowsill. But would giving her such a nice gift be proper?

Who knew? He sure didn't. Life at a stage stop didn't exactly prepare a man for courting a woman. And he was sure now that he wanted to court Sophie. Wanted to give her the life she never had. A life where she was free to run her own home as she pleased and not be restricted by overly controlling parents.

A sudden idea burst into his thoughts. He hadn't seen Sophie today, since he'd walked the children to school this morning instead of taking them to her house. Maybe she'd be willing to join him at the café for lunch. He spun around and grabbed the envelope. First, he'd post this letter, so it would be sure to make the next train, and then he'd go to Sophie's and ask her to dine with him.

Josh whistled as he walked, feeling more lighthearted than he had in a long time. Then his steps slowed. If he wanted to court Sophie, he could hardly afford to stop working at the bank, at least for now. But then, if he knew she was waiting for him at home, he could endure anything his job threw his way. He picked up his pace again. He was putting the horse before the cart. First, he needed to see if Sophie would allow him to court her. Then he could decide about the bank.

He stepped into the mercantile and almost plowed into two women standing just inside the doorway. He halted quickly, grabbing the door frame to slow his momentum. "Forgive me, ladies."

Kate McMillan turned around, and Sophie peered over her shoulder. Josh's heart leapt at seeing her. He smiled and tipped his hat. "Morning."

A pretty blush colored Sophie's cheeks, but her eyes didn't light up as they usually did. Was she displeased to see him? Or maybe sorry that he'd interrupted her conversation with her friend?

"I was just leaving, Mr. Harper," Kate said. "And no need to apologize when I was blocking the entrance."

"As was I." Sophie peered at him for a moment, but the closeness they'd experienced the evening before was gone.

Josh didn't know what to say—or do. "I...uh...wonder if I might have a word with you, Miss Davenport?"

If his use of her formal name bothered her, she didn't react. She glanced at Kate, who nodded and nudged her chin in his direction in some kind of private female code. Sophie looked as if she didn't want her friend to leave. He wasn't sure if he should wait for her to answer him or go ahead and mail his letter.

"All right," Sophie finally whispered.

Josh stood a bit straighter, although his gut had started churning. Kate smiled and continued on her way. He was ready to ask Sophie to dine with him, but now he couldn't seem to get the words out. "I...uh...would you mind...uh...waiting while I pay to post this letter?"

She shook her head. "No, I don't mind. I'll wait out on the porch, so as not to block any other customers who might want to come in." A teasing grin appeared, then hid behind her tightened lips, and then it appeared again, like a child playing hide-and-seek.

Feeling reassured, Josh winked at her, then spun toward the counter, eager to finish his business.

After standing in line behind a woman with a large order, he paid the required coin for postage and then hurried outside. He stopped quickly and stepped back inside the doorway. Sophie was talking to Wade Barnes, who leaned against a post, standing entirely too close to her. Josh heard her giggle. His jaw tightened. What was Wade Barnes doing in town in the middle of the week? Didn't the man have a ranch to run?

⌒

Wade Barnes' dimples winked at Sophie as he held out a brown cone of paper, twisted closed at the top.

Sophie frowned. *Not another gift.* They were making her uncomfortable. "What's that?"

"Horehound."

She tried not to shudder, but she loathed the taste of horehound and wondered how anyone could call the nasty stuff "candy." "That's kind of you, but you know I can't accept gifts from you."

He shrugged, but his grin stayed in place. "Give it to the children."

Though she didn't care for the candy, she was surprised by her disappointment that the gift hadn't been meant exclusively for her—even if she couldn't accept it. "The children. Of course."

Mr. Barnes straightened, looking so tall that his hat might scrape the porch roof. "If I thought you'd accept it, I'd say keep it for yourself."

Her heart trilled at the comment. Other than the vegetables Mr. Barnes had brought the last time she'd seen him, and the flowers Josh had once given her as an apology, no man had ever given her a gift—except for her father, of course. There was something exhilarating about knowing the gift had been meant for her. She accepted the bag. "Thank you for your kindness. The children will enjoy the candy."

"How about I walk ya home, if that's where you're headed?"

Saying no to a man with such a charming, hopeful expression was difficult. "I'm waiting for someone."

"Let me give ya this before they arrive, then." He stepped aside to reveal a small canvas bag sitting on a bench.

"What is that?"

"A peck of strawberries."

"Strawberries?" She approached the bag, untied the twine, and peeked inside. A sweet, fruity fragrance teased her senses. "Mmm, I love strawberries. Wherever did you find them?"

"They grow wild on my ranch. There's something else at the house. Shall we?" Mr. Barnes offered his arm, and Sophie slipped her hand around his solid muscle, thinking of strawberries with cream for dessert. Perhaps she could bake a pound cake to go with them. She hadn't had strawberries since last year and couldn't wait to sample one.

As they walked, Mr. Barnes tipped his hat to each female they passed, receiving smiles or blushes in return. Sophie doubted anyone would gossip about her walking with him, since no one seemed to notice she was there.

His steps slowed as they neared her door. "I came by earlier, but ya weren't here. I brought a ham and a couple of chickens—for the kids." His ever-present grin widened, as if he'd pulled a joke on her. "I hope ya don't mind that I took it inside and put it on the kitchen counter. I didn't want to leave it outside, in case some dogs caught wind of it."

Three gifts? "Really, Mr. Barn—"

"Wade, remember."

"All right, Wade. Please stop bringing gifts—for the children and for me. It's very kind of you but not necessary."

"I like doing things for ya, Sophie." He brushed his hand over hers.

Sophie released his arm and opened her door. "I need to go. Thank you for the candy—and the other things—and for walking me home."

Wade nodded, but he didn't move. "The Busbys are hostin' a shindig at the town square on Saturday night." He leaned in close. "Scuttlebutt has it their oldest boy's asked an Olathe gal to marry him, so there's to be a party so they can make an announcement. But, shh." He lifted his index finger to his lips. "It's a secret."

Sophie raised her eyebrows. "If it's a secret, how did you find out about it?"

Wade just grinned. "Can't tell. So, will ya go with me? To the dance?"

Her heart jumped. Her first invitation to a social—and by a handsome man. But as quickly as her spirits lifted, they plummeted back down. "I can't, but I thank you for asking."

"Why can't ya?"

"Because my mother is arriving on the Friday train." She dreaded telling him that she would be leaving, but she had to. "I'll be returning to St. Louis on Monday, so you will need to pick up Mikey this weekend."

His grin wilted, and he toed a loose board with his boot. "Why do ya have to leave? You're a grown woman. Ya don't have to do what your mama says anymore."

She couldn't explain—didn't want to explain—about her childhood and the restrictions her parents had put on her life. And though she agreed with what he'd said about her mother, she didn't like his tone. "I'm sorry."

"Shucks. I had my heart set on dancin' with ya."

"It would have been fun." She could have given the girls the new dresses she'd been working on while they were at school, and Mikey could have worn his new shirt. But the dance wasn't on her horizon. "I really must go. There are things I need to do before the children come home. I hope you'll stay in town long enough to spend a little time with Mikey before you head home."

Wade scowled and shook his head. "I'd better get going myself if I want to get back to my place before dark. Besides, there's no telling what those hands of mine will do while I'm gone."

After he tipped his hat and handed her the bag, she slipped inside, shutting the door. If only her mother wasn't coming this Friday. One extra day was all she would need to attend her first dance. If her mother was in town, she would forbid Sophie to go. She dropped onto the sofa, disappointment making her legs weak. Something in her pocket crinkled, and she reached in and pulled out the telegram. Her mother wasn't even in the same town, but she'd effectively squelched Sophie's hopes again.

She dreaded seeing her mother and having to tell her that Aunt Maude was dead. As bad as it would have been to inform her father, confessing to her mother what she'd done would be much worse. She would find some way to blame Sophie and would say that if she hadn't come to Windmill, Aunt Maude might still be alive. And, since she wasn't, Sophie's mother wouldn't be staying in Windmill to help care for her but would instead escort Sophie home. She cringed at the thought of her mother treating her like a child in public. It was deplorable enough when she did it at home.

Sophie wadded up the paper. What if she refused to leave? The house was hers, after all. She just needed to figure out a way to pay off the mortgage. Maybe she could try talking to Josh again. Surely there was something that could be done.

Josh! Sophie lurched up. She'd completely forgotten that he wanted to talk to her about something. Oh, she felt awful. What must he think about her, making cow eyes at Wade Barnes and going off with him, leaving Josh at the store? She shook her head. What did it matter? She'd be gone in a few days anyway.

Chapter Nineteen

Sophie hadn't even reached the kitchen when someone knocked at her door. *Josh*. She owed him an apology for allowing Wade to charm her into letting him walk her home. Shame slowed her steps. Being attracted to a man—two men—was such a foreign concept that she barely knew how to act. With her palm on the door handle, she closed her eyes and took a steadying breath, hoping that Josh wasn't angry.

But when Sophie pulled open the door, she found Pearl McMillan standing there.

"Oh! Oh! Who was that man? Isn't he the most handsomest fellow you've even seen? And those dimples." She fanned her face with her hand. "I nearly swooned when he winked at me. How do you know him?" Pearl danced about like a butterfly flitting from flower to flower. Sophie had never seen her so excited.

"That's Mikey's father, Wade Barnes."

"He's married?" She stamped her foot. "Oh, pooh. I'm gonna have to move to Kansas City to find an eligible man."

Sophie bit back a smile. "I imagine the good Lord can provide you a man right here in Windmill." She stepped back and gestured for Pearl to enter, wondering what the girl wanted. Sophie had several decisions to make and needed time alone.

"Ma sent me over to cheer you up. She said you got some bad news today."

Sophie smiled. Leave it to Kate. "Come in to the kitchen, and I'll heat some water for tea. And, just so you know, I've never heard

Mikey or his father mention a Mrs. Barnes, so I don't believe Mr. Barnes is married."

Pearl gasped and clapped her hands, then quieted. "Do you have your cap set for him?"

Sophie nearly dropped the teapot. It clanked on the counter, and she spun around, a hand on her chest. "Me? Why would you think that?"

The girl shrugged. "I don't know. It is a bit odd for him to visit in the middle of the day, if he isn't your beau."

"He was in town and had bought a sack of horehound for the children. It's on the dining table, if you'd like a piece."

"Oh, yes. I love horehound." Pearl hurried through the door.

Sophie took a set of cups and saucers from the shelf and placed them on the counter, as she considered Pearl's question whether she'd set her cap for Mikey's father. Yes, she was attracted to Wade's personality and charm, and she soaked up his attention. But was she interested in a relationship with the man?

And what about Josh?

As she thought about the two men, she realized that she liked them both but did not feel the same toward them. Wade was charming and intriguing; he made her feel like a girl with her first infatuation. Josh was handsome, too, but less flirty, more solid. He made her feel like the grown woman she was. And a grown woman had no business entertaining the affections of two men.

"Mmm. Delicious!" Pearl reentered the kitchen. She dragged out a chair, its legs screeching, and dropped into it. "I can't get that man off my mind. Where does he live?"

Leaning back against the counter, Sophie shrugged. "I don't know. He said that he owns a ranch a ways from town, which is why he doesn't get to see Mikey all that often."

"Barnes." Pearl pressed her index finger across her lips and gazed up at the ceiling for a long moment. "I've lived here most of my life, but I don't remember ever hearing of a rancher named Barnes."

The water had boiled, so Sophie prepared the tea and carried it to the table. She set a plate of sliced bread in front of Pearl. "Sorry I don't have any sweets today."

"Tea is fine. Thank you."

Sophie thought about her mother's telegram. Maybe Pearl was the solution to one problem. "Did your mother explain why I was upset?"

Pearl shook her head and pinched off the corner of a piece of bread. "No, she didn't."

"I got a telegram from my mother, saying she will be arriving in three days to take my place here, and that I should be prepared to go back home."

"Oh, no!"

Sophie nodded and picked at a crusty spot of oatmeal she'd missed when cleaning up from breakfast. "I'm afraid it's true."

"But why is she planning to stay?"

Sophie nibbled her lower lip. "She doesn't know my aunt is dead."

Pearl's eyes widened. "You still haven't told your parents?"

"No. I knew they'd insist I return home."

"But I don't want you to go." The ever-present light in Pearl's eyes dimmed. "We've just become friends. I don't want to lose you already."

"I know. I feel the same."

"You're plenty old enough to live on your own. Why don't you just tell your mother that you want to stay?"

Pearl made it sound so easy, but she didn't know how forceful Ellen Davenport could be. If only Sophie could stay. If not for the issues surrounding the mortgage and her need for a source of income, she might consider it. But she'd quickly learned that the money earned from caring for the children was not nearly enough to live on. How had her aunt gotten by on her own for so long?

A knife clattered on Pearl's saucer, pulling Sophie's attention back to her guest. She studied the young woman for a moment. Though a bit flighty, Pearl was a good person—one Sophie thought she could depend on. "I wonder, Pearl, would you consider watching the children after I leave—just until school is over?"

The jam-covered bread on its way to Pearl's mouth halted. Pearl's brown eyes widened. "Me? Watch all those young'uns?"

Sophie smiled and nodded. "I know you'd treat them well, and it would be good experience for when you become a mother—which may not be far off, considering you're seventeen."

Pearl held up one hand. "Thank you for your nice words, but I couldn't watch so many at one time. I don't know how my sister manages with so many students. She's told me horror stories about that Mikey boy. No, I'm afraid not."

Sophie tried not to let her disappointment show. What was she going to do? She could hardly ask the parents to come and get their children when the school term wasn't over yet. She stared out the window. The Bible instructed children to obey their parents, but there was no guidance about what to do when a woman was no longer a child. She didn't want to upset her parents, and yet she couldn't return to her dreary existence. *What am I to do, Lord?*

⌒

Josh paced his office. He dreaded picking up the children after work. Sophie had run off with that Wade Barnes and never given him another thought. Maybe he'd been too hasty in wanting to ask to court her. Could she have developed feelings for Barnes? The thought twisted his gut.

What should he say to her this evening? Should he even mention that she'd left without hearing what he needed to say to her? His stomach grumbled, reminding him that he'd skipped lunch and come straight back to work. He'd been too frustrated to eat. Not that he'd achieved much, since all he could think of was that snake charmer Barnes flashing his roguish smile as he walked away with Sophie on his arm.

Josh paused at the window. Why had he never heard of Wade Barnes? He'd checked the bank's file and been disappointed to learn that the man had never borrowed money. If he had, Josh would at least know where his ranch was located.

Something about the man irritated him like sandburs on trousers. What was it? He raked his mind, searching, struggling to grasp the thought he needed. Suddenly, like a lantern lit in a dark room, the thought burst into his mind. Josh snapped his fingers. "That's it." Sophie had said that Barnes owned a ranch a fair distance from town, but Barnes had also mentioned his monthly pay. If he owned a ranch, he wouldn't get paid.

Josh hurried across the lobby to David Samuels' desk. The man finished the note he was writing and looked up. "Mr. Samuels, do you have any record of a Wade Barnes ever having an account at the bank?"

"Hmm. The name doesn't sound familiar."

Mr. Samuels was an expert with names and numbers, and he'd been at the bank since it opened. He would probably be the bank manager now if he wasn't such a meek-mannered man—a good temperament for an office worker, but not for a president who had to turn people away when they couldn't come up with enough collateral for a loan.

"Could I do some research and get back to you?"

"Sure. But make it a priority. This is important."

Mr. Samuels lifted his brows but didn't question Josh further. He nodded. "Yes, sir. I'll get right on it."

"Thanks. I'm going to run an errand. Be back soon."

If anyone knew about Barnes, the marshal or Doc Walton would. He'd check with them first. He could only hope that if his suspicions were correct, Sophie would listen to him and not get upset.

～

When the door knocked again, Sophie went to open it. Once again, she expected to see Josh, but the same man who'd given her the telegram earlier stood there, holding another piece of paper.

"Guess this is your lucky day, Miss Davenport." A frown replaced his smile. "Well, maybe not. I don't guess this is good news, but then, I shouldn't have said anything." His large ears turned crimson.

"Let me get my handbag." Mercy! Two telegrams in one day. Who could this one be from? Probably her father, confirming her mother's news. She retrieved a coin from her purse and hurried back to the door, her feet driven faster by her curiosity.

She paid the clerk and closed the door. Her hand shook as she read the missive, and then a smile broke through her worry when she read that her grandmother had broken her ankle, and Mother would be staying in Boston indefinitely. Instantly, guilt heaped onto her shoulders. She shouldn't smile when her grandmother had been injured, but her broken ankle couldn't have come at a better time.

Sophie pivoted in a circle like a schoolgirl. She had been granted a reprieve!

She stopped suddenly. That meant she would be here for the dance!

She gazed up at the ceiling. "Thank You, Father! I mean, thank You that I can stay longer, not for Grandmother's broken ankle. Please relieve her discomfort."

She rushed up the stairs, thinking of what she needed to do to finish the girls' dresses. Mikey's new shirt was complete, although she'd thought his first time wearing it would be to church rather than a social. She went to the wardrobe in her aunt's room—a perfect hiding place for the small dress she'd started for Amanda from one of Aunt Maude's old gowns. She still needed to hem it and stitch some lace that she'd removed from one of her own dresses onto the cuffs and collar. Grabbing a chair, she hauled it over to the window, then climbed up to retrieve her aunt's sewing basket from the top of the wardrobe. Joy flooded her. She wouldn't attend with Wade, but she and the children would go to the dance.

God had made a way for her to attend the social.

Maybe He'd make a way for her to stay in Windmill.

⟲

Josh fidgeted at Sophie's door like an anxious schoolboy. David Samuels' search had yielded no information about Wade Barnes, and Josh's trip to the marshal's office had been a waste of time, since the man hadn't been there. He'd hoped to talk with Sophie about his suspicions, but he wouldn't do so until he had some actual facts.

Hazel opened the door, much to Josh's disappointment. He gazed past her but caught no glimpse of Sophie.

Toby jogged toward him, smiling. "Uncle Josh! Can I go on home?"

Josh nodded at his nephew, his mind fully absorbed with Sophie. "Is Miss Davenport available?"

Hazel shook her head. "Her and Amanda are upstairs." The girl's eyes suddenly lit up. "Miss Sophie made me and Amanda new dresses to wear to the dance, and Amanda's trying hers on now. Corrie's up there too. Want me to holler at her?"

"Yes, if you would, please." Josh's disappointment made his shoulders feel as if they were made of lead. He dropped into one of the rickety rockers, which screeched under his weight. He couldn't imagine how Sophie had managed to find time to sew two dresses while doing everything else she had to do.

She was aware of the time he usually came by to pick up the children. Was she purposely avoiding him? Had she already decided to allow Barnes to court her?

Josh punched one fist into his other hand. He'd never been besotted over a woman before and didn't like the emotions swirling through him. Most times, he was able to easily fix a problem. His parents were resourceful and had taught their sons to be the same, but dealing with a woman—well, he just wish he'd been better prepared. But then he remembered how Ethan had been run through the wringer when he'd first realized his affections for Sarah—at the same time their brother Aaron had started to court her.

Footsteps thudded on the stairs inside, echoing out the open window. The door opened, and Corrie stepped out, her eyes glowing. "Oh, Uncle Josh, you should see the dresses Miss Sophie made. They're so pretty."

Josh nodded, his niece's chatter buzzing his thoughts like a pesky mosquito.

"Can I have a new dress too?"

When he didn't respond, the girl took his cheeks in her hands and turned his face toward her. "Did you hear me? I need a new dress—for the dance."

Josh blinked, suddenly angered with himself. He'd let his feelings for Sophie interfere with his attention to Corrie. He stood and took her hand. "That's a fine idea. Let's collect Toby and go see if the store has something in your size."

"Yahoo!" Corrie skipped the short distance back to his house.

The child's excitement lifted Josh's spirits. He was making too big of a deal about Barnes. If the man was insincere or a scoundrel, he would show his true colors sooner or later. Josh needed to entrust Sophie and his relationship with her to God's hands. If they were meant to be together, He would make it happen.

Barnes or no Barnes.

⌒

Saturday evening, the lively music from the social drifted in through Sophie's window as she braided Amanda's hair. "Hold still, sweetie, or your braids will be crooked."

"I'm just so excited. I've never been to a dance before."

Sophie wondered what Amanda would say if she knew this was her first dance too. Excitement bubbled through her at the thought of dancing and socializing. She tied a bow that matched the blue of Amanda's dress.

Hazel primped in front of the mirror. Her frock fit her slim figure well, but it was long enough to allow her room to grow.

"There." Sophie smiled at Amanda. "Turn around and let me see how you look."

The girl's cornflower blue eyes twinkled, and she spun one way and then the other, her skirt swirling.

"Beautiful!"

Amanda giggled.

"Let's go see if Mikey's ready."

They walked down the hall to the door to the boy's room. "Time to go," Sophie announced.

The door slowly opened. Mikey stood with his head down, not looking at all pleased. "How come I gotta dress up? I ain't dancin'. I'm just goin' 'cause they got food."

Sophie folded down his collar. "Don't say 'ain't.' And you have to dress up because we're attending the social and you need to look nice."

"Shucks."

Sophie pressed down the boy's ever-present cowlick, but it sprang up again. "At any rate, you look quite handsome."

Mikey's cheeks turned bright red. He brushed his hand down his new shirt, obviously proud of it, despite his fussing about having to dress up. Sophie's heart warmed. How long had it been since he'd worn something new?

"Try to keep it clean so you can wear it to church tomorrow."

He nodded, then slipped around her and trotted down the stairs. Amanda and Hazel followed. Sophie hurried into her room and took a final look at her dress in the mirror. The light blue short-waisted Basque bodice flared at her hips, accentuating her womanly shape, while the skirt fanned out, except where it was bunched up on the sides with a bow, revealing her sapphire-blue flounced underskirt. She donned her hat and gloves, then descended the stairs at a more sedate pace than the children, even though she was just as excited.

Still, apprehension twisted her stomach into knots. Would Josh be there? Would Wade? And if so, would he be upset that she had shown up after turning down his invitation? Would anyone ask her to dance? And if someone did, would she know what to do? She'd never danced before—not taken a single lesson. That thought dimmed her enthusiasm for a moment, but no matter. She would have an enjoyable time, whether she danced or not.

Amanda and Hazel waited on the porch, bouncing on their toes, but Mikey was almost to the square already. She took the girls by the hand and crossed the street, thankful once again that her mother had been kept in Boston. She hoped tonight would be an event that she would remember for a long time.

Chapter Twenty

Josh tugged on his frock coat, wishing he could forget about tonight's social, but Corrie was so excited that he couldn't refuse to attend. The girl loved any occasion to dress up and look pretty. Toby, on the other hand, sat in the chair in Josh's bedroom, grumbling.

"How come I gotta wear my Sunday clothes when it ain't even Sunday?" Toby squirmed around until his head rested on one arm of the chair and his legs dangled over the other.

Josh smiled—his first smile in three days, ever since Sophie had ignored his request to talk and walked home on the arm of Wade Barnes. Josh fiddled with his tie, thinking on how little he'd found out about Mikey's father. Even the marshal didn't know the man, which made Josh wonder if "Wade Barnes" was an alias.

He glanced in the mirror, noting his tie, which hung at an angle like a sinking ship. He yanked out the bow and retied it, making sure it was straight this time. He wasn't sure why he was going to so much trouble to look nice, when he'd rather stay home and work in his shop. After getting snubbed by Sophie and then not seeing her for several days, he was ready to pound out his frustrations on a piece of wood.

"Let's go, Toby. I'm as ready as I'll ever be."

The boy slid off the chair, looking like he was going to a funeral.

"Most of your friends should be there, and you know there will be food."

Toby's eyes brightened. "I'm real hungry."

Grinning, Josh nudged the child out the bedroom door. "You just had supper less than an hour ago."

"So?" Toby trotted down the stairs.

As Josh reached the bottom step, his gaze landed on his niece. At nine years old, she was half grown and already a beauty.

Corrie shoved her hands to her hips. "It's about time you two got ready. They're playin' the third song already. I'm missin' everything."

Josh waved her out the door, choosing not to mention that the social would go on for several hours, as long as the rain held off. He glanced hopefully up at the gray clouds that had settled over the town just past lunchtime. If it rained, he could come home early and change back into his comfortable clothes. He quirked his mouth sideways as a shaft of guilt speared him. He shouldn't wish for inclement weather at a time of celebration. Mumbling a prayer for God to forgive his bad attitude, he wove his way around several parked buggies and followed the children to the square.

A good-sized crowd had already gathered, and half a dozen couples sashayed to the lively fiddle music. Food tables lined the exterior of the windmill, and people stood in small clusters nearby, visiting. His eyes, as if they had a will of their own, searched the crowd for Sophie. Would she come?

His heart leapt when he spotted her standing with the McMillan family. She looked beautiful in her fancy blue dress, but it was her hair that held him immobile. She had pulled part of it up in the back but let the rest hang loose in a mass of waves that washed over her shoulders. He'd decided to back off from pursuing her after she'd run off with Wade Barnes, but seeing her here, looking so lovely, made him reconsider.

He felt a tug on his coat and glanced down.

"Can we eat now?" Toby pointed to the food tables.

"Not yet, but you can go find your friends. Just don't leave the square, and stay off the windmill." The boy had taken off as soon as he'd said the word "friends." Josh shook his head, grinning. Corrie stood with two of her schoolmates, watching the dancers and swaying to the music. He didn't envy Aaron for having to deal with all of the young men that were sure to come courting his pretty daughter.

Not wanting to appear too eager, Josh nonchalantly worked his way toward Sophie, stopping to talk with several of his customers. Mrs. Lambert explained that she'd just returned from out of town, taking care of her mother, who had a goiter. In the next few minutes, Josh learned more than he cared to know about the ailment. By the time he excused himself and looked for Sophie, she was dancing—if one could call it that—with a cowboy he didn't recognize.

Josh hated the jealousy that swarmed him. He had no claim on Sophie. Someone walked up and stopped next to him.

"Why don't you ask her to dance?"

He sidled a glance at Kate McMillan. Was his attraction to Sophie obvious to everyone? "Who are you referring to?"

Kate grinned, her eyes twinkling. "I never took you for a dunce, Josh."

Her unexpected comment made him smile.

"If you're as interested in Sophie as I suspect you are, you need to let her know. You had a close call this week."

Josh frowned at her cryptic comment. Was she referring to Barnes? Had the man asked to court Sophie? Just the thought made his gut twist.

"I guess she didn't tell you about the telegram from her mother. She was due to arrive yesterday and expected Sophie to be packed."

He spun to face Sophie's friend, his hopes shriveling like his garden under the relentless summer sun. "She's leaving? When?"

"Not just yet. She got a reprieve, but she doesn't think it will be much longer before she has to go back to St. Louis."

Tension tightened every muscle in his body. Sophie couldn't leave. He needed more time—time to show her how he felt. To tell her the dreams he'd imagined in the wee hours of the night, when sleep eluded him because he was thinking of her.

"Like I said, you need to tell her." Kate patted his arm, then strode off to join a cluster of women.

He'd gotten the message, but Kate had given no clue as to whether she thought Sophie would accept his offer of courtship. He straightened and watched as Sophie's dance partner escorted her to the sidelines again. The man tipped his hat and walked away, and Josh moved forward, pushing through the crowd. Just as he reached the dance area, someone called to Sophie. She turned away from Josh and started walking to meet Wade Barnes. The man said something to her, and she nodded, then took his arm and moved back toward the dancers.

Josh blew out a sigh and turned away. Corrie rushed toward him, squeezing between two men. "Uncle Josh, will you dance with me?"

He smiled and nodded, although being near Sophie and Wade wasn't his idea of a pleasant time. Corrie took his hand, pulling him back the way he didn't want to go.

"Have you seen your brother?" Maybe if he kept his gaze on Corrie, he could get through this dance.

"He's playing marbles with some boys over there." She swatted her hand before recapturing his palm. Josh glanced that way but failed to spot his nephew.

The delightful smile on his niece's face made him feel like pond scum for even considering saying no. They joined the other dancers and formed a circle, with Corrie on his right side. The musicians started playing the lively tune of "Skip to My Lou." Tom McMillan stood in the center of the circle, slowly turning, looking for a female to choose as his partner. He stopped at Corrie, bowed, then held out his hand. She giggled and glanced up at Josh, then stepped forward, obviously delighted to be the first chosen.

Halfway through their second dance, Corrie's pace slowed, and Josh steered her to the sidelines. His niece was ready to rejoin her friends, and he needed something to wash down the dust in his throat.

Carrying two cups of citrus punch, he worked his way back to where he'd last seen Sophie. She stood with two other women, smiling and fanning her face with her hand. Perfect. Josh made a beeline for her, then suddenly felt out of sorts as he approached. What if Barnes had already cajoled her into letting him court her?

Josh forged on, never having been one to give up easily. All three ladies looked his way as he drew near. He nodded at the two other women, then focused on Sophie, glad to see she appeared no worse for the wear after three dances. "I thought you might be thirsty."

The smile she rewarded him with made all of his doubts flee, and he handed her the cup. Remembering the other women, he turned. "It's Miss Marks and Mrs. Woods, right? Would one of you like this other glass of punch?"

The women blushed but politely declined, and then both of them headed for the refreshment table. When he looked back at Sophie, her cup was nearly empty. He took several sips of his, quickly finishing it off. He didn't know what to say. Had she even realized that she'd left him back at the store the other day?

"It's a nice evening, isn't it?" Sophie's eyes lifted upward. "As long as it doesn't rain."

Josh glanced at the pewter sky. "The breeze is nice, but I could do without the humidity."

Sophie nodded.

Josh released a sigh. Wonderful. Their conversation had been reduced to talking about weather. It certainly was a safer topic than Wade Barnes.

The fiddler returned after his short break, tuned up, and then began the soothing strums of a waltz. The thought of taking Sophie in his arms was more refreshing to Josh than the punch. He took her empty cup, then gazed at her with a smile. "Save this dance for me." He jogged over to the table reserved for dirty dishes and placed both cups on it, then scanned the crowd until he saw both Corrie and Toby playing with friends.

Before he could make it back to Sophie, a trio of eager-looking bachelors surrounded her. She shook her head, her eyes lighting up when she saw Josh. He shouldered past two burly cowboys. "Sorry, gents, but the lady promised this dance to me." He couldn't help grinning when they groaned.

Josh led Sophie to the dance floor and held her close—as close as proper decorum allowed—with one hand lightly clinging to her tiny waist. He loved the feel of her small, gloved hand in his. He could easily understand her father's need to protect her, even if he didn't agree with the man's underhanded methods. He gazed down at her, putting Wade Barnes from his mind, and allowed the possibilities of the future to consume him. Possibilities that included this sweet but stubborn woman.

She met his gaze for a moment, smiled, and then looked away. Something troubled her, if he wasn't mistaken. If she wanted to talk, that was fine with him; if not, he'd remain silent and make a memory that he was certain he'd review over and over in the evenings to come.

As the waltz ended, Sophie looked up again and smiled. "Thank you for the dance, Josh." She nibbled her lip for a moment. "I wonder...would it be possible for us to talk somewhere? I owe you an apology."

Instantly intrigued, he nodded. "Of course. Would you like to take a closer look at the windmill?"

"Yes, that sounds nice."

As they left the dance area, several men elbowed their way toward them. Josh held up his hand. "Gentlemen, the lady needs to take a break."

One man moaned, and the other scowled. "Ain't right for you t'hog one of the only unmarried wimmen here."

Josh shrugged. "Be that as it may, the lady is no longer dancing. Please excuse us."

When the men stepped aside, Josh led Sophie to the refreshment table. The wind whipped at the tablecloth, threatening to yank it out from under the glasses. Away from the crowd, he noticed how the breeze had increased. The air was still humid, but it had cooled somewhat. "Shall we have another drink before our walk?"

"Yes, that's a wonderful idea. It is rather muggy. Do you think we're in for a storm?"

Josh glanced at the sky once more. Tall white clouds bubbled up like froth, lined underneath with dark gray. "I would say that's likely."

"At least you won't have to water your garden." Sophie picked up a glass of punch and handed it to him.

"That's true, although it means I'll have to think up another chore for Toby to do when he gets into trouble."

She giggled, turning his insides to mush. He'd never been in love before. Was that what he was experiencing? He watched her look around as she delicately sipped her drink. He could have finished off the puny contents of his cup in one swig, but he forced himself to use the manners his ma had drilled into him. Sophie's long tresses swayed with each gust of wind, tempting him to reach out and touch them. His fingers twitched, and he lifted his hand.

She spun around, eyes twinkling. "This is such a grand event. I never knew a dance could be so much fun."

He dropped his hand to his side, stunned. "What do you mean? Surely you've been to a social before."

Her lips tightened, and she shook her head. "I'm afraid not. My parents wouldn't allow it. They were afraid all the excitement would set off an episode.

She'd told him that she'd been kept at home much of her life, but he never dreamed her parents would keep her away from all social events. "I'm sorry, Sophie. I know they did what they thought was best, but I wish things could have been different for you."

"Thank you. I think that's one of the nicest things anyone has ever said to me."

He stared at her, amazed how someone who'd been a prisoner in her own home for most of her life had turned out to be such a kindhearted woman. He set her empty cup on the table next to his, then offered his arm. Smiling, Sophie accepted, and he walked her around behind the windmill, where the noise of the crowd and the music were somewhat muffled.

Sophie ran her hand along the windmill's white wood base. "Who built it?"

Josh released her and leaned back against the wood. "It's a rather sad story. Are you sure you want to hear it on this festive day?"

Her gaze turned serious, and she nodded.

"The way I heard it, a Dutch immigrant lost his only son when he got disoriented in a snowstorm one night. He built the windmill as a tribute to his son, and so no one else would ever have to suffer the pain of loss as he had. The purpose of the windmill was so the townsfolk could go up to the top and set up lanterns in the windows to help family members and travelers find their way after dark."

A *v* formed between Sophie's thin, brown eyebrows. "That is a sad story, but it was a nice idea he had to save others from a similar pain."

"Yep, it was. And now the town is named for it."

"What was the town originally called?"

"Why don't you guess?"

Her eyes twinkled, and she glanced at the town square. She drew her lower lip between her teeth in an enticing manner that held his gaze captive. "Um...Windy City? Windblown?"

Josh grinned. "No, but those are good guesses. You're sort of on the right track."

Her mouth quirked to one side, and she tapped her upper lip with her index finger. "I know—Sunflower! I haven't seen any yet, but don't you have a lot of those here?"

"Yes, but they don't usually bloom until mid to late summer. Anyway, no, that's not correct." Josh enjoyed this game—he liked seeing Sophie's playful side.

After a moment, she shrugged. "I could guess all night and not get it right. So, what was it?"

"Grassland."

"Well, that does make perfect sense, with all the tall grass around here. Windmill is much more charming, though, don't you think?"

She gazed up at him, and all he could do was stare back. He'd never seen eyes so dark in a face so fair—a face that resembled porcelain. Black lashes fanned her beautiful eyes, enhancing them even more. A pretty pink blush tinged her cheeks the color of the wild columbine that grew on his family's ranch. Josh licked his lips; the desire to kiss her almost pushed him forward, but it was far too soon. He wasn't even sure that she felt anything for him other than friendship.

Sophie's throat moved as she swallowed and looked away, as if studying the clouds on the horizon. Her skirts flapped in the stiff breeze, and she held them down with both hands. When she raised her face to his, her expression was serious, all playfulness gone. "Josh, I'm sorry about leaving the store the other day when you said you wanted to talk to me. That was rude."

Part of him was glad that she had realized she'd gone off and left him, but he couldn't hold a grudge for long. Didn't want to, even though he'd been jealous of Barnes at the time. "It's all right."

She shook her head. "No, it's not. I'm sorry."

He grinned. "I forgive you."

Her face brightened. "Thank you." She coughed into her hand.

Josh realized that the wind, as well as the dancers, had stirred up quite a bit of dust. "Are you all right?"

"I'm fine, thanks."

A small group of people circled the windmill and came into view. Mayor Wilkes nodded at Josh. Elmer and Juanita Busby followed close on his heels, along with their son, Pete, and a pretty young woman Josh hadn't seen before. Her eyes glistened with excitement.

The mayor pulled a key from his pocket, and Josh tugged Sophie away from the door to the windmill. "Looks like we're in for a storm, so the Busbys want to get on with their announcement," Mayor Wilkes explained as he unlocked the door. He opened it and entered, and the Busby family followed.

Josh looked at Sophie. "Shall we go around front and see what's happening?"

"Yes, let's. Besides, I need to check on the children."

She took his arm, and he led her around to the front of the windmill. He'd sobered at her mention of the youngsters. He'd been so engrossed with Sophie that he hadn't thought to check on Toby or Corrie for at least twenty minutes. He searched the crowd, relieved to see them standing near the food table with Hazel and Amanda.

"I see the girls, but do you see Mikey? I'm too short to see through this crowd."

Josh searched for the boy but couldn't find him. "No, but as soon as the announcement is over, I'll help you look for him. It shouldn't take more than a few minutes."

Sophie nodded, seeming satisfied. "Do you know those people who went inside the windmill with the mayor?"

With chagrin, Josh realized his etiquette blunder. "I do, and forgive me for not introducing you." As they found a spot in front of the windmill, far enough back that they wouldn't get a crick in their necks from looking up during the announcement, Josh filled her in on the Busbys.

Sophie leaned in close, eyes dancing. "Do you really think that young couple is getting married?"

"That would be my guess."

She clapped her hands. "Oh, this is so exciting. I've never been to an engagement celebration, other than my sister's—and that was in our home."

A loud clap of thunder boomed, and Sophie jumped. Squeals followed as almost every head turned to the sky. Lightning zig-zagged across the expanse like an unsocial curmudgeon determined to put an end to the festive evening.

"Ladies and gentlemen." The mayor put his fingers in his mouth and let out a loud whistle. "Everyone, please, could we have your attention?"

A few people started for their buggies, but most stayed. Evidently satisfied, the mayor continued. "Regretfully, we may have to call an early close to this delightful evening. But you're welcome to stay as long as the rain holds off."

He motioned for Elmer and Juanita to come forward. "The Busbys, here, would like to make an announcement."

Elmer, a tall man dressed in his Sunday best, took his wife's hand and gazed lovingly at her, in a way that created a yearning in Josh. He glanced at Sophie, who was mesmerized by the goings-on. Was she the woman God had created especially for him? Was it possible that, in spite of their differences, Sophie's trouble with asthma, and her issues with her parents, they could fall in love?

Excited by the possibility, Josh reset his focus on the landing around the windmill.

"Most of you know our boy, Pete." Elmer motioned for his son to come forward. "Well, we're proud to let you all know that he's found a bride—Angela Cummings, of Olathe. They plan to marry on May twenty-ninth, and we hope you all will come and help us celebrate."

Congratulations and cheers rang out from every direction. Men and women clapped, and several hats sailed through the air. Pete put his arm around his fiancée and pulled her to his side, looking proud and so much in love that Josh longed to feel the same. His stomach quivered at the possibilities. He patted Sophie's hand where it rested on his arm, and she gazed up, almost glowing in her excitement. He smiled, and she grinned back.

Lightning illuminated her face as it skittered across the darkening sky. Josh sighed, dreading to see an end to the evening.

Sophie glanced skyward. "I suppose we should round up the children and get them home before the rain starts."

"But you didn't get to eat anything."

Sophie shrugged, looking only mildly disappointed. A raindrop splattered on her forehead, and she jerked, blinking several times. "Time to go."

She turned and headed for the table where the children had congregated. At least they'd gotten some of the tasty treats. Josh had a hankering for some pie, but he'd waited too long. Toby and the girls ran up to them.

"It's startin' to rain." Hazel wrapped her thin arms around her waist. "My parents already started for home, so I'm staying with you, Miss Sophie."

"I'm cold." Corrie huddled against Josh.

Sophie's gaze searched in every direction. A man rushed passed with a woman in tow, bumping her. Josh reached out to steady her. She looked at the children. "Have any of you seen Mikey lately?"

"I think he went home." Shivering, Toby raised his arms for Josh to pick him up. "S-said he was b-bored."

Women cleared the tables of any remaining food, while families started for their wagons. Josh felt bad for those who had a long drive home, as it looked likely they were in for a soaking. Thunder boomed again, and lighting flickered across the sky. The girls screeched, and Hazel took off running. Toby tucked his face against Josh's shoulder, still shivering.

"Let's go." Josh took hold of Sophie's arm and guided her through the crowd. They jogged the short distance to Sophie's house, reaching her porch just as the rain let loose.

"I feel...." Sophie wheezed. "So bad...for those...people."

Josh frowned. Why hadn't he considered that running might not be good for her?

"I'm fine." She placed a hand on his arm. "Just let me...catch... my breath."

Nodding, he felt some of the tension leave his shoulders.

The front door flew open, and Hazel rushed out, eyes wide. "Somebody's in the house. The lantern's lit, and I heard footsteps upstairs."

Chapter Twenty-one

Someone was in her house? Sophie's heart lurched, and she tugged Hazel into her arms. "Are you sure it isn't Mikey?"

Hazel shook her head. "He's in the kitchen. When I heard footsteps overhead, I ran for the front door."

Josh shouldered his way past Sophie and then set Toby down. "Let me see who it is. You all stay here."

"But I'm getting wet." Amanda moved away from the edge of the porch and pressed against the house. The sky flashed, and the rain pounded like a hundred hammers on the roof and ground.

"What if we wait in the kitchen?" Sophie took Toby's hand.

Josh pursed his lips but nodded. "I suppose that would be fine. Keep everyone in there, out of sight, and stay away from the stairs. I'll take the intruder out the front door."

"All right. Come along, children. The storm should mask our footsteps, but no talking." Sophie tiptoed across the parlor, hurried past the stairs with a quick glance up to the second story, then hustled through the dining room and into the kitchen. Her heart beat in time with the drumming of the rain.

Would the children be safe if the intruder escaped from Josh and ran their way? She glanced around for some place to hide. Going out the back door was out of the question. The pantry would work, although it was a small space for so many. As she turned toward it, she noticed the door ajar. Then she remembered

Mikey was supposedly in the kitchen. She hurried over and tugged the door open. Mikey was reaching up to a shelf above his head but spun around when he heard her. Just like before, canisters, crocks, and jars had been moved from their normal places.

"What are you doing?"

"Nothin'. I was just hungry."

"Hungry? Didn't you eat anything at the dance? I saw you over by the food tables several times."

"So? Them ladies wouldn't give me much. I'm still hungry."

Sophie eyed the pantry again. There was nothing in there that the boy could eat that didn't have to be prepared first. Mikey was up to something. She faced him again. "Why don't you tell me the truth? What are you looking for?"

The boy's face turned white under his blanket of freckles. Then his forehead furrowed and his lips puckered. "You don't believe me! Nobody ever does."

He pushed past her, ran to the door, shoved it open, and disappeared into the storm.

Sophie hurried to the porch, heedless of the rain, and ran into the yard. "Mikey, come back!"

She knew calling him was futile. He wouldn't return until he was ready. She breathed a prayer, then stepped back inside and shut the door. She had the other children to be concerned about.

"Come, children. I want you to wait in the pantry until Josh has escorted the stranger out."

Toby dashed through the door, as if it was a game, but the girls were less eager.

"What about you, Miss Sophie?" Corrie asked.

She brushed her hand over the girl's damp hair. "Don't worry. I'll be just outside the door. Now, go on. You won't be in there for long. Hazel, take the lantern."

Amanda's lower lip quivered. "I'm scared."

Hazel put an arm around her. "C'mon. We'll pretend were hiding from Indians, and if they find us, they'll scalp us, so we hav'ta be quiet."

Amanda's eyes grew wide, but she let Hazel lead her into the pantry, and Corrie followed. Sophie closed the door, plunging the kitchen into darkness. Overhead, she heard thumps and thuds, as if someone was moving furniture—or two men were fighting. Concern for Josh pushed her through the dark dining room to the bottom of the stairs. Someone had lit the lantern in the second-story parlor, and a faint light cast its beam over the upstairs landing.

The floor creaked, and a man stumbled into view. Sophie stiffened. She tightened her grip on the railing. The man wasn't Josh. Where was he? Was he injured? Suddenly the intruder stumbled sideways, and if he hadn't grasped the railing, he would have fallen down the stairs. Sophie hid in the shadows, worrying about Josh. Lightning flashed, giving her a glimpse of the man's profile. She gasped. "Wade?"

He stumbled down the stairs. "Hey there, purty lady. Been lookin' for ya."

"Looking in my house? Upstairs?"

"Nah." He grinned. "I was huntin' fer Mikey."

Indignation boiled up in Sophie like a thunderhead on a hot, humid day. "You have no right to come in here without permission. I insist that you leave."

He slipped on the final step and nearly fell down, but he righted himself at the last second. "Don't go gettin' all riled up." He belched.

Sophie covered her nose. Had the man been drinking? "Where's Josh?"

Wade snarled his lip up on one side. "That sissy banker?"

Shoving her hands to her hips, Sophie fought the anger surging through her. She would have pummeled the man if she'd thought it would help. "He's no sissy. Where is he?"

"Here."

Sophie looked upstairs, relieved to see Josh coming down.

"Get on out of here, Barnes, before I fetch the marshal." Josh halted on the last step, standing close to Sophie.

She couldn't help wondering if he'd chosen to remain on the step because it made him taller than Wade, who also had to outweigh Josh by fifty pounds. The light from upstairs faintly illuminated the room, making it barely possible to see, although Josh's face remained in the shadows.

"I was just huntin' that boy o' mine." Wade reached for the stair railing and missed, and would have fallen if Josh hadn't grabbed his arm.

"Get the door, Sophie." Josh nodded at her across Wade's back.

She hurried and did as requested, then stood out of the way. She had never thought of Wade Barnes as a man given to drink, or one who'd be so rude as to come into her home without her permission, especially to go upstairs. Disappointment clung to her like prairie sandburs, not so much because of how he'd acted as because she'd been naive enough to nearly succumb to his charms.

Josh propelled Wade toward the door, but at the last minute, he leaned toward Sophie. His foul breath wafted over her. "How's about a li'l kiss?"

Sophie gasped and stepped away.

Josh yanked him back, shoving the man's arm behind him and up toward his shoulder. Wade ground out a groan.

"After all them gifts I gave her, a kiss ain't much to ask."

"All you're getting is the boot and then a jail cell with your name on it."

Horrified, Sophie dropped onto the couch. Josh shouldered the bigger man outside, and she heard a loud splat. Too ashamed to move, she buried her face in her hands. Wade actually expected her to reward his gifts with kisses? What would she have done if Josh hadn't accompanied her home? Would Wade have forced himself on her? If anyone had seen him upstairs, her reputation would be in tatters.

She shivered. Tears stung her eyes. Perhaps she had no business living alone. Perhaps her parents had been right when they'd said she wasn't fit to live on her own.

"Miss Sophie," Hazel whispered loudly from the dining room.

"Oh!" The children! She shoved up from the couch, shut the door and locked it, and hurried through the house.

Toby stuck his head out of the pantry. "Can we come out?"

"Toby! Get back in here!" Corrie cried.

"Yes, it's all right." Sophie hated that she'd been wallowing in self-pity so much that she hadn't even remembered the children. "Let's get you upstairs and out of those wet clothes." She motioned them out.

"What about me an' Toby?" Corrie asked.

"It's late. I wonder if your uncle would mind if I put you to bed upstairs. I don't know how long he'll be tied up at the marshal's office."

"He won't mind." The girl's eyes danced, as if she thought sleeping in another house was a great adventure.

"What about me?" Toby gazed up, his brow crinkled.

Sophie smiled and tweaked his nose. "You can sleep in Mikey's room."

"But he's not here. I don't want to sleep there alone."

"Why not?" Corrie nudged her brother. "You sleep alone in your room at Uncle Josh's house."

The boy quirked his mouth but didn't seem to have a response to his sister's wisdom.

Thirty minutes later, the children were all snuggled down in dry clothing, prayers said. Sophie carried the lantern downstairs to the parlor and set it on the side table. She had changed into another dress, glad to be rid of the dampness. She walked to the window, pulled back the curtain, and peered out. How had Josh made out with Wade? And where was Mikey?

The town was dark, except for a few dim lights shining from windows in the distance. She couldn't tell if the rain had stopped, but it no longer pounded on the roof. Doubting that Josh would return to his house without stopping to pick up his niece and nephew, Sophie sat on the sofa to wait and pray that Mikey had found someplace dry to spend the night. Surely, he would come back tomorrow. She yawned. This day had been one of her favorites—until Wade had gone and ruined it.

⌒

Josh slogged back to Sophie's house, glad to have Barnes locked up. He would sleep well knowing the man couldn't trouble Sophie any more. Barnes had sure put a damper on the fine evening Josh and Sophie had been having. He'd enjoyed dancing with her, even though her steps had been unsure at times, and she'd managed to stomp on his toes more than once. He smiled at the memory.

At Sophie's house, a light shone through the thin fabric of the front window's curtain. He worked his way through the muck the rain had made of the streets, then stomped on the first step of her porch, hoping to dislodge some of the mud. He would have to clean his boots good when he got home.

He knocked on the door and waited. Sophie didn't answer, so he knocked again, a bit harder. Finally, he heard the click of the lock and saw the handle turn. Sophie's hair was mussed, and her eyes held the half-glazed appearance of someone not fully awake, yet she looked charming. He wanted to run his hand over her head and smooth down the wayward wisps of hair, but after the scare she'd had this evening, she probably wouldn't welcome a man's touch. He blew out a sigh. What would it be like to wake up next to her and see her like this each morning?

"Josh?"

"I've come to get Corrie and Toby and to see how you're faring." Since she'd been asleep, he assumed she was doing all right.

She brushed several strands of hair from her face and yawned. "I must have fallen asleep. Do you want to come in?"

He grinned. "You must not be fully awake to ask me that question at this hour. If anyone sees me just standing on your porch this time of night, tongues will wag."

"Oh." She glanced up and down the street.

"Relax, Sophie. Most everyone's tucked away in their homes, and Wade Barnes is in jail. He's swearing that Mikey let him in the house."

"What does that have to do with anything?"

"The marshal says if Mikey did, he'll have to let Barnes go on Monday morning, unless you find something is missing. Is the boy asleep?"

Sophie shook her head, and her lower lip trembled. "I don't know where he is. He got upset at me when we first got back from the dance and ran outside."

Unease twisted in his gut. Mikey might be a mischief-maker, but he was a young boy and shouldn't be out at night, especially with the damp weather. "Where do you think he might have gone?"

"I have no idea. No—wait! What about the fort you made for Toby?"

Josh straightened. "It's worth checking. I'll go have a look. Is there anything you need?"

Sophie gazed up at him, then frowned. "You're bleeding." She reached out toward his mouth but didn't quite touch him.

He couldn't resist capturing her hand with his. "It's stopped. I cleaned it up at the marshal's office."

"Did Wade do that?"

Embarrassed, Josh released her hand and kicked his boot against the rocker, knocking off another chunk of mud. "Yep. He came barreling out of one of the bedrooms upstairs and knocked me into the wall. I didn't even know he was in there."

"I'm glad it's not too bad." She tugged her shawl tighter. "I can't thank you enough for helping me tonight. I don't know what I would have done if I'd come home alone, with just the children, and found him upstairs."

He longed to take her in his arms, to reassure her. But he was wet. Muddy. And he had no right to do such a thing. Instead, he stepped back. "Where are my two shadows?"

Sophie smiled. "Upstairs, asleep. I wanted to get them out of their wet clothes, and I didn't know how long you'd be. I hope that's okay."

"It's fine. I'll go check and see if I can find Mikey. Do you need any water? I could pump some while I'm out there."

She nibbled her lip. "I don't know. Probably."

"Why don't you meet me at the back door?"

Sophie yawned again and then frowned, as if she didn't understand.

"So you can give me the bucket, and I can fill it before I go home."

"Oh. All right." She stepped back and started to close the door.

"Be sure to lock up."

She glanced at him again, one side of her face dimly illuminated by the flickering lantern. Her gaze locked with his, and he couldn't move. Her soft breathing and a steady drip of water were the only things he could hear.

"I truly appreciate what you did tonight—and the fact that you refused to come inside a few minutes ago. I wasn't fully awake, or I wouldn't have asked. I mean, it's not that you aren't welcome, but...you understand."

Resisting as much as he could for one evening, he cupped her soft cheek in one hand, then let go. "I know. Get the bucket, Sophie."

Sophie smiled, shut and locked the door, then hurried through the house. She grabbed the bucket off the kitchen cabinet, opened the back door, and waited. Though it was early May, the rain had chilled the air, and a cool breeze drifted in. Sophie shivered, dreading the thought of Mikey wandering about alone on such a chilly, damp night.

Wade had sorely disappointed her in showing her something other than his charming side. He had trespassed in her home, struck Josh, attempted to kiss her in his drunken state, and then insulted her. Josh, on the other hand, had been a perfect gentleman, protecting her with no thought of harm to himself. He had boldly come to her rescue, overpowering a man much larger than himself and then having him locked up, so that she would be safe. And now, he was out in the dankness, clothes soaking wet, searching for Mikey. In spite of the differences they'd had at times, she'd come to realize Josh Harper was an honorable man—a man she could trust. And, if she wasn't mistaken, he had developed an attraction to her. Sophie smiled. Perhaps there was hope for a happy future for her, after all—and perhaps it included a handsome, blue-eyed banker.

Movement at the back of the yard drew her attention. She set the bucket down and carried the lantern to the door, illuminating the steps and the area just beyond them. Josh walked into view, his arm around Mikey. The poor boy was soaking wet and shivering. She hoped he wouldn't take sick.

Sophie opened the door and smiled at the pair, grateful to Josh and hoping to reassure the boy that she wasn't upset. "Come on in here. You need to get out of those wet clothes."

Mikey hung his head and wouldn't look at her. Heedless of his sopping condition, she wrapped her arms around him and laid her cheek against his head. He was nearly as tall as she, and yet he was just a child—a child with no mother and whose father was in jail.

"I'm sorry," he mumbled.

It was the first time he'd apologized for anything.

"It's all right. Go on upstairs and change into your night-clothes. Toby is sharing your room tonight."

Mikey cocked one eyebrow at that but nodded and headed for the stairs. Sophie turned back to Josh, who looked cold and miserable. "You need to go home and get dry too."

He nodded and reached past her for the bucket. "Just let me get your water."

When he turned his back, Sophie closed the door and hurried to the stove. She checked the water in the teakettle and found it to be lukewarm. Quickly, she fixed Josh a cup of tea, hoping it would help warm him a little.

Moments later, he knocked on the door, then opened it and peeked in. "Here you go." He stepped just inside the door and set the bucket on the counter.

Sophie crossed the room and held out the teacup.

Josh glanced at it, then met her eyes.

"It's not very hot, and it's a bit weak, but I wanted to thank you for all you've done tonight, and I hope it might help warm you a bit."

Smiling, he accepted the cup and took a sip. "Mmm. Thank you."

She reached out and touched his arm. "No, Josh. Thank you. I really don't know what I would have done if I had come home alone and found Wade upstairs."

Josh finished off the tea in two more sips. "I wondered about that too. In the state that he was in, there's no telling what he might have been capable of. I want you to avoid him as much as you can, Sophie. I don't believe he's been truthful about owning a ranch, for one thing. Don't let him in the house again. And don't let him catch you alone."

Sophie bristled at his unexpected set of commands, no matter that they were issued with her safety in mind. It was an order—and she'd thought she was done with being ordered around by others when she left home. The comfortable atmosphere evaporated. She'd been bossed around by her parents her whole life, and she didn't need Josh telling her what to do, even if she agreed with the wisdom in keeping her distance from Wade. She hiked her chin. "I'm quite capable of deciding for myself what to do about Mr. Barnes, and it's no business of yours."

Josh's affable attitude disappeared behind a scowl. He set the cup on the counter and took hold of her shoulders. "Listen to me, Sophie. I've done some checking around on Barnes. I know pretty much all of the landowners in this county, and many in the surrounding ones, and I'd never heard of Wade Barnes until you met him. No one I've talked to knows a rancher named Barnes. Even the marshal didn't know who he was when I took him over there. Do you realize how uncommon that is in a town this small?"

Indecision battled with stubborn independence. It *was* odd that no one knew of Wade, but still, it wasn't Josh's place to establish parameters for her relationship with the man. She crossed her arms, feeling as if she were back in St. Louis, being lectured by her parents.

"Sophie, don't get all riled up. There's something else Barnes said that didn't sit right with me. Took a while, but I finally figured it out. The day I repaired your door, he made a comment about Mikey eating up his whole paycheck. Why would a man who owns a ranch be drawing pay?" Josh caught her gaze, held it, and gave her shoulders a squeeze. "He lied to you. Invaded your home and tried to assault you. Stay away from the man. You hear?"

Sophie knew he was right, but all the years of being ordered around came to a head. She jerked from his grasp and stepped back. "I think you'd better leave."

"What?" Confusion engulfed his features. "Didn't you hear a word I said? Barnes is dangerous—deceitful. He lied to you."

"Do you know that for certain?" She had to be sure. The man was Mikey's father, after all. Was it even safe for the boy to be with him?

Josh's lips puckered. "I know he's not told you the whole truth."

Sophie crossed her arms. "It's not that I don't believe you, but I need to be sure."

Pain slashed the determination on Josh's face, and he looked down. Guilt gnawed at Sophie. Had she pushed him too far?

"It sounds as if you don't believe me. I'd better go." He stepped out the door, then turned. "I'll come and get the children early tomorrow morning, so don't worry about feeding them breakfast."

And then he was gone.

Sophie wanted to call him back, but another part of her wanted to throw the teacup at him. Why did Josh have to *order* her not to see Wade? It's not that she wanted to be near the man again, because she didn't, especially after what Josh had said. She just couldn't bear another person telling her what to do. Her father bossed her. Her mother dictated what she could and couldn't do. Even her younger sister would order her around at times. Windmill was her chance to be free of all of that.

So, why did she feel so lousy?

Chapter Twenty-two

Josh pumped the treadle lathe with his foot as he held the chisel against the spinning bur oak. The lone lantern flickered, the light dancing with the darkness, illuminating the wall and his work space. He pressed gradually harder, causing the wood to take on a spindle shape. He loved working with his hands like this and creating beautiful things from pieces of raw wood. This was his thinking time—his praying time. And if he ever needed to pray, it was tonight.

He'd been unable to sleep after the way his evening with Sophie had ended, and with the children gone, he'd decided to get up and work for a while until his irritation had been chiseled smooth. Why had Sophie gotten so angry, when all he'd done was try to offer her some advice about Wade Barnes?

Josh reached the end of the wood and leaned back, giving his leg a rest. In spite of his grumpy mood, he ran his hand across the wood, brushing off the sawdust and enjoying the faint scent of the fresh-cut oak.

Women! Why had God created them so complicated? Why couldn't He have brought a meek, mellow woman into his life instead of a stubborn, easily agitated one? And after her reaction tonight, he was questioning whether she cared for him at all.

He walked to the door, opened it, and surveyed Sophie's house. All lanterns were out now, and the house was dark. He huffed a snort. She must not be having any trouble sleeping. Returning to his work, he placed another piece of raw wood into the lathe, then prepared to carve it to match the one he'd just finished. Once the rocker was complete, he planned to give it to Sophie.

A peace offering—that's what he was making.

Surely, when she saw the work he'd put in to making her a solid rocker—one that wouldn't creak and groan when she sat in it, like the two on her porch did—she would realize how much he cared for her. And he did, even if she'd gotten upset with him tonight.

In truth, that was partly his fault. He knew how her parents had forced her to abide by what they thought best for her—and he knew how much that annoyed her. He should have known she would get upset at his telling her to stay away from Barnes, even if he was right. He should have handled things differently.

Next time, he would. He was a man who learned from his mistakes, and he wasn't about to make this one again.

⌒

Sophie lay in bed, wide awake, staring at the fingers of moonlight that reached through the window and crept across the wall. She shouldn't have reacted to Josh like she had. Guilt swirled in her stomach like rotten milk. With a loud sigh, she slipped from the bed, and walked over to the window. The three-quarter crescent moon cast a faint glow across her backyard. All was dark at Josh's house, but a light shone through the window of his shed.

Was he out there working, unable to sleep, like she? Was he angry that she'd defended Wade and then had gotten upset at him for being bossy?

He had every right to be.

The more she thought on things, the more she realized how childish her actions had been. Having no experience with men, she'd succumbed to Wade's charming personality and soaked up his attention like a shaded flower seeking the sun. She hadn't used the good sense God had given her, even when she'd felt something wasn't quite right. If she was going to get by on her own, she couldn't afford to ignore His gentle nudging.

Closing her eyes, Sophie bowed her head. "Forgive me, Lord, for not heeding Your prompting that something wasn't right where Wade was concerned. Thank You for protecting the children and me from him, and for allowing Josh to be there just when I needed him. Please help him to forgive me, and give me the courage to ask his forgiveness, once again. Please, Father, show me a way to stay in Windmill. I don't want to go back to St. Louis."

Feeling better, she checked on the children, then returned to her bed, her bare feet cold from the chilly floor. Tomorrow, after church, she would prepare something special to show Josh the sincerity of her apology. She yawned and lay back on the bed, ready to rest. Today, her emotions had run the gamut, from sad to happy, excited to fearful. She'd attended her first dance and had delighted in taking a turn with several men, but her favorite had been the waltz she and Josh had shared. That would be something she'd remember for a long time.

The next morning, when Josh knocked on her door to pick up the children, Sophie had a smile waiting. But with the need to get the children back home to change clothes, eat breakfast, and still get to church on time, there was no opportunity to talk. His return smile gave her hope that last night's tiff left no lasting repercussions. That afternoon, when things weren't so rushed, she planned to apologize.

After Josh had left with Corrie and Toby, Sophie took a moment to breathe in the fresh morning air, crisp and clean after last night's rainfall. There was still a slight chill, but the dazzling sun would soon chase it away. Sophie felt hopeful. Happy. If only things could stay this way.

Footsteps thudded on the stairs behind her. She took a final glance up the street at the peaceful town, the quiet marred only by the church bell's clang. With a sigh, she closed the door and hurried back to the kitchen to finish breakfast while the children tended to their ablutions outside. She stirred the porridge and removed it from the heat, disappointed that because of her time spent ushering Corrie and Toby out to their uncle and then lollygagging at the front door, the gooey substance had since stuck to the bottom of the pan. She dished the porridge into four bowls, stirred in a little molasses and milk, then set the dishes on the table.

Hazel clomped in from the backyard with Amanda on her tail. The younger girl closed the door.

"Where's Mikey?"

"In bed." Hazel pulled out her chair. "He wouldn't get up."

Amanda's chair screeched as she dragged it across the floor, and then she sat, waiting to eat.

"Hazel, why don't you bless the food, and I'll run up to check on him?" Sophie didn't wait for a response but hurried upstairs. She dearly hoped Mikey wasn't in a bad mood today. If he didn't hurry, they would all be late for church.

She knocked on his door and waited. After a few seconds and no response, she pushed it open and peered in. She quirked her lips. He *was* still in bed. She crossed the room and drew back the curtains, allowing a shaft of bright sunlight to flood the room.

"No, don't. That hurts my eyes." Mikey rolled over to his other side, away from the window.

"If you'll get up, your eyes will quickly get used to the light." She tried to think of something that might motivate him. "Your porridge is getting cold."

"I don't want any."

Concern pushed Sophie's feet forward. She'd never heard the boy turn down food before. "Are you ill?"

"Don't feel good. I'm cold." He sneezed twice, then huddled under the ragged quilt.

Alarmed, Sophie touched his face. His skin felt hot. What should she do? Get the doctor?

Yes, the doctor. She pulled the quilt off the bed that Toby had slept in and laid it across Mikey. "I'll be back in a few minutes. You try to rest."

As she reached the stairs, her steps slowed. If she hadn't been sharp with Mikey when she'd found him in the pantry last night, he wouldn't have gotten upset and gone out into the rain, and he wouldn't be sick now. Other than her aunt, she hadn't tended a sick person before—and Aunt Maude had died under her care. Sophie pressed her hand to her mouth. "No. Please, Lord. Don't take Mikey too."

She hurried downstairs to the kitchen, chastising herself for fretting. Mikey was a strong boy, not a sick, elderly woman. Comparing the two was an exercise in foolishness. The girls had almost finished eating. "Hazel, Mikey is sick, and I'm going for the doctor. You and Amanda go on to church when you've finished breakfast. Sit with the McMillans." She started to turn, then noticed Amanda's hair wasn't yet braided. "Amanda, run up and get your brush and ribbons."

Hazel stood and set Amanda's empty bowl in her own. "I can do her hair if you want to go on."

Sophie smiled and gave the girl a quick hug. "Thank you."

She hurried down the street, praying the doctor was at home, and that whatever the diagnosis, Mikey's would be a mild case and he would recover soon.

She knocked on the Waltons' door several times, waiting for what seemed hours but surely was only a minute or two. A wheeze squeaked out as she struggled for breath after walking so fast. She pressed her hand to her chest. Footsteps hurried her way, and then the doctor answered, looking as if he'd just climbed from his bed. He hoisted a suspender strap over his shoulder and pushed his glasses up his nose, squinting at her.

"Miss Davenport, are you ill?"

She shook her head. "Not me. Mikey."

"What's wrong with the boy?" Doc Walton relaxed against the door frame, his expression softening. "He's not faking sickness again to keep from going to Sunday services, is he?"

"I don't believe so. He felt terribly hot."

Doc straightened immediately. "I'll be ready in a few minutes. Go on home, if you want, and I'll be there shortly."

"Thank you." As Sophie turned to leave, she reached up to straighten her bonnet. Her hand relaxed instantly. She'd been in such a rush, she'd forgotten to wear one. Her mother would be aghast at her deplorable manners. Ducking her head, she hurried home, hoping not to run into anyone she knew. The businesses she passed were all closed, but several couples ambled toward the church. At least she didn't have to worry about running into the miserable bank teller today. As she walked past the building, she glanced between the bars, but all she saw was the reflection of the street in the shiny glass.

Hearing footsteps behind her, she looked back and saw Josh and the children walking toward her.

He smiled and tipped his hat. "I didn't expect to see you again so soon."

"Mikey is ill, and I had to go get the doctor."

"I'm sorry to hear that. But I can't say I'm surprised. He was wetter than a rat in a rain barrel when I found him." Josh frowned. "Did you not find Doc Walton?"

"I did; he'll be down shortly." She suddenly realized that Josh had been as wet as Mikey. "How are you feeling? You seem all right."

An engaging smile brightened Josh's expression, and his sapphire eyes twinkled. "Is that concern I detect?"

Sophie hiked her chin, secretly delighted he was teasing her. "So what if it is? If you take sick, then it's likely that Corrie and Toby will, too, and then I'll have more patients to tend to."

Josh sobered slightly. "That sounds as if you'd take care of me if I were ill. I rather like that idea."

Sophie's eyes widened at the implications of his statement. Her caring for a sick, unmarried man would be highly inappropriate, no matter how much she might like him. "I...uh...well, just remember what happened to my last patient."

All jesting fled from Josh's gaze. He turned to the children. "You two head on over to the church and find us a seat. I'll be right there."

"Will Mikey be all right?" Toby asked.

Sophie smiled, hoping to soothe his concern. "Yes, I believe so, but it would be nice if you two prayed for him to recover."

Toby nodded. "He can be mean sometimes, but I don't want nuthin' to happen to him."

"C'mon, Toby." Corrie took her brother's hand, gave Sophie and Josh a curious glance, then continued down the boardwalk.

Josh watched them for a moment, then took hold of Sophie's upper arms. "You know you had nothing to do with your aunt's death, don't you?"

When she didn't respond, he continued, "I sincerely hope you don't think you did. Miss Maudie was far sicker than she let on."

"I know." Breaking eye contact, Sophie watched a couple with two small children on their way to church. She sighed, thinking again about her aunt. "But I should have done more. Maybe if I hadn't been so focused on the children—"

"Don't." Josh took hold of her hand, instantly snapping her attention back to him.

"You had your hands so full that you were burning the candle at both ends—and in the middle. You did all that you could, and there's no sense in thinking otherwise."

His defense of her meant more to her than she could express. Not even Blake had stood up for her. Tears blurred her eyes, and love for this man blossomed and took wing. "That means a lot, especially since I know how concerned you were at first about leaving the children with me."

Josh winced, and a red hue covered his ears. "I didn't know you then, and little realized how determined you were." He squeezed her hand, gazing into her eyes.

"Thank you." Her stomach swirled with delightful sensations. "I need to get back to check on Mikey. And to make sure the girls got off to church."

"I saw the girls up ahead when we left our house, so I'm sure they made it. Is there anything I can do to help you?"

Sophie shrugged. "I don't know what to do."

"Ma always made us chicken soup when we were sick. How about I go see if the Purdys know where I could get a fresh hen today?"

Sophie smiled. "That would be nice."

Josh looked past her. "Here comes the doc."

Tugging her hand from his, Sophie started for home but then stopped and turned back to him. "Josh, I'm sorry about the way I acted last night. You were right about Wade. I was merely being stubborn and didn't like you ordering me to stay away from him."

"So, you don't have feelings for the man?"

She thought for a moment. "Only feelings of mortification for the naive, schoolgirl infatuation I had with that charlatan."

"That's all? Nothing more?"

"No. Why do you ask?" Sophie's pulse took off like a runaway buggy. Dare she hope that Josh was at least a tiny bit jealous that she'd been attracted to Wade? That would mean he felt something for her.

"Because I...uh...." He glanced up, then stepped back. "Morning, Doc."

"Josh. If you were hoping to carry Miss Davenport home again, I'm sorry to say she's not the patient today."

Sophie's face instantly heated. Talk about mortification. "I need to go." She hurried toward the house but was still within earshot when Doc Walton chuckled.

"You'd better lasso that one before she gets away," he said to Josh.

Sophie opened the door, wishing Doc would mind his own business. If only he had been delayed another minute, Josh might have finished his statement.

Chapter Twenty-three

Sunday afternoon, Sophie carried a bowl of steaming chicken broth and a glass of cold milk on a tray to Mikey's room. She was so grateful that Josh had not only located a hen but also taken the time to kill and pluck it so that she wouldn't have to. Her heart warmed just thinking about his kindness.

Mikey's eyes opened, and he scooted to the head of the bed and sat up. He coughed several times, then blew his nose on a handkerchief. "What's that?"

"It's chicken broth. Mothers have been feeding it to their sick children for centuries."

Mikey gave her an odd stare, and then one corner of his mouth lifted in a tiny smile.

She placed the tray on the room's only table, then handed a cloth napkin to Mikey. "Cover your nightshirt with this."

He did as ordered.

She scooted a chair up beside the bed, then picked up the bowl of soup and the spoon, preparing to sit.

"I can feed myself."

A twinge of disappointment rushed through Sophie. She had hoped that by caring for Mikey like a real mother might, she could win the boy's trust. "All right. If you want to." She transferred the milk to the table, moved the tray to his lap, and then lowered the bowl and spoon onto it.

While Mikey slurped the broth, Sophie set about tidying his room. She opened the window to allow in the warm breeze, as Doc

Walton had instructed her to do. Then she folded the extra quilt and laid it on the other bed.

"So, Doc said I just got a cold?"

Turning back to him, she smiled. "Yes, I was so relieved. I—" She could hardly tell him she was worried he might die, like her aunt.

"This soup's good—what little I can taste."

She dropped into the chair next to the bed. "I'm glad you like it."

"Your cookin's better than when you first came here."

Sophie attempted to brush down the boy's mussed hair, but his cowlick was as stubborn as the child. At least Mikey didn't pull away, like he often did when she tried to touch him. That was progress.

Emboldened, she voiced the question she'd often wondered to herself. "Would you tell me what happened to your mother?"

Mikey's eyes widened, but he continued eating. "She died. When I was seven. We lived in Kansas City then."

She brushed her hand across the boy's cheek. "I'm sorry. That must have been a difficult time for you and your father."

Mikey frowned, as he often did at the mention of Wade. She wished the father and son had a better relationship, but she wouldn't be the one to make that happen. Josh was right—the more she stayed away from Wade, the better. How could she have been so naive about the man?

"Wade tricks lots o' folks into believin' him, so don't feel bad."

Sophie stared at Mikey, amazed that he'd all but read her thoughts. His hazel eyes stared back at her with sincerity, not belligerence. His freckles stood out against his skin, which was paler than normal. "You must look a lot like your mother."

He shrugged and held up the tray, his bowl now empty. "Ma said she was Irish."

She returned the tray to the table and handed Mikey the glass of milk she'd brought him. "That certainly explains your coloring."

He stared into the cup. "Her name was Darcy, and she told me her family came over on a boat from Ireland. I ain't never even seen the ocean."

"It's quite beautiful, but the voyage to cross it is long."

"Have you been to Ireland?"

Sophie shook her head. "No, but we did go to England when I was a child, to visit my great-grandmother."

The memory was a very special one, as it was the only traveling she'd ever done, other than making the trip to Kansas. If she had to return home, would she ever travel again?

"I'm going when I get bigger. Maybe I can find some o' my kin."

"What about your father? Doesn't he have any family living?"

Mikey stared in the direction of the window and shook his head.

"That's too bad." Sophie stood and returned the chair to its place next to the table. "I'd better get started on the laundry before the day gets too hot."

Mikey handed her the half-emptied glass and slid back down in the sheets. "I should tell you—" He broke into a round of harsh coughs.

"Shh. You need to rest. Remember what the doctor said?"

He nodded and closed his eyes, then sneezed twice.

"We can talk later." She gathered up the boy's dirty laundry and laid it on the tray, then carried it to the door. As she walked out, Mikey cleared his throat.

"I'm glad you came here."

Sophie smiled as warmth flooded her. "I am too."

Monday afternoon, Sophie used her sleeves to brush at the sweat running down her temples. She should have started the laundry earlier in the day, but she'd spent some time reading *Journey to the Center of the Earth* to Mikey. She smiled as she hung up the boy's freshly scrubbed shirt. He'd been so engrossed in the book and hadn't wanted her to stop, even agreeing to attempt to continue reading on his own. Knowing how much he disliked school, she doubted he'd be able to get far.

With the sun directly overhead, the heat was nearly unbearable. Back home in St. Louis, she'd had the luxury of choosing when to work outside—and that was usually in the morning, while her garden was still partly shaded. At least her aunt's wide-brimmed straw hat helped shade her face. Her mother would have apoplexy if she returned with a tan.

Behind her, Sophie heard the loud whoosh of rushing water. She spun around, and her heart stopped. Wade Barnes stood there, holding her rinse pot, now empty.

"I hope ya were done with that." He shrugged. "Guess I should've asked before dumping it."

The warm ground soaked up the water quickly, leaving only glistening droplets behind. Sophie considered what she should do. Josh had warned her not to be alone with Wade, but she'd thought he was still in jail.

"Why are you here, Mr. Barnes?"

He grinned and leaned against the porch railing. "I came to see if you were still mad at me."

"Of course I am." She lifted her chin. "You had no business being in my house without permission, especially upstairs."

He rubbed his jaw and looked contrite, but she wasn't about to fall for his charm again. "I'm right sorry about that. I had too much to drink and must've gotten confused as to where I was."

She tugged a pair of Amanda's stockings from the basket, then had second thoughts about hanging them up in front of Wade. Needing something to still her shaking hands, she grabbed two of Mikey's socks. She reached up to hang one, but it dropped to the ground.

Wade pushed off the railing and started toward her. "I'll get that."

Sophie lifted her palm to stop him. "Don't. You need to leave."

He halted and placed both hands on his hips. "How come?"

"Because it isn't proper for you and me to be alone—and I need to finish my chores."

"I could help." He flashed that trademark grin.

Sophie was relieved to realize it no longer had an effect on her. "Please, you need to go."

"What if I don't want to?"

Sophie swallowed the lump in her throat. Her mind raced. If he had nefarious purposes in mind, she would be hard-pressed to defend herself.

"It's that Harpy guy that's set ya against me, isn't it?" All hint of charm fled, leaving behind a man Sophie didn't know.

"I suppose you mean Josh Harper?" She wasn't about to admit that he was exactly right about what had happened.

"You leave her alone."

Sophie jerked her head up to see Mikey leaning out her bedroom window. Relief made her limbs weak for a second, but then she realized the boy would be little help against his robust father. She took a step backward while Wade was distracted. Then she turned and made a dash around the side of the house.

Hard footsteps thudded behind her, and a harsh hand grabbed her arm and yanked her to a halt. "Where do ya think you're going?"

"Stop!" Mikey cried from the back door.

Wade spun her around and pressed her against the house, holding her there with his body. Sophie struggled, but she was no match for the big man. He laughed, sending a chill down her spine.

She tried to breathe, but her lungs felt as if they'd been filled with muck. She couldn't catch her breath. Gasping for air, she wheezed.

Help me, Lord. Please. And don't let Mikey see.

A ruckus outside his office door pulled Josh to his feet.

"Hey, you can't go in there," the bank teller shouted.

Footsteps slapped against the wood, and then his door flew open. A young boy stood there, bent over and coughing. He lifted his head, his eyes frantic.

Josh was so surprised that it took him a moment to recognize the barefoot boy in his nightshirt as Mikey.

Mr. Franklin hurried toward the boy and grabbed his arm, hauling him backward.

"Let him go." Josh rushed to intervene.

Mikey doubled up his fist and punched the teller in the stomach. The man howled and released him.

Mikey spun back toward Josh, struggling for breath. "Wade." He swiped his arm in the air, pointing behind him.

Josh frowned, trying to make sense of his gestures. "Wade what?"

"Miss Sophie's house." The boy fell to his knees, barking harsh coughs.

Wade was at Sophie's? Alarm surged through Josh. He raced past the boy.

"That hoodlum hit me." Franklin reached for Mikey again.

"Touch him and you're fired." Josh sent him a glare, and Franklin stepped back. "Mr. Samuels! Come help this boy. I need to go."

Mr. Samuels jumped up and rushed across the room.

"Get him over to the doc's, if you will."

Mr. Samuels nodded, and Josh ran past him. He didn't bother knocking on Sophie's door. If Barnes had her, every second mattered. Josh stopped in the center of the dim house and listened, hearing nothing. Dread heaped on him. Was he too late?

"Stop that!" a masculine voice shouted from out back.

Josh glanced out the window behind the dining table and saw Barnes, with Sophie pulled against him. Anger, and the desire to protect her, nearly overwhelmed him. He searched for a weapon and saw nothing but a skillet on the stove. He grabbed it and raced out the back door.

Sophie's loud wheezing must have been what had annoyed Wade enough to yell at her to stop. Josh despised the man even more. He hurried down the steps, hoping they wouldn't creak and give him away. Wade's back was to him. Josh couldn't take the chance that he was armed. As much as he hated attacking the man from behind, he raised the iron skillet and conked it against Wade's head, hoping it was hard enough to knock him out but not hard enough to kill him.

The varmint released Sophie, then turned slowly toward Josh, a stunned expression on his face. He took one step, and then his eyes rolled back, and he tumbled like Goliath to the ground.

Sophie bent over, struggling for each breath. Relief filled her eyes, and she reached for Josh. He dropped the skillet and hurried to her, pulling her into his arms. He blinked back tears of gratitude that God had gotten him there before she'd been badly hurt.

He held her, loving the way she felt in his arms. "Shh. You're all right now. Try to relax."

Sophie clung to him, quivering like a rabbit he'd once found in one of his brother's snares. He drew her against his chest and rested his chin on top of her head, love flooding him. "Thank God you're all right."

After a few moments, she patted his shoulder, and he relaxed his hold and took a step back. Sophie attempted to smile, but her wheezing continued. She glanced at Wade and shivered.

"Do you want to go inside?"

Shaking her head, she pointed to the steps. Josh guided her over, but she paused when she came upon the skillet. She looked up again, amazement in her eyes. "You hit him? With that?"

Josh shrugged and felt a bit chagrined. "Yep."

"I will forever love that frying pan." She smiled, then continued to the steps and sat.

Footsteps pounded around the side of the house, and Marshal Stephens ran into view, gun in hand. Mikey followed with Doc Walton on his heels. The marshal holstered his gun and strode over to Barnes' limp body. Mikey settled on the step next to Sophie, coughing.

Doc paused beside her. "Are you all right?"

She nodded, her wheezes lessening. "Better check him, though. Got the wrong end of a skillet." She glanced at Josh, her eyes dancing.

He smiled, feeling like he'd defeated an army and not just one man—albeit a larger man than he.

"Doc, you'd best make sure this fellow's still breathing." Marshal Stephens stood and walked over to Josh. "Tell me what happened—before you walloped this feller, I mean."

Josh quickly explained, the marshal nodding the whole time. When Josh finished, the marshal pulled a folded paper from his pocket, unfolded it, and handed it to Josh. It was a wanted poster.

"Got that right after the train left, about ten minutes after I let that rascal go."

The picture was of Wade Barnes, but the name was Wilbur Bradley. He'd kept his initials and taken an alias. Josh's hand shook as he read the list of the man's offenses. Robbery. Assault. Murder. "Looks like he'll be in jail for a long while."

The marshal snorted. "He ain't ever gettin' out."

Barnes moaned and drew up one leg. Doc Walton stepped back and motioned for the marshal. "He'll live. He'll have a mighty fierce headache for a while, but it's nothing he doesn't deserve."

The marshal eyed Josh. "You wanna help me lug him back to jail?"

"Sure. Just give me a moment." He nudged his chin toward Sophie, and the marshal nodded.

Josh picked up Sophie's straw hat, which must have gotten squashed during her tussle with Barnes. Just the thought turned his stomach. What if he hadn't been in his office when the boy had showed up?

Mikey still sat at Sophie's side, so there'd be no talking privately with her. Josh put one foot on the lowest step and leaned down so he'd be at eye level with her. At least her wheezing had subsided. "How are you?"

"Fine." She smiled. "I can't thank you enough for coming when you did. He—" Her voice broke, and her eyes shimmered with unshed tears. She closed them for a moment and sat up straighter. Mikey reached out and laid his hand over hers. Sophie smiled at him, then wrapped her arm around his shoulders. "I had two gallant knights come to my rescue today. I can't thank you both enough."

Josh knew she spoke the words partly for the boy, but she kept her gaze locked on his, and he felt a hundred feet tall. He'd always hated being smaller in stature than both his brothers, especially his younger one, but stature couldn't hold a candle to determination. Sophie had proven that. He wanted to hold her again, but not with an audience, and the boy needed her attention. "I'll see you later, then."

She smiled and nodded, conveying to him a secret message— that she was looking forward to the visit. Josh tipped his hat to her, then grabbed Barnes—or whoever he was—and helped the marshal lift the wobbly man to his feet. At least he'd never have to worry about the criminal bothering Sophie again.

With Barnes returned to his cell, the marshal dropped the key in his pocket and lowered himself onto the edge of his desk.

"What will happen to the boy with his pa in jail for good?" Josh asked.

The marshal quirked his lips, then shrugged. "Guess he'll have to go to a children's home somewhere. With the trouble he's caused here, I can't imagine anyone in town wantin' to take him in."

Josh nodded, feeling bad for Mikey. The boy had endured a tough life. He needed a family like the Harpers to love him and teach him right from wrong. With school ending on Thursday, Aaron, and possibly Ma and Pa, would come to town for the end-of-the-year program. Maybe he'd talk to his family and see if they had any ideas.

One thing was for certain: Sophie would be heartbroken when the boy left.

Chapter Twenty-four

If not for the children leaving, this would have been the best week of Sophie's life. With the exception of tonight—Thursday—Josh had spent time with her every evening, either talking on the porch or walking on the prairie, with the children close at hand. Today, his family had arrived about noontime to eat with Corrie and Toby at the school picnic, to which all parents were invited. Many of the townsfolk had come to see the end-of-school program. Sophie had felt like a proud mother watching the girls sing a song and Hazel recite a poem. Mikey had participated in reciting the multiplication tables, and he had actually behaved himself. Yes, she'd been proud, but it was a bittersweet time.

She closed the book she'd been reading to Mikey as they sat on the porch.

"Can I go see Toby? He's leaving tomorrow."

Sophie nodded. "Be sure to ask Josh if he can play."

"Yes'm."

She smiled and watched him scurry next door. When he reached the porch, he looked back and waved. She repeated the gesture, thinking how much he'd changed since his father had gone to jail. Nothing had been said as to what was to become of him. If she knew she would be staying in Windmill, she would see about adopting him, but her parents would never allow such a thing if she returned home.

If she returned home. That was the big issue. The time had come to write to her father and explain about his sister's death. She would do that tomorrow. By next week, she expected him to arrive to get her. She didn't want to go. Didn't want to leave her friends. Didn't want to leave Mikey.

Or Josh. Especially Josh.

But unless Josh declared his love and asked her to marry him, she feared she'd be returning to St. Louis.

The rocking chair made an annoying creak whenever she moved, so she stopped. Everything in this house needed repair, yet there was no money to make that happen. She had hoped to find a hidden treasure but found nothing. With the children gone, except for Mikey, she would be receiving no more money for watching them. Short of sewing, she could think of no way to generate an income—and without a way to earn money, she couldn't stay.

Laughter echoed out of Josh's house. She'd been glad to meet his parents, his other brother, Ethan, and Ethan's two-year-old son, Jeff. Sarah, Ethan's wife, had stayed home with their baby son, Mark, only ten days old, and Sarah's aunt Emma had also remained behind to help care for him. Josh's family was so different from hers, and they treated her as if she were normal. Not a pariah.

Something clunked beside the house, and Sophie jumped. It was probably just the boys, sneaking up to scare her. "I know you're there, so you might as well come out."

Something banged against the porch rail, and Sophie jumped up, spying Josh. "What in the world? Josh, what have you got there?"

He came around front and set a brand-new rocking chair on the porch. He beamed. "Haven't you seen a rocking chair before? I know you're not used to seeing one so fancy, but those old things you're so fond of sitting in are rockers, you know."

She gave him a playful shove. "You're funny." Then she stood and ran her hand over the exquisite floral engraving. "This is beautiful. Did you buy it as a gift for your mother?"

"Uh, no…and no."

"What?" Sophie looked up.

"No, I didn't buy it. I made it."

She gasped. "You did? I never knew you were so talented."

He waggled his brows. "There are many things you don't yet know about me, Miss Davenport. But, to answer the rest of your question, this is not for my ma. It's for you."

"Me?" Sophie drew her hand up to her chest. "Why would you want to give *me* such a fine gift?"

"Because you desperately need a new rocker—and because I want you to have it."

"This is what you've been working on in your shop, isn't it?"

He blinked, revealing his surprise. "How did you know?"

"I can see your shed from my bedroom window, and the light has been on in the evenings lately."

"And here I thought it was a secret."

Sophie glanced around, glad no one was on the street, and stepped closer. "It is a wonderful surprise, but I shouldn't accept it. Not proper, you know."

He shrugged. "Rules, schmules. Us country folk don't conform to all those hoity-toity regulations you city folk do."

"Well, in that case, thank you. I love it."

Josh's eyes captured hers, and she couldn't look away. Her chest tightened, and her breaths came faster—not because she was having an asthma episode, but because she'd come to care for this man more than she'd ever thought possible.

He brushed his hand down her cheek. "Sophie, surely you know—"

A scream next door made them both jump. The screen door flew open, and Corrie ran out, followed by her father. Aaron grabbed the girl and tossed her up in the air, as if she weighed no more than a baby. She squealed her delight. Then her father hugged her.

Josh touched the back of Sophie's hand, and she turned it over so he could grasp it. He blew out a loud sigh. "It seems we're never alone."

Aaron noticed them and started ambling their way. He halted suddenly and frowned. Sophie glanced up to see Josh nudging him away with his chin.

"Come and see the amazing rocking chair your brother made."

Aaron glanced at Josh again, as if uncertain of the welcome, but when Corrie trotted over, he followed. Aaron let out a low whistle through his teeth. "Nice work. Did you really do all of this?"

Josh nodded, his eyes shining with pride.

"Why are you working in a bank if you can make furniture this nice?" Aaron asked.

"I was thinking that too." Sophie scooted the new chair back and sat, taking delight in the fact that it made no sound at all.

Josh rested his hip against the porch rail. "I've considered making furniture, but I wasn't sure if I could make a living at it. It takes quite a while to build something, and wood isn't easy to come by here."

"We've got plenty on the ranch, plus we recently acquired the Mortonsons' place, and you know they have a small forest on their land."

Josh appeared to be thinking. "I don't know. I'd have to be sure I could make a living before leaving the bank."

"Tomorrow or Saturday, let's ride over and take a look at the place." Aaron flipped one of Corrie's braids. "C'mon, short stuff. Time to get ready for bed."

"I'm not short; Toby is."

Josh chuckled. "See what I've been dealing with for months?" When his brother and niece had gone inside, he turned back to Sophie. He lifted one finger. "Stay right here for a minute."

He jumped over the porch rail and ran around the side of the house. Sophie wondered what he was up to, but she enjoyed relaxing, cushioned in her new chair. She'd never received a finer gift.

Josh jogged back around the porch, then stopped in front of her, holding out a small wooden box. "I dropped this while wrestling with the chair."

She studied the box, which was about four inches by six. An engraved vine with tiny flowers wove around the outside of the lid, leaving the smooth middle untouched. She'd never seen such delicate handiwork, not even in the boutiques of St. Louis. "It's lovely, but what's it for?"

"Here. Open it." He set the box in her hand, then demonstrated how the front lifted up.

"It's a tiny cedar chest!" Splashes of color met her gaze instead of the brown she'd expected. "Flowers?"

"I picked some of the ones I had blooming and pressed them. Now you can keep them forever."

Tears blurred her eyes. "I don't know what to say. It's too much, Josh."

"No, it's not. I want you to have it."

She shouldn't keep it, but she hugged it to her chest, knowing the hours he'd spent creating the beautiful box just for her. "I'll cherish it forever."

Josh's wide grin made her glad she hadn't refused his gifts.

"Are you sure you don't want to come over and visit with my folks? They all loved you."

But do you love me? she desperately wanted to ask. "I enjoyed spending time with them at the picnic, but you need your own time with them."

"I'll be with them all weekend."

Sophie's heart slipped down a few notches. "So, you *are* going home? I'd thought you might stay, since Aaron came for the children."

"There are some things I need to talk over with my folks, but tonight isn't the right time."

"I understand." Disappointment stole her joy. She'd hoped they might have more time together, now that Hazel and Amanda had gone home, but she wouldn't keep him from his family.

"Why don't you and Mikey come to the ranch too?"

Her gaze zipped to his. "I can't. You know that."

"You could if you wanted to."

She did want to, but she'd already made plans to work on a quilt with Kate. "It wouldn't be right for me to go to your home, even with all of your family there."

Josh blew out a sigh and stood. "I understand, and you're probably correct." He bent down and put both hands on the arms of the chair.

Sophie leaned her head back against the rocker and swallowed.

"But when I return, you and I are having a talk."

About what? she wanted to ask. But all she could do was nod. If she moved as much as a hair, their noses would touch.

Josh's gaze dropped to her lips, and he suddenly reared back, as if she'd bitten him. "Good night, Sophie."

She watched him stride home and duck into his house without a second glance. She sighed. Josh had left her so confused. If he cared for her, why didn't he just say so?

At least he hadn't asked her to trade gifts for kisses—not that she would have minded.

⌒

Friday morning dawned gray and humid. The drab clouds reminded her of the storm that had ended her wonderful evening at the dance. Josh was leaving and wouldn't return until Monday. And he was taking her heart and energy with him. She gazed out the girls' window, where she could see the roof of the depot and the smoke of the engine. It hadn't yet pulled out. If she hurried, she could make it.

But, no. She'd made her decision, and it was the right thing to do. If Josh asked her to marry him, then she would go with him to visit his family.

She closed the window, looked around the spotless room, then moseyed out to find something to do until it was time to go to Kate's. Mikey was still asleep, and probably would be for a while, since the sky was so dark. She needed to wash the girls' bedding, but that could wait until Monday.

The one place she hadn't yet searched for treasure was the attic. She'd never had time to venture up there. Mind made up, she hurried down the hall to her bedroom to retrieve the two-piece ladder she'd discovered one day while sweeping under the bed.

Down on her hands and knees, she reached under the bed and pulled out one part of the ladder. As she stretched for the second part, someone pounded on her door. She jumped, bumping her head on the underside of the bed. She rose and hurried downstairs, rubbing the sore spot.

She pulled the door open and gasped. "Father? W-what are you doing here?"

He strode inside and looked around—quite disgusted, if she wasn't wrong. "I've come to take you home. Your mother insists." He dropped his satchel onto the sofa. "This place is atrocious. Why did Maude allow it to fall into such disrepair?"

Sophie twisted her hands, then gripped the top of her rocker—the one Josh had made—to still them. She'd dragged the rocker inside last night, not wanting to risk someone stealing it. If only Josh were here to stand beside her. "Auntie had little money to get by on. She certainly didn't have enough to do repairs to the house."

"Well, where is she? And why are you answering the door? Doesn't she have a butler?" He gazed down at her skirt. "What have you been doing?"

Sophie looked down and noticed the dust clinging to her smudged apron. "I was getting something out from under the bed and encountered some Kansas dust. It's impossible to keep it out, the way the wind blows here."

He paced to the kitchen then back, scowling. "Where is everyone? Do the servants have the day off?"

She took a breath to calm her nerves. Her hour of confession had come. "There are no servants, Father. Aunt Maude couldn't afford any."

Her father's frown deepened. "I don't understand. Who's been taking care of this place?"

Sophie pressed her hands to her stomach. "I have."

"You? What do you mean?"

"Perhaps you should sit down."

"I've been sitting for two days. Tell me what's going on."

"Tea! I bet you're dying for a cup." She rushed past him, but he grabbed her arm.

"Stop stalling and tell me everything."

She closed her eyes, saying a quick prayer for strength, then nodded. "When I arrived, Aunt Maude was far worse off than we thought. She'd broken her arm, but she'd also fallen outside on a chilly day. She took sick and never recovered."

"What are you saying?"

"Your sister is dead."

His eyes widened, and he pulled out a chair from the dining table and sat. "When?"

"The week after I arrived."

His nostrils flared, and Sophie prepared for his eruption.

"What! Why didn't you notify me?"

Sophie dropped into the closest side chair. "Because we had her service and buried her the same day she passed. You couldn't have been here in time, even if you'd known."

Scuffling sounded at the top of the steps. Mikey leaned over the banister and peered down, his hair going in five different directions. "Who's doin' all that yellin'?"

"It's all right," Sophie called to him. "My father has arrived."

"Your pa?" Mikey trod down in his bare feet and nightshirt.

"Whose urchin is that?"

"Father, please. There's no call to be rude. That's Mikey, and he lives here."

Father's face turned the color of pickled beets.

Sophie smiled at the boy. "Run on upstairs and get dressed. I'll have your breakfast ready soon."

Mikey looked as if he was unsure whether to leave her, but then he scampered back upstairs.

"What is he doing here, Sophia?"

"Aunt Maude took in some children, whose parents are local ranchers and farmers, and let them stay at her house so they could attend school. The parents paid for their room and board. That's how she'd been getting by."

He ran his hand through his thinning hair. "I don't believe it. I wrote her several times after Sam died and asked if she needed help. She always said no."

"She was proud and stubborn, like you."

"How have you managed all this time?" He stared at her for a long moment. "You mentioned making breakfast. Are you saying you know how to cook?"

"I didn't have a choice. We needed to eat. I did have a couple of minor episodes, but nothing I couldn't manage. I've learned to cook many things and have made friends here. I don't want to leave."

He snorted a laugh. "Learning to cook and tending a boy doesn't mean you are prepared to live on your own."

"And yet I have lived on my own, and not while tending one child but five."

"Five!" He shook his head. "Be that as it may, you're not staying. Your mother would have my head."

Sophie lurched to her feet, desperate to make him understand. "But I have managed, and without your help—other than the money you gave me when I left town."

"I sent you more money."

"And I sent it back."

He pursed his lips. "That banker I hired to keep an eye on you sure wasn't worth his salt."

Sophie's knees almost went out from under her. He'd hired Josh to keep an eye on her? No.

Her father stood. "I'm going back to the depot to find out when the next train leaves for St. Louis. You might as well start packing." He slammed the door as he left.

Sophie fell onto the chair. Her insides felt as if they'd been bored out with a knife. Not only had she been taken in by Wade, but Josh had tricked her too.

Mikey plodded downstairs. "Did he say you're leavin'?"

Sophie reached for the boy's hand, but he stepped back. "I don't want to, but what else can I do?"

"Stay here. Be my ma."

Sophie's broken heart shred into tattered strips. "I would love to do that with all of my heart."

"Then stay! Don't let him take you. Please." Mikey swiped at a tear.

"I can't. I have no way to support myself."

"Josh will take care of you. Can't you tell he loves you?"

Her lips trembled. "You're wrong. He's been working for my father."

Mikey grabbed the back of the chair her father had sat in and threw it to the ground, the loud clatter echoing through the house.

"Your pa's the one that's lyin'. I heard Josh tell his brother."

If only it were true. But without Josh and his love, she couldn't stay, no matter how much this town—this prairie—called to her.

"I'm sure Josh will let you stay with him, Mikey."

The boy shook his head. "You're a liar—just like everyone else." He spun and ran to the door, threw it open, and fled.

Sophie rushed to the door. "Mikey. Come back!"

Her last thread of control broke, and she collapsed on the floor, watching the last of her dreams die.

Chapter Twenty-five

Josh couldn't stop grinning. He was on his way back to Windmill to ask Sophie to marry him. His parents had loved her and told him not to let anything stop him, if he felt she was the woman God wanted him to wed—and she was. He knew that now without a doubt.

His whole family had also encouraged him to follow his heart about building furniture. The prairie passed in a blur, and the whistle signaled their arrival in Windmill. Josh rose, anxious to get off the train and start his future with the woman he loved.

There was one other thing he and Sophie had to talk about—Mikey. He was sure she would agree with his proposal to adopt the boy and raise him as their own. In fact, that had been the hardest detail for him to accept, because it meant he and Sophie would never be alone as newlyweds. But he knew in his heart it was God's will. The boy had no one else.

The train slowed, the brakes screeched, and they shuddered to a stop.

The conductor chuckled. "Just let me get that door open before you try running through it, Mr. Harper."

Josh grinned.

"I'm surprised you're so anxious to get back to work. Aren't you gonna miss those youngsters?"

"Yes and no. I love them, but it's time their father took charge over them for a while."

The door opened, and the conductor set the step in place. "See you next trip."

Josh nodded at the man and then wove his way through the small crowd on the platform. He'd just reached the steps when he saw Mikey running up the other set of stairs at the far end of the depot.

"Wait, Miss Sophie," the boy cried. "Don't go."

Josh's heart clenched. Sophie was leaving?

⌒

Numb to the bone, Sophie allowed her father to lead her to the train. She'd said her tearful good-byes to Kate and her family yesterday and asked that they not come to the depot to see her off. She couldn't bear another good-bye.

All her hopes—her dreams—had evaporated, and she was returning to her prison. Why had God allowed her to come so far and learn so much, only to leave this place she'd grown to love?

And Mikey. She'd searched for the boy whenever she could manage to get away from her hovering father, but she hadn't been able to find him. She hated leaving, not knowing what had happened to him. Kate and Tom had promised to hunt for him, but if Mikey didn't want to be found, he wouldn't be. Her heart ached for the lonely child.

Her father cleared his throat. "It's time, Sophia. Put on your happy face. We don't want people to think I'm abducting you against your will."

"But you are. You just don't see it."

That halted him, and for the first time, she read indecision in his expression.

"Miss Sophie!"

She spun around. "Mikey!"

The boy ran to her, tears coursing down his dirty cheeks. He hugged something—a velvet bag—to his chest. "Don't go. Please. I found this." He shoved the bag toward her. "Wade wanted me to find the treasure, but I hid this from him."

"Get away from her, boy." Her father reached for Mikey's shoulder, but Sophie stepped in front of him.

"Don't touch him!"

He paused at her uncommon demand. "We'll miss the train."

Turning her back to him, she hugged Mikey. "What's in this bag that's so important?"

Mikey wiped his eyes with his sleeve, his cheeks pale beneath the grime. "It's Miss Maudie's treasure."

Sucking in a gasp, she opened the drawstring, reached into the soft bag, and drew out several rocks—no, gems. Two rubies and a huge emerald and a number of diamonds. "Where did you find these?"

"In the hidey-hole in the stairs."

"Sophie! What are you doing here?"

She spun around to face Josh. In the excitement of seeing Mikey, she'd forgotten about his return. She frowned. He was the last person she wanted to see.

Her father came alongside her. "And who's this? Someone else you must talk with?"

"No, Father. I have nothing to say to him."

The light in Josh's eyes dimmed, and she read the confusion on his face. She might as well enlighten him. "This is Josh Harper, the man you hired to spy on me."

"What? No, wait!" Josh cried.

"Your uncle was certainly wrong about you." Her father wrinkled up his face in a scowl that would cause most men to cower, but Josh didn't.

"Is that what you told Sophie? Did you also tell her that I returned your checks and refused to do your spying?"

Hope surged through Sophie. "You did?"

"Of course. Did you actually think I'd stoop that low?"

"I didn't know what to think. You left without saying anything. I thought maybe you didn't care for me as much as I'd hoped."

He clutched her shoulders, his eyes filled with a light she hadn't seen before.

"Hey, there. Unhand my daughter."

Mikey rushed behind her and shoved her father in the stomach. "You leave them alone, you big bully."

Put in place by a ten-year-old, her father stepped back.

Josh gave her a gentle shake. "Look at me, Sophie."

"All aboard!"

"Don't you dare leave until you hear what I have to say."

"Sophia, we have to go."

She glanced at her father and shook her head. "No, Father. Not yet."

He curled his lips and crossed his arms.

She looked back at Josh.

"I love you, Sophie, and I hope you feel the same. I'd ask your father for permission to marry you, but I think we both know what he'd say."

Sophie blinked, and the depot faded from view. Her grumpy father disappeared. Only Josh was there. "You're serious? You want to marry me?"

"With all of my heart. And if you say no and board that train, you might as well shoot me, because I'll be a dead man."

She giggled. "That's silly. I'd never shoot you. Although I did contemplate it for the briefest of moments when Father said you were his spy."

"I never for a moment considered spying on you, and I didn't even know you that well then. His letter arrived at the same time as the draft he sent you. I returned it and told him under no circumstances would I follow his instructions."

She smiled. "You did?"

"Yes. So, will you marry me?"

Sophie glanced at her father. She longed to say yes, but she also desperately wanted his blessing. "Father, you heard everything—except that I love Josh with all of my heart. I want to marry him, but I would like your blessing."

He waved his hand in the air. "I don't even know the man."

"Don't you? He had enough character to refuse to spy on me and to return your check, two facts you neglected to tell me, and which caused me severe pain. And I know you—I doubt you would have written to him in the first place unless someone you respected had vouched for his character."

He squirmed. "Oh, all right, then. His uncle told me he was a fine, upstanding man, but Mr. Harper's refusal angered me."

"His action should have garnered your respect."

"Well…." He shrugged. "Maybe it did a little."

"A *little?*" Sophie grinned. She knew he was waffling.

"Oh, fine. You can marry him if you want. Just know your first visit home will be to attend my funeral, because your mother will shoot me when she finds out."

Sophie wrapped her arms around the burly man. "I love you, Father."

"Hmpf. Don't know if you noticed, but we missed our train."

The locomotive whistled, as if to confirm his statement, as it headed out of town.

Sophie turned to Josh, her heart pumping as fast as the train's wheels. "Josh Harper, there's nothing I'd love more in this world than to marry you."

"Yee-haw!" Josh tossed his hat in the air. It plopped against the depot ceiling, but that was the last thing she noticed because he kissed her.

And it was the most wonderful thing she'd ever experienced. Far too soon, he pulled away, but he kept his arm firmly around her.

"So, does this mean you're not leaving?" Mikey ducked his head, as if afraid she might not answer the way he wanted her to.

She lifted his chin with her finger. "I'm not going anywhere."

The boy's worried look fled, and the biggest grin she'd ever seen brightened his whole countenance. Then his eyebrows dipped. "Can I still stay with you?"

Josh cleared his throat. "Um, actually, I was wondering if you might want to live with me—at least until Sophie and I marry."

"You want me?" The wonder in his voice was almost Sophie's undoing.

She tugged him over and wrapped her arm around his thin shoulders. "You bet we do. Both of us."

Her father coughed into his fist. "And what about me?"

Mikey reached out and took hold of her father's hand. "You can come too, as long as you're not grumpy."

Sophie and Josh both chuckled.

"I'm not grumpy, am I?"

Leaving her fiancé, she took her father's arm. "Yes, Father, you are sometimes."

That evening, Sophie and Josh sat on the porch, she in her new rocking chair, he in the creaky one.

"I can tell if I want to keep my sanity, I'm going to have to make another rocker."

"Might as well make *two* more. Mikey will need one." She nibbled on her lip. "I didn't speak out of turn, did I, when I hinted at keeping him?"

Josh took her hand and squeezed it. "No. I think you read my thoughts. He needs a family, and we're it."

Sophie waved at a man driving his wagon out of town. "I'm glad. I was so worried when he ran away and Father was making me leave town."

"That's some tale the boy told of Wade Barnes finding him on the streets of Dallas and duping him into helping him steal from people. I still can't believe they went so far as to pretend to be family so that Mikey could live here and search the house."

"And don't forget that Wade tried a search of his own. I'm sure now that's why he was upstairs—and why I kept finding holes in the walls and things out of place."

"It's rather bizarre, especially since there really was a treasure. What do you plan to do with it?"

Sophie gazed at the man she loved. "Well, first off, it isn't mine. It's ours."

Josh rewarded her with a smile and a kiss on the back of her hand.

"I don't really know what to do. I thought I might sell the jewels and use some of the money to fix up this house so we could live in it. What do you think?"

"Hmm. There's not much room for a workshop, and you'd have to listen to hammering all the time."

"What do you have in mind?"

"I know of this pretty piece of land that's for sale   recently repossessed—with a beautiful view, a nice-sized creek that runs through it, and plenty of land for some horses and cattle, with room for half a dozen kids to roam."

Something caught in Sophie's throat. "Half a dozen?"

Josh winked. "Give or take a few."

She laughed. "Perhaps tomorrow we could take a drive and go look at this land. We need to make a quick decision before the bank reclaims this house."

Josh chuckled, then stood and tugged her to her feet. "Have no fear, fair lady. I know the man who runs the bank—at least for now."

He leaned in for a kiss, and Sophie met him halfway.

The front door of Josh's rented house flew open, and Mikey charged out. "I won. I beat that old curmudgeon at checkers."

Sophie shook her head. "Do you think we'll ever get a chance to experience a kiss that lasts more than a few seconds?"

The look Josh gave her set a fire in her stomach to smoldering.

"You can count on it, my dear."

About the Author

Vickie McDonough grew up reading horse stories and dreaming of marrying a rancher. Instead, she married a computer geek who is scared of horses. But those old dreams find new life as she pens stories of ranchers, lawmen, and others living in the Old West. Vickie is an award-winning author of twenty-eight books and novellas. Her novel *Long Trail Home* won the 2012 Booksellers' Best Award for Inspirational Fiction. *End of the Trail* won the Oklahoma Writers Federation Inc. Award for the 2013 Best Fiction Novel. Her books have also won the Inspirational Reader's Choice Contest, Texas Gold, and the ACFW Noble Theme contest, and Vickie has been a multiyear finalist in the American Christian Fiction Writers' BOTY/Carol Awards.

Call of the Prairie follows *Whispers on the Prairie* in Pioneer Promises, Vickie's first series with Whitaker House.

Vickie and her husband live in Oklahoma. Married for thirty-eight years, they have four grown sons, one daughter-in-law, and a precocious eight-year-old granddaughter. When she isn't writing, Vickie enjoys reading, gardening, antique shopping, collecting quilted wall hangings, watching movies, and traveling. She recently took a stained glass class and is working on several projects.

To learn more about Vickie's books, readers may visit her Web site at www.vickiemcdonough.com or find her on Facebook, Twitter, and Pinterest. Vickie also co-moderates and contributes regularly to the Christian Fiction Historical Society blog: http://christianfictionhistoricalsociety.blogspot.com.